Texas! Chase

Texas!
Chase

Sandra Brown

Bantam Books • New York

2010 Bantam Books Hardcover Edition

Published in the United States by Bantam Books, an imprint of The Random House Publishing Group, a division of Random House, Inc., New York.

BANTAM BOOKS and the rooster colophon are registered trademarks of Random House, Inc.

Originally published in paperback in the United States by Doubleday, a division of Random House, Inc., in 1991.

ISBN 978-0-553-80404-1

Printed in the United States of America on acid-free paper

www.bantamdell.com

2 4 6 8 9 7 5 3 1

Dear Reader,

I'm thrilled that you're reading this classic love story, because of all the books I've written, the Texas! trilogy are among my personal favorites.

I didn't set out to write a trilogy. In fact, I didn't set out to write anything except a regular-length Loveswept romance. But when I "saw" Lucky Tyler sitting in that East Texas bar, staring into his whiskey, none too happy about the fistfight about to take place—"There was going to be trouble, and, hell, he just wasn't in the mood for it."—I immediately fell in love with him. I didn't know he had an older brother until Chase entered the scene to help Lucky fight his way out of a jam. Sage soon announced herself, and I felt I was onto something. What started as one short romance expanded into a family saga told in three parts.

Since 1990, the Tylers' stories have been printed around the world in numerous languages. People from all points on the globe find Lucky, Chase, and Sage as entertaining and endearing as I did when they introduced themselves to me. Fans often tell me they reread these books often because they miss the Tylers. I don't find that hard to believe, because I miss them, too!

I hope you have as much fun reading this book as I did writing it.

Sandra Brown

Texas! Chase

Prologue

"Chase, please, let's get out of here. We shouldn't bother her."

The hushed words had to penetrate pain and narcotics to reach her. Somehow they did. Marcie Johns pried open her swollen eyes. The hospital room was dim, but the scant daylight leaking through the drawn blinds seemed painfully brilliant. It took a moment for her eyes to adjust.

Chase Tyler was standing at the side of her bed. With him was his younger brother, Lucky, whom she recognized though they'd never met. Chase was staring down at her with unstinting intensity. Lucky seemed apprehensive.

Though she couldn't be specific about the time of day, she believed it to be the morning following the fatal auto accident. Earlier, the efficient hospital staff had moved her from an intensive care unit into this standard room at St. Luke's Methodist Hospital.

She had been examined by a team of doctors, each of

whom specialized in a different field, and had been informed that her injuries were serious but not critical. She had suffered a concussion, a broken arm and collarbone, and shock.

She was grateful to be alive and relieved that her prognosis for a full recovery was positive. But no one had mentioned Tanya. From the moment she regained consciousness in the intensive care unit, she had frantically asked questions about Tanya. At last they told her: Tanya Tyler had died upon impact in the crash. A Texas Tech student, home for summer vacation, had run a stop sign and hit the car broadside.

Marcie had been wearing her seat belt. Even so, she'd been hurled to the side and momentum had brought her up and forward. Her head had crashed into the windshield. Her face was bruised and abraded. Both eyes had been badly bruised. Her nose and lips were battered and swollen. Her shoulder was in a cast designed to keep her broken arm elevated. The impact that had done so much damage to her had instantly killed Chase's wife.

In less than twenty-four hours, Chase had undergone a physical change as drastic in appearance as Marcie's injuries. His handsome features were now ravaged by grief. He was disheveled, unshaven, bleary-eyed. If she hadn't known him for most of her life, if his face hadn't always been dear to her, Marcie might not have recognized him.

She had been retained as the Tylers' real estate agent, but had been working strictly with Tanya. They had looked at several properties over the course of a few weeks, but Marcie's enthusiasm for one particular house had been contagious. Tanya had fallen in love with it and was eager to see if Chase's opinion would match hers.

Chase Tyler and Marcie Johns had gone through thirteen grades of public schooling together, but hadn't seen each other for years, until yesterday when she and Tanya had unexpectedly called on him at the office of Tyler Drilling Company.

"Goosey!" He had stood and rounded his desk to greet her with a handshake, then a quick, hard hug.

"Hi, Chase," she had said, laughing at the ancient nickname. "It's good to see you."

"Why haven't you been to any of our class reunions?" His smile made her believe him when he added, "You look fantastic."

"I can't believe you're calling her by that horrid name," Tanya had exclaimed.

"You didn't take any offense, did you?" Chase asked.

"Of course not. If I could bear it as a sensitive, self-conscious adolescent, I can bear it as a mature adult. As for the class reunions, I lived in Houston for several years, but it was never convenient for me to make one."

He gave her an approving once-over. "You're really looking terrific, Marcie. The years have been more than kind. They've been generous. I hear your business is going great guns, too."

"Thank you, and yes, I've enjoyed being in business for myself. The economy has slowed things down the past year or two, but I'm hanging in there."

"Wish I could say the same," Chase had remarked good-naturedly.

"Oh, but I understand you've got something *very* special to celebrate."

"I told her about the baby," Tanya informed him. "And she's convinced me that even though our budget is tight, we can afford a house, and that now is an excellent time to buy. It's a buyer's market," she had told him, repeating what Marcie had told her earlier.

"Should I be reaching for my checkbook?" he had asked teasingly.

"Not yet. Marcie and I want you to come see the house she showed me yesterday. I think it's perfect. Will you come?"

"What, now?"

"Please."

"Sorry, sweetheart, but I can't," Chase had said.

Tanya's animated face became crestfallen.

"If it were any other time, I would, but I'm expecting a rep from the insurance company. He was supposed to be here right after lunch, but called to say he was running late. I need to be here when he arrives."

Marcie remembered saying, "I read in the morning papers that your brother has been cleared of those ridiculous arson charges."

"Is there another problem, Chase?"

"No," he had said, reassuringly pressing Tanya's hand between his. "We just need to go over the inventory of all the equipment we lost and discuss our claim."

She sighed with disappointment. "Well, maybe tomorrow."

"Or even later today," he had offered. "Why don't you go look at the house again, and if you're still excited about it, call me. Maybe I can meet you there after he leaves. That is, if you're free, Marcie."

"I blocked out the entire afternoon for Tanya and you."

Tanya, smiling again, had thrown her arms around Chase's neck and kissed him soundly on the mouth. "I love you. And you're going to love this house."

With his arms around her waist, he had hugged her tight. "I probably will, but not as much as I love you. Call me later."

Following them to the doorway, he had waved them off.

That was the last time Tanya and Chase had seen each other, touched, kissed. Marcie and Tanya had gone without him and had spent another hour touring the vacant house.

"Chase is going to love this," Tanya had said as they walked through yet another spacious room. Her excitement had been as keen as that of a child with a secret. Her smile had been so sweet. Her eyes had sparkled with exuberance over life in general.

Now she was dead.

At the sight of her grieving widower, Marcie's sore chest muscles contracted around her heart. "Chase, I'm sorry," she wheezed. "So sorry."

She wanted to reach out and touch him, and she tried to before realizing that her arm and collarbone were unmovable in their cast. Had he come to rebuke her for being a reckless driver? Did he blame the accident on her? *Was* she to blame?

"We . . . we never even saw him." Her voice was thin and faint and unfamiliar to her own ears. "It was just . . . a racket and . . ."

Chase lowered himself into the chair beside her bed. He barely resembled the man he'd been the day before. Always tall, with a commanding presence, he was now stooped. Lines seemed to have been carved into his face overnight. His gray eyes, characteristically intense, were bloodshot. Not only did they look bereaved, there was no life behind them. They reflected no light, as though he were dead, too.

"I want to know about Tanya." His voice cracked when he spoke her name. He roughly cleared his throat. "What kind of mood was she in? What was she saying? What were her last words?"

Lucky groaned. "Chase, don't do this to yourself."

Chase irritably threw off the hand Lucky placed on his shoulder. "Tell me, Marcie, what was she doing, saying, when . . . when that bastard killed her?"

Lucky lowered his forehead into one of his hands and massaged his temples with his thumb and middle finger. He was obviously as upset as his brother. The Tylers were a close family, never failing to bolster, defend, and protect one another. Marcie understood the concern they must feel for Chase. But she could also empathize with Chase's need to know about the final moments of his young wife's life.

"Tanya was laughing," Marcie whispered.

Pain medication had slowed and slurred her speech. Her brain had trouble conveying the correct words to her tongue, which felt thick and too large for her mouth. It was a struggle to get the words out, but she tried very hard to make herself understood because she knew Chase would cling to every careful word she managed to speak.

"We were talking about the house. She . . . she was so excited about . . . about it."

"I'm going to buy that house." Chase glanced up at Lucky, his eyes wild and unfocused. "Buy that house for me. She wanted the house, so she's going to have it."

"Chase—"

"Buy the damn house!" he roared. "Will you just do that much for me, please, without giving me an argument?"

"Okay."

His wild and loud outburst was jarring to Marcie's traumatized system. She recoiled from this, another assault, to her injured body. Yet she readily forgave him. In his own way he had been just as traumatized as she by the accident.

To anyone who had seen Chase and Tanya together, it was instantly apparent that they had shared a special love. Tanya had adored him, and he had cherished Tanya, who had been pregnant with their first child. The accident had robbed him of two loved ones.

"Right before we went . . . through the intersection, she asked me what color I thought . . ." A shooting pain went through her arm, causing her to grimace. She badly wanted to close her eyes, surrender to the anesthetizing drugs being dripped into her vein, and blot out consciousness and the anguish that accompanied it.

More than that, however, she wanted to help alleviate Chase's pain. If talking about Tanya would ease his pain, then that was the least she could do. She would continue talking for as long as she could hold out against her own discomfort and the allure of unconsciousness.

"She asked me . . . what color she should paint the bedroom . . . for the baby."

Chase covered his face with his hands. "Jesus." Tears leaked through his fingers and ran down the backs of his hands. This tangible evidence of his grief caused Marcie more agony than the brutal car crash.

"Chase," she whispered raggedly, "do you blame me?"

Keeping his hands over his eyes, he shook his head. "No, Marcie, no. I blame God. He killed her. He killed my baby. Why? *Why?* I loved her so much. I loved—" He broke into sobs.

Lucky moved toward him and again laid a consoling hand on his brother's shaking shoulders. Marcie detected tears in the younger man's eyes also. He seemed to be battling his own heartache. Recently Lucky had made news by being charged with setting fire to a garage at Tyler Drilling. The charges had been dropped and the real culprits were now in custody, but apparently the ordeal had taken its toll on him.

She searched for something more to say, but words of comfort were elusive and abstract. Her befuddled mind couldn't grasp them. It didn't really matter. Anything she said would sound banal.

God, how can I help him?

She was an overachiever to whom helplessness was anathema. Her inability to help him filled her with desperation. She stared at the crown of his bowed head, wanting to touch it, wanting to hold him and absorb his agony into herself.

Just before lapsing into blessed unconsciousness, she vowed that somehow, someday, some way, she would give life back to Chase Tyler.

Chapter One

"We've got a bunch of mean bulls tonight, ladies and gentlemen, but we've also got some cowboys who're rough and ready to ride 'em." The announcer's twangy voice reverberated through the cavernous arena of the Will Roger's Coliseum in Fort Worth, Texas.

"Eight seconds. That's how long a cowboy has to sit on top of that bull. Doesn't sound like much, but it's the longest eight seconds you can imagine. There's not a cowboy here who wouldn't agree to that. Yessiree. In the world of rodeo, this is the most demandin', most dangerous, most excitin' event. That's why we save it till last."

Marcie looked toward her two guests, pleased to see that they were enjoying themselves. Bringing them to the rodeo had been a good idea. What better way to introduce them into pure, undiluted Texana? It was like a baptism of fire.

The announcer said, "Our first bull rider tonight comes from Park City, Utah, and when he's not bull riding, Larry

Shafer likes to snow ski. Here's a real thrill-seekin' young man, ladies and gentlemen, coming out of chute number three on Cyclone Charlie! Ride 'im, Larry!"

The couple from Massachusetts watched breathlessly as the Brahman bull charged out of the chute with the cowboy perched precariously atop his bucking back. Within a few seconds, the cowboy/skier from Utah was scrambling in the dirt to avoid the bull's pounding hooves. As soon as he'd gained his footing he ran for the fence, scaled it, and left it up to the two rodeo clowns to distract the bull until it ran through the open gate and out of the arena.

"I never saw anything like that," the woman said, aghast.

"Do these young men train to do this?" her husband wanted to know.

Marcie had only recently become interested in bull riding and her knowledge was still sketchy. "Yes, they do. There's a lot of skill involved, but a lot of chance, too."

"Like what?"

"Like which bull a cowboy draws on a particular night."

"Some are more contrary than others?"

Marcie smiled. "All are bred to be rodeo animals, but each has his mood swings and personality traits."

Their attention was drawn to another chute where the bull had already lost patience and was bucking so violently the cowboy was having a difficult time mounting. The woman from Massachusetts fanned her face nervously. Her husband sat enthralled.

"Ladies and gentlemen, it looks like our next cowboy is going to have a time of it tonight," the announcer said.

"Anybody here want to take his place?" After a pause he chuckled. "Now, don't all of y'all volunteer at once.

"But this cowboy isn't afraid of a tough bull. In fact, the rougher the ride, the better he seems to like it. He rodeoed for years before retiring from it. Took it up again about a year and a half ago, not the least bit intimidated that he's a decade older than most cowboys who ride bulls.

"He hails from East Texas. Anybody here from over Milton Point way? If so, put your hands together for this young man from your hometown, Chase Tyler, as he comes out of chute number seven on Ellll Do-ra-*do*!"

"Oh, my God!" Unaware of what she was doing, Marcie surged to her feet.

The announcer raised his voice to an eardrum-blasting volume as the gate swung open and the mottled, gray bull charged out, swinging his hindquarters to and fro and, moving in opposition, thrashing his head from side to side.

Marcie watched the cowboy hat sail off Chase's head and land in the dirt beneath the bull's pulverizing hooves. He kept his free left arm high, as required by the rules of the sport. It flopped uncontrollably as the bull bucked. His entire body was tossed high, then landed hard as it came back down onto the bull's back. He kept both knees raised and back, held at right angles to either side of the bull, rocking back and forth, up and down, on his tailbone.

The crowd was wildly cheering, encouraging Chase to hang on. He managed to maintain his seat for about five seconds, though it had seemed like five years to Marcie. Before the horn sounded, the beast ducked his head so far down it almost touched the ground, then flung it up again. The movement had so much raw power behind it, Chase was thrown off.

He dodged the stamping hooves by rolling to one side. A clown, wearing baggy pants held up by suspenders, moved in and batted the bull on the snout with a rubber baseball bat. The bull snorted, stamped, and the clown scampered away, turning to thumb his nose at the animal.

It looked as though it were all in fun and the crowd laughed. The seriousness of the clown's job became instantly apparent, however, when the tactic failed to work.

The bull swung around, slinging great globs of foamy slobber from either side of its mouth, its nostrils flared. Chase, his back to the bull, picked up his hat from the dirt and slapped it against his chaps. A warning was shouted, but not in time. The bull charged him, head lowered, over a ton in impetus behind the attack.

Chase sidestepped quickly enough to keep from being gored by a pair of vicious-looking horns, but the side of the bull's head caught him in the shoulder and he was knocked down. Everyone in the audience gasped when the pair of front hooves landed square on Chase's chest.

Marcie screamed, then covered her mouth with her hands. She watched in horror as Chase lay sprawled in the reddish-brown dirt, obviously unconscious.

Again the clowns moved in, as well as two spotters on horseback. They galloped toward the bull. Each was standing in his stirrups, leaning far over his saddle horn, swinging a lasso. One was successful in getting the noose over the bull's horns and pulling the rope taut. His well-trained mount galloped through the gate, dragging the reluctant bull behind him while one brave clown swatted his rump with a broom. The second clown was kneeling in the dirt beside the injured cowboy.

Marcie scrambled over several pairs of legs and feet in her haste to reach the nearest aisle. Rudely she shoved past anyone who got in her way as she ran down the ramp. When she reached the lower level, she grabbed the arm of the first man she saw.

"Hey, what the—"

"Which way to the . . . the place where the people come out?"

"Say, lady, are you drunk? Let go of my arm."

"The barns. The place where the performers come from. Where the bulls go when they're finished."

"That way." He pointed, then muttered, "Crazy broad."

She plowed her way through the milling crowd buying souvenirs and concessions. Over the public address system she heard the announcer say, "We'll let y'all know Chase Tyler's condition as soon as we hear something, folks."

Disregarding the AUTHORIZED PERSONNEL ONLY sign on a wide, metal, industrial-size door, she barged through it. The scent of hay and manure was strong as she moved down a row of cattle pens. Breathing heavily through her mouth, she almost choked on the dust, but spotting the rotating lights of an ambulance across the barn, she ran even faster through the maze of stalls.

Reaching the central aisle, she elbowed her way through the curious onlookers until she pushed her way free and saw Chase lying unconscious on a stretcher. Two paramedics were working over him. One was slipping a needle into the vein in the crook of his elbow. Chase's face was still and white.

"No!" She dropped to her knees beside the stretcher and reached for his limp hand. "Chase? Chase!"

"Get back, lady!" one of the paramedics ordered.

"But—"

"He'll be fine if you'll get out of our way."

Her arms were grabbed from behind and she was pulled to her feet. Turning, she confronted the grotesque face of one of the rodeo clowns, the one whom she'd last seen bending over Chase.

"Who are you?" he asked.

"A friend. How is he? Have they said what's wrong with him?"

He eyed her suspiciously; she obviously wasn't in her element. "He's prob'ly got a few broken ribs, is all. Had the wind knocked out of him."

"Will he be all right?"

He spat tobacco juice on the hay-strewn concrete floor. "Prob'ly. I reckon he won't feel too good for a day or so."

Marcie was only moderately relieved to hear the clown's diagnosis. It wasn't a professional opinion. How did he know that Chase hadn't sustained internal injuries?

"Shouldn't've been ridin' tonight," the clown was saying as the stretcher was hoisted into the back of the ambulance. "Told him he shouldn't get on a bull in his condition. Course I guess it wouldn't matter. That bull El Dorado is one mean sum'bitch. Last week over in—"

"What condition?" Frustrated when he only gazed at her

in puzzlement through his white-rimmed eyes, she clarified her question. "You said 'in his condition.' What condition was Chase in?"

"He was half-lit."

"You mean drunk?"

"Yes, ma'am. We had us a pretty wild party last night. Chase hadn't quite recovered."

Marcie didn't wait to hear any more. She climbed into the back of the ambulance just as the paramedic was about to close the doors.

He reacted with surprise and an air of authority. "Sorry, ma'am. You can't—"

"I am. Now we can stand here and argue about it or you can get this man to the hospital."

"Hey, what's the holdup?" the other paramedic shouted back. He was already in the driver's seat with the motor running.

His assistant gauged Marcie's determination and apparently decided that an argument would only waste valuable time.

"Nothing," he called to his cohort. "Let's go." He slammed the doors and the ambulance peeled out of the coliseum barn.

"Well, I'm glad you made it back to your hotel safely."

Marcie, cradling the receiver of the pay telephone against her ear, massaged her temples while apologizing to the gentleman from Massachusetts. She had probably lost a sale, but when she saw Chase lying unconscious in the dirt, her guests had been the farthest thing from her mind. Indeed, she hadn't even remembered them until a few minutes ago while pacing the corridor of the hospital.

"Mr. Tyler is an old friend of mine," she explained. "I didn't know he was appearing in this rodeo until his name was announced. Since his family isn't here, I felt like I should accompany him to the hospital. I hope you understand."

She didn't give a damn whether they understood or not. If she had been entertaining the President and First Lady tonight, she would have done exactly the same thing.

After hanging up, she returned to the nurses' station and inquired for the umpteenth time if there had been an update on Chase's condition.

The nurse frowned with irritation. "As soon as the doctor—Oh, here he is now." Glancing beyond Marcie's shoulder, she said, "This lady is waiting for word on Mr. Taylor."

"Tyler," Marcie corrected, turning to meet the young resident. "I'm Marcie Johns."

"Phil Montoya." They shook hands. "Are you a relative?"

"Only a good friend. Mr. Tyler doesn't have any family in Fort Worth. They all live in Milton Point."

"Hmm. Well, he's finally come around. Got swatted in the head pretty good, but thankfully no serious damage was done."

"I saw the bull land on his chest."

"Yeah, he's got several broken ribs."

"That can be dangerous, can't it?"

"Only if a jagged rib punctures an internal organ."

Marcie's face went so pale that even the freckles she

carefully camouflaged with cosmetics stood out in stark contrast. The doctor hastily reassured her.

"Fortunately that didn't happen either. No bleeding organs. I've taped him up. He'll be all right in a few days, but he's not going to feel very chipper. I certainly don't recommend that he do any bull riding for a while."

"Did you tell him that?"

"Sure did. He cussed me out."

"I'm sorry."

He shrugged and said affably, "I'm used to it. This is a county hospital. We get the psychos, the derelicts, and the victims of drug deals gone awry. We're used to verbal abuse."

"May I see him?"

"For a few minutes. He doesn't need to be talking."

"I won't talk long."

"He's just been given a strong painkiller, so he'll likely be drifting off soon anyway."

"Then if it's all the same to you," Marcie said smoothly, "I'd like to stay the night in his room."

"He'll be well taken care of," the nurse said stiffly from behind her.

Marcie stood firm. "Do I have your permission, Dr. Montoya?"

He tugged on his earlobe. Marcie gave him the direct look that said she wasn't going to budge from her position. Buyers, sellers, and lending agents had had to confront that steady blue stare. Nine times out of ten they yielded to it. Earlier that night, the paramedic had found it hard to argue with.

"I guess it wouldn't hurt," the resident said at last.

"Thank you."

"Keep the conversation to a minimum."

"I promise. Which room is he in?"

Chase had been placed in a semiprivate room, but the other bed was empty. Marcie advanced into the room on tiptoe until she reached his bedside.

For the first time in two years, she gazed into Chase Tyler's face. The last time she had looked into it, their positions had been reversed. She'd been lying semiconscious in a hospital bed and he had been standing beside it, weeping over his wife's accidental death.

By the time Marcie's injuries had healed and she was well enough to leave the hospital, Tanya Tyler had been interred. A few months after that, Chase had left Milton Point for parts unknown. Word around town was that he was running the rodeo circuit, much to the distress of his family.

Not too long ago, Marcie had bumped into Devon, Lucky's bride, in the supermarket. After Marcie had introduced herself, Devon had confirmed the rumors circulating about Chase. Family loyalty had prevented her from openly discussing his personal problems with an outsider, but Marcie had read between the lines of what she actually said. There were hints about his delicate emotional state and a developing drinking problem.

"Laurie is beside herself with worry about him," Devon had said, referring to Chase's mother. "Sage, Chase's sister—"

"Yes, I know."

"She's away at school, so that leaves only Lucky and me at the house with Laurie. She feels that Chase is running away from his grief over Tanya instead of facing it and trying to deal with it."

Chase had also left the foundering family business in the hands of his younger brother, who, if rumors were to be believed, was having a hard time keeping it solvent. The oil business wasn't improving. Since Tyler Drilling depended on a healthy oil economy, the company had been teetering on the brink of bankruptcy for several years.

Marcie put to Devon the question that was never far from her mind. "Does he blame me for the accident?"

Devon had pressed her arm reassuringly. "Never. Don't lay that kind of guilt on yourself. Chase's quarrel is with fate, not you."

But now, as Marcie gazed into his face, which looked tormented even in repose, she wondered if he did in fact hold her responsible for his beloved Tanya's death.

"Chase," she whispered sorrowfully.

He didn't stir, and his breathing was deep and even, indicating that the drug he had been given intravenously was working. Giving in to the desire she'd felt while lying in pain in her own hospital bed, Marcie gingerly ran her fingers through his dark hair, brushing back wavy strands that had fallen over his clammy forehead.

Even though he looked markedly older, he was still the most handsome man she'd ever seen. She had thought so the first day of kindergarten. She distinctly remembered Miss Kincannon's calling on him to introduce himself to the rest of the class and how proudly he had stood up and spoken his name. Marcie had been smitten. In all the years since, nothing had changed.

The mischievous, dark-haired little boy with the light-gray eyes, who had possessed outstanding leadership qualities and athletic prowess, had turned into quite a man. There was strength in his face and a stubborn pride in his square chin that bordered on belligerence, inherent, it seemed, to the Tyler men. They were noted for their quick tempers and willingness to stand up for themselves. Chase's lower jaw bore a dark-purple bruise now. Marcie shuddered to think how close he had come to having his skull crushed.

When he was standing, Chase Tyler topped most men by several inches, even those considered tall by normal standards. His shoulders were broad. Marcie marveled over their breadth now. They were bare, as was his chest. The upper portion of it had been left unshaven, and she was amazed by the abundance of dark, softly curling hair that covered it.

The tape that bound his cracked ribs stopped just shy of his nipples. Marcie caught herself staring at them, entranced because they were distended.

Thinking he must be cold, she reached for the sheet and pulled it up to just beneath his chin.

"Jeez, did he die?"

The screech so startled Marcie that she dropped the sheet and spun around. A young woman was standing just inside the threshold of the door. Her hand, weighted down with costume jewelry and outlandishly long artificial fingernails, was splayed across breasts struggling to be free of a tight, low-cut sweater. A cheap, fake-fur coat was draped over her shoulders. The coat was longer than her skirt, which came only to midthigh.

Chase moaned in his sleep and shifted his legs beneath the

sheet. "Be quiet!" Marcie hissed. "You'll disturb him. Who are you? What do you want?"

"He's not dead?" the girl asked. In a manner Marcie thought looked incredibly stupid, the woman rapidly blinked her wide, round eyes several times. That was no small feat considering her eyelashes were gummy with mascara as thick and black as road tar.

"No, he's not dead. Just very badly hurt." She assessed the girl from the top of her teased, silver hair to the toes of her bejeweled, silver boots. "Are you a friend of Chase's?"

"Sort of." She shrugged off the fake fur. "I was supposed to meet him at this bar where everybody goes after the rodeo. I was getting pissed because he didn't show, but then Pete— you know, the clown—said that Chase got trampled by a bull. So I thought I ought to come check on him, see if he's okay, you know."

"I see."

"Did they say what's wrong with him?"

"Several of his ribs are broken, but he'll be all right."

"Oh, gee, that's good." Her eyes moved from the supine figure on the bed to Marcie. "Who're you?"

"I'm his . . . his . . . wife."

Marcie wasn't sure what prompted her to tell such a bold-faced lie. Probably because it was convenient and would swiftly scare off this woman. She was certain that in his more sane and sober days, Chase would have had nothing to do with a tramp like this. His marital status certainly didn't break the girl's heart. It merely provoked her.

She propped a fist on one hip. "That son of a bitch. Look, he never told me he was married, okay? I was out for kicks, that's all. Nothing serious. Even though he is kinda moody, he's good-looking, you know?

"When I first met him, I thought he was a drag. I mean, he never wanted to talk or anything. But then, I figured, 'Hey, what the hell? So he's not a barrel of laughs, at least he's handsome.'

"Swear to God, we only slept together three times, and it was always straight sex. Nothing kinky, you know? I mean, missionary position all the way.

"Between you and me," she added, lowering her voice, "it wasn't very good. He was drunk all three times. As you well know, the equipment is *im*-pressive, but—"

Marcie's mouth was dry. She drew upon reserves of composure she didn't know she had. "I think you'd better go now. Chase needs his rest."

"Sure, I understand," she said pleasantly, pulling her coat back on.

"Please tell his friends that he's going to be okay, though his rodeo days might be over. At least for a while."

"That reminds me," the girl said. "Pete said to tell him that he's leaving in the trailer for Calgary tomorrow. That's where he's from, you know? I think it's somewhere in Canada, but I always thought Calgary had something to do with the Bible." She shrugged, almost lifting her breasts out of the sweater's low neckline. "Anyway, Pete wants to know what to do with Chase's stuff."

Marcie shook her head, trying to make sense of the woman's nonsensical chatter. "I suppose you could mail it to him at home."

"Okay. What's the address? I'll give it to Pete."

"I'm not—" Marcie broke off before she trapped herself in her lie. "On second thought, please ask Pete to leave everything with the officials at the coliseum. I'll pick up Chase's things there tomorrow."

"Okay, I'll tell him. Well, see ya. Oh, wait!" She dug into her purse. "Here's Chase's keys. His pickup is still parked in the lot at the coliseum." She tossed the key ring to Marcie.

"Thank you." Marcie made a diving catch before the keys could land in Chase's vulnerable lap.

"I'm really sorry about, you know, balling your husband. He never told me he was married. Men! They're all bastards, you know?"

Marcie couldn't quite believe the woman had been real and stood staring at the door for several moments after it closed behind her. Was Chase reduced to seeing women like that to ward off his loneliness and despair brought on by Tanya's death? Was he punishing himself for her death by sinking as low as he could go?

Marcie moved to the narrow closet and placed the key ring on the shelf beside the chamois gloves he'd been wearing when he was thrown from the bull. His battered hat was there, too. She noticed a pair of scuffed cowboy boots standing on the closet floor.

His clothes had been hung on the few hangers provided. The light-blue shirt was streaked with dirt. His entry number was still pinned to it. His faded jeans were dusty. So was the cloth bandanna that had been tied around his neck. She touched the leather chaps and remembered their flapping against his legs as they sawed up and down against the bull's heaving sides.

The recollection caused her to shiver. She shut the closet door against the memory of Chase's lying unconscious in the dirt.

Returning to the bed, she noticed his hand moving restlessly over the tight bandage around his rib cage. Afraid he might hurt himself, she captured his hand and drew it down to his side, patting it into place beside his hip and holding it there.

His eyes fluttered open. Obviously disoriented, he blinked several times in an attempt to get his bearings and remember where he was.

Then he seemed to recognize her. Reassuringly, she closed her fingers tightly around his. He tried to speak, but the single word came out as nothing more than a faint croak.

Still, she recognized his pet name for her. Right before drifting back into oblivion he had said, "Goosey?"

Chapter Two

He was giving a nurse hell when Marcie walked into the hospital room the following morning. He suspended the invective long enough to do a double take on Marcie, then resumed his complaining.

"You'll feel so much better after a bath and a shave," the nurse said cajolingly.

"Get your hands off me. Leave that cover where it is. I told you I don't want a bath. When I feel good and ready, I'll shave myself. Now, for the last time, get the hell out of here and leave me alone so I can get dressed."

"Dressed? Mr. Tyler, you can't leave!"

"Oh, yeah? Watch me."

It was time to intervene. Marcie said, "Perhaps after Mr. Tyler has had a cup of coffee he'll feel more like shaving."

The nurse welcomed the subtle suggestion that she leave. With a swish of white polyester and the squeak of rubber soles, she was gone. Marcie was left alone with Chase. His face was as dark as a thundercloud. It had little to do with his stubble or the bruise on his jaw.

"I thought I had dreamed you," he remarked.

"No. As you can see, I'm really here. Flesh and blood."

"But what the hell is your flesh and blood doing here?"

She poured him a cup of coffee from a thermal carafe and scooted it across the portable bed tray toward him, guessing correctly that he drank it black. Absently, he picked up the cup and sipped.

"Well?"

"Well, by a quirk of coincidence," Marcie said, "I was at the rodeo last night when you danced with that bull."

"What were you doing in Fort Worth in the first place?"

"Clients. A couple is moving here from the Northeast. They're going to live in Fort Worth, but have been shopping lake-front property near Milton Point for a weekend retreat. I drove over yesterday to do some stroking. Last night I treated them to a Mexican dinner, then for entertainment, took them to the rodeo. They were exposed to a few more chills and thrills than I bargained for."

"A thrill a minute," he grumbled, wincing as he tried to find a more comfortable position against the pillows stacked behind him.

"Are you still in pain?"

"No. I feel great." The white line encircling his lips said otherwise, but she didn't argue. "That explains what you were doing at the rodeo. What were you doing here? In the hospital?"

"I've known you for a long time, Chase. There was no one else around to see about you. Your family would never have forgiven me if I hadn't come with you to the hospital. I would never have forgiven myself."

He set aside his empty coffee cup. "That was you last night, squeezing my hand?" She nodded. Chase looked away. "I thought . . . thought . . ." He drew a deep sigh, which caused him to grimace again. "Crazy stuff."

"You thought it was Tanya?"

At the mention of her name his eyes sprang back to Marcie's. She was relieved. She no longer had to dread speaking his late wife's name aloud for the first time. It was out now. Just like going off the high-diving board, the first time was the hardest. It got easier after that.

But seeing the pain in his eyes, as though he had been poked with a deadly needle, Marcie wondered if Chase would ever get over Tanya's tragic death.

"Would you like some more coffee?"

"No. What I would like," he enunciated, "is a drink."

Though it was no laughing matter, Marcie treated it as a joke. "At eight o'clock in the morning?"

"I've started earlier," he muttered. "Will you drive me somewhere to get a bottle?"

"Certainly not!"

"Then I'll have to call somebody else." At great expense to his threshold of pain, he reached for the telephone on the nightstand.

"If you're planning to call Pete the clown, it won't do you any good. He's leaving for Calgary today."

Chase lowered his hands and looked at her. "How do you know?"

"A friend of yours told me. She came here last night to see

about you when you didn't show up for your postrodeo date. Big hair. Big boobs. I didn't get her name."

"That's okay. I didn't either," he admitted. Marcie said nothing. He studied her calm face for a moment. "What, no sermon?"

"Not from me."

He harrumphed. "Wish you'd talk to my family about preaching. They love to preach. They're all in on the act of saving me from myself. I just want to be left the hell alone."

"They love you."

"It's my life!" he cried angrily. "Where do any of them get off telling me how to live it, huh? Especially Lucky." He snorted in an uncomplimentary way. "Until Devon came along, he had the busiest zipper in East Texas. Nailed anybody who moved and probably a few who didn't. Now he's so bloody righteous it's sickening."

"But I believe his . . . er, zipper is as busy as ever." That brought his eyes up to hers again. "Every time I see Devon, she's smiling."

Her composure was incongruent with the bawdiness of the topic. In light of that, it was difficult for him to remain angry. Although his scowl stayed in place, a fleeting grin lifted one corner of his lips. "You're all right, Goosey. A real good sport."

She rolled her eyes. "Every woman's secret ambition."

"I meant that as a compliment."

"Then thanks."

"While we're still on good terms, why don't you exercise your super brain, do the smart thing, and leave me where you found me?"

"What kind of friend would I be if I deserted you in your time of need?"

"It's because we've always been friends that I'm asking you to leave. If you stick around for long, something really terrible might happen. Something I'd hate."

"Like what?" she asked with a light laugh.

"I'm liable to make us enemies."

Her expression turned serious. "Never, Chase."

He grunted noncommittally. "Pete's heading home, you say?"

"That's right."

"He's got all my stuff in his trailer."

"Taken care of." She took a cup of custard from his bed tray and peeled back the foil seal. "He dropped everything off at the coliseum on his way out of town early this morning. I picked it all up there."

Without realizing he was doing so, he opened his mouth when she foisted a spoonful of custard on him. "You went to all that trouble for me?"

"No trouble."

"Did you call my family?"

"No. I wanted to ask you about that first."

"Don't call them."

"Are you sure that's what you want?"

"Positive."

"They'll want to know, Chase."

"They'll find out soon enough. When they do, they'll make an issue of it."

"Well, they should. You could have been killed."

"And wouldn't that have been a tragedy?" he asked sarcastically.

She stopped spooning in the custard. "Yes. It would have been."

He looked ready to argue the point, but turned his head away instead and with annoyance, pushed back the bed tray. "Look, Marcie, I appreciate—"

"What happened to Goosey?"

He looked her over carefully. The carrot-colored hair she'd had in kindergarten had mellowed to a soft red, shot through with gold. It was still naturally curly and had a mind of its own, but she had learned to arrange it artfully.

For years she had vainly tried to tan. She used to pray that all her freckles would run together. After several severe sunburns and weeks of unsightly peeling, she had eventually given up on that futile endeavor. She had decided that if she couldn't have the sleek, golden tan of beach bunnies, she would go in the opposite direction and play up her fair complexion to its best advantage. It now appeared almost translucent and was often remarked upon with envy by women her age who had basked in the sun for years and were now paying for their gorgeous tans with lines and wrinkles.

Eyeglasses had been replaced by contacts. Years in braces had left her with a perfect smile. The beanstalk body had finally sprouted and filled out. She was still strikingly slender, but it was a fashionable, not an unfortunate, slimness. The curves beneath her expensive and chic clothing weren't abundant, but they were detectable.

Marcie Johns had come a long way from the awkward

bookworm all the other kids had called Goosey. While the popular girls in her class had gone out for cheerleader and drum majorette, she had been captain of the debate team and president of the Latin club.

Her more curvaceous classmates had been crowned Homecoming Queen and Valentine Sweetheart; she had received awards for outstanding scholastic achievements. Her parents had told her that those were much more important than winning popularity contests, but Marcie was smart enough to know better.

She would have traded all her certificates of merit for one rhinestone-studded tiara and a crowning kiss from the president of the class, Chase Tyler. Few realized that their class valedictorian pined for anything other than scholastic recognition. Indeed, who would have even thought about it? Goosey was Goosey, and no one had ever given her a second thought beyond how smart she was.

Chase did now, however. Summing up her appearance, he said, "Somehow the name Goosey doesn't fit a well-put-together lady like you."

"Thank you."

"You're welcome. Now, as I was saying—"

"You were brushing me off."

Chase raked his hand through his unruly hair. "It's not like I don't appreciate all you've done, Marcie. I do."

"It's just that you want to be left alone."

"That's right."

"To wallow in your misery."

"Right again. Now, unless you're prepared to stand there

while I come out of this bed with nothing more on than a bandage around my ribs, I suggest you say your farewells and leave."

"You can't be serious about leaving the hospital."

"I am."

"But the doctor hasn't even seen you this morning."

"I don't need him to tell me that I've got a few cracked ribs. Nothing a day or two in bed won't cure. I'd rather pass the time somewhere else, someplace where whiskey isn't so scarce."

He struggled into a sitting position. The pain took his breath. Tears sprang to his eyes. He made a terrible, teeth-gnashing face until the worst of it subsided.

"How are you going to get to this 'place'?" she asked. "You can't drive in your condition."

"I'll manage."

"And probably kill yourself in the process."

He swiveled his head around and speared her with his eyes. "Maybe I should take a safe-driving lesson from you."

He couldn't have done or said anything that would hurt her more. She almost bent double against the assault of his harsh words. The blood drained from her head so quickly, she felt faint.

The second the words were out of Chase's mouth, his head dropped forward until his bruised chin rested on his chest. He muttered a litany of expletives. Beyond that, the silence in the room was thick enough to cut with a knife.

At last he raised his head. "I'm sorry, Marcie."

She was nervously clasping and unclasping her hands as

she stared sightlessly into near space. "I wondered if you blamed me for the accident."

"I don't. I swear I don't."

"Maybe not consciously. But deep down—"

"Not at all. It was a thoughtless, stupid thing to say. I told you I'd make an enemy of you. I can't . . ." He raised his hands helplessly. "Sometimes I get so furious about it, I turn nasty and victimize whoever happens to be around me at the time. That's why I'm not very good company. That's why I just want to be left alone."

His emotional pain was so starkly evident, it was easy to forgive him for lashing out at her. He was like a wounded, cornered animal that wouldn't allow anyone to get close enough to help him. For the two years since Tanya's death he had been licking his wounds. They hadn't healed yet. Left alone they never would. They would only fester and become worse. Chase was no longer capable of helping himself.

"Do you insist on leaving this hospital?"

"Yes," he said. "If I have to crawl out."

"Then let me drive you home. To Milton Point."

"Forget it."

"Be reasonable, Chase. Where will you go? If you were staying with that clown and he's left for Canada, where will you go?"

"There are plenty of other rodeo folks I can stay with."

"Who might or might not take proper care of you." She moved closer and laid her hand on his bare shoulder. "Chase, let me drive you to Milton Point."

Jaw stubbornly set, he said, "I don't want to go home."

What he didn't know was that Marcie could be as stubborn as he. Her personality had an inflexible streak that few ever saw because she only exercised it when given no alternative. "Then I'll call Lucky and discuss with him what I should do with you."

"The hell you will," he roared. He came off the bed, reeling from his weakened condition when his feet hit the floor. "Leave my family out of this. I'll manage just fine by myself."

"Oh, sure. You can barely stand up!"

Gritting his teeth in frustration and pain, he said, "Please go away and leave me alone."

Marcie drew herself up to her full height. "I didn't want to bring up such a delicate subject, Chase, but you leave me no choice. There's the matter of the money."

That took him aback. For a moment he merely stared at her blankly, then, drawing a frown, he growled, "Money? What money?"

"The money it took to admit you to this hospital and get treatment. I didn't think you would want to be admitted as a charity patient, so I paid for everything."

"You what?"

"You had no insurance card in your wallet. We didn't find a significant amount of money there either, so I footed the bill."

He gnawed on his lower lip, his agitation plain. "The entry fee was several hundred dollars, but if I hadn't put it up, I couldn't have ridden in the rodeo. I was low on cash."

"Then it's lucky for you I happened along, isn't it?"

"You'll get your money."

"That's right, I will. As soon as we get to Milton Point you can withdraw it from your bank account or borrow it from your brother."

"Marcie," he said, ready to argue.

"I'm not leaving you to your own devices, Chase. According to sources who know you well, you've been drinking too much. How can your body heal if you take no better care of it than that?"

"I don't give a damn whether it heals or not."

"Well, I do."

"Why?"

"Because I want my five hundred seventy-three dollars and sixty-two cents back." Having said that, she marched to the door and pulled it open. "I'll send a nurse in to help you get dressed." She lowered her eyes pointedly, reminding him that he was indeed naked except for the white swathe of bandaging around his rib cage.

"What about my truck?"

Marcie kept her eyes on the road. Pellets of ice were falling intermittently with the rain. "I took care of it."

"Are we towing it or what?"

He had refused to lie down in the backseat of her car as she had suggested. But ever since leaving the hospital, his head had been reclining on the headrest. Her car was roomy and plush because she used it to drive clients around in. Soft music was playing on the stereo radio. The heater was controlled by a thermostat. Chase was surrounded with as much comfortable luxury as possible. His eyes had remained closed, though he wasn't asleep.

They were only half an hour into a two-and-a-half-hour car trip. Morning rush hour was over, but the weather, deteriorating by the minute, was making driving hazardous. Precipitation had increased, a nasty mix of rain and sleet that frequently plagued north Texas during January and February. The Fort Worth Livestock Show and Rodeo always seemed to herald it in.

Marcie had her eyes glued to the pavement just beyond her hood ornament and kept a death grip on the steering wheel while maintaining minimum speed as she navigated the labyrinth of freeways that encircled downtown Dallas. Unfortunately it fell directly in the path between their starting point and their destination.

"I hired someone to drive your pickup to Milton Point later this week," she said in answer to Chase's question. "By the time you're able to drive, it'll be there."

"*You* hired someone to drive *my* truck?"

"Uh-huh," she replied, concentrating on the eighteen-wheeler whizzing past her at a speed that set her teeth on edge.

"Still competent, aren't you?"

"The way you said that leads me to believe you don't mean it as a compliment."

"Oh, I commend your competency. It's just that most men are intimidated by self-sufficient, overachieving women." He rolled his head against the cushion so he could look at her. "Is that why you never got married? Never could meet your match in the brains department?"

She didn't feel inclined to discuss her private life with him, especially since she detected a derisive quality to his seemingly harmless question.

"You ought to try to sleep, Chase. You're fighting the pain medication they gave you before we left."

"What do they call that?"

"Demerol."

"No, I mean when a woman wants to be a man. Some kind of envy. Oh, yeah, penis envy."

Despite the traffic and glazed highway, she looked across at him. His smug expression was intolerable. She longed to come back with the swift and sure retort.

Marcie turned her full attention back to the road. She swallowed with difficulty. "Actually, Chase, I was engaged to be married once."

His snide smile faltered. "Really? When?"

"Several years ago, while I was living in Houston. He was a realtor, too. We worked out of the same office, although he was in commercial real estate and I was in residential."

"What happened? Who broke it off, you or him?"

She evaded the direct question. "We had dated for several months before becoming engaged. He was very nice, intelligent, had a good sense of humor."

"But you weren't compatible in the sack."

"On the contrary. We were very compatible."

He tilted his head to one side. "It's hard for me to imagine you in the sack."

"What a nice thing to say," she remarked, her tone implying just the opposite.

"I guess because you didn't date much in high school."

"It wasn't because I didn't want to. Nobody asked me."

"All you were interested in was getting straight A's."

"Hardly."

"That's what it looked like."

"Looks can be deceiving. I wanted to be beautiful and popular and go steady with a superjock just like every high school girl."

"Hmm. Back to the guy in Houston, why didn't you marry him?"

She smiled sadly. "I didn't love him. A week before the wedding I was trying on my gown for a final fitting. My mother and the seamstress who was doing the alterations were fussing around me. The room was filled with wedding gifts.

"I looked at myself in the mirror and tried to relate that bride to myself. The gown was gorgeous. My parents had gone all out, but it wasn't *me*.

"I tried to imagine walking down the aisle and pledging undying love and devotion to this man I was engaged to. And in a blinding instant I knew I couldn't do it. I couldn't be that dishonest. I was fond of him. I liked him very much. But I didn't love him.

"So I calmly stepped out of the white satin creation and informed my mother and the flabbergasted seamstress that the wedding wasn't going to take place after all. As you can imagine, my announcement created quite a commotion. The next few days were a nightmare. All the arrangements, flowers, caterer, everything had to be canceled. The gifts had to be returned to their senders with notes of apology."

"What about him? How'd he take it?"

"Very well. Oh, at first he argued and tried to talk me out of it, passing off my reservations as prewedding jitters. But after we had discussed it at length, he agreed that it was the right thing to do. I think he realized all along that . . . well, that I didn't love him as I should."

"That was a helluva thing to do, Marcie."

"I know," she said with chagrin. "I'm certainly not proud of it."

"No, I mean it *was* a helluva thing to do. It took real guts to break if off at the eleventh hour like that."

She shook her head. "No, Chase. If I'd had any guts, I would have admitted to myself, before involving an innocent man, that it just wasn't destined for me to get married."

They were silent for a while, which suited Marcie fine since the road had gone a stage beyond being glazed and was now like the surface of an ice rink.

Before long, however, Chase moaned and laid a hand against his ribs. "This is hurting like a son of a bitch."

"Take another pill. The doctor said you could have one every two hours."

"That's nothing but glorified aspirin. Stop and let me buy a bottle of whiskey."

"Absolutely not. I'm not stopping this car until I get to your place in Milton Point."

"If I wash the pill down with whiskey, it'll go to work faster."

"You can't bargain with me. Besides, it's stupid to mix alcohol and drugs."

"For godsake, don't get preachy on me. Pull off at the next exit. There's a liquor store there. It won't take a sec for me to go in—"

"I'm not letting you buy any liquor while you're with me."

"Well, I didn't ask to be with you, did I?" he shouted. "You ramrodded your way into my business. Now I want a drink and I want it now."

Marcie eased her foot off the accelerator and let the car coast toward the shoulder of the highway. Gradually she applied the brake until it came to a full stop. She uncurled her stiff, white fingers from around the padded-leather steering wheel and turned to face him.

He wasn't expecting the slap. Her cold palm cracked across his bristled cheek.

"Damn you!" Her whole body was trembling. Unshed tears shimmered in her eyes. "Damn you, Chase Tyler, for being the most selfish, self-absorbed jerk ever to be born. Look at my hands."

She held them inches in front of his nose, palms forward. "They're wringing wet. I'm scared to death. Haven't you realized that it isn't easy for me to drive under any circumstances, but especially under conditions like this?" She gestured wildly toward the inclement weather beyond the windshield.

"I'm afraid that every car we meet is going to hit us. I live in terror of that happening to me again. Even more so when I have a passenger sitting where Tanya was sitting.

"I was in that car, too, Chase, when that kid ran the stop sign. To this day I have nightmares where I experience the sound of squealing tires and feel the impact and taste the fear

of dying all over again. I had to undergo weeks of therapy before I could even get behind the steering wheel of a car again.

"If you didn't need to get home immediately, I would be
holed up in my hotel room in Fort Worth until the next sunny,
dry day. I wouldn't think of risking my life or anyone else's
by driving in this ice storm."

She paused and drew in a shuddering breath. "You're
right, you didn't ask for my help, but I felt I owed you this
much, to get you safely home to your family where you can
properly recuperate."

She doubled up her fist and shook it at him. "But by God,
the least you could do is shut up and stop your infernal belly-
aching!"

Chapter Three

"... still don't think we should wake him up. If he didn't wake up when we came barging in, as much noise as we were making, he needs this sleep."

Marcie, with both arms curled around loaded supermarket sacks, paused outside the door of Chase's apartment. Through it, she could hear voices.

"But how else are we going to find out how he got here, Mother? And how do we know how many of those pills he's taken? That could be the reason he's sleeping like a dead man."

"Lucky, relax," a third voice said, "the pill bottle was almost full. He couldn't have taken many. Laurie's right. For the time being, he's better off asleep."

"That's a wicked-looking bandage around his chest," Laurie Tyler said. "Obviously he needs bed rest. We can wait until he wakes up on his own to find out who brought him home."

"Probably his current squeeze," Lucky muttered.

Marcie had heard enough. She managed to grip the doorknob and turn it, staggering inside under the weight of the grocery sacks. Three heads came around to gape at her with astonishment.

"Ms. Johns!"

"Hello, Mrs. Tyler."

She was flattered that Laurie Tyler knew her. Though she'd been in Chase's class all through school, they hadn't had the same circle of friends. Following her release from the hospital, Marcie had considered going to see Laurie and apologizing for Tanya's death. She had ultimately decided against it, thinking that it would be a difficult meeting each of them could do without.

"Lucky, take those sacks from her," Laurie ordered, shoving her dumbfounded younger son forward.

"Marcie, what the hell are you doing here?" Lucky relieved her of the grocery sacks and set them on the bar, which separated the small kitchen from the living area of the apartment.

Marcie dropped her purse and keys into a chair littered with unopened mail and discarded articles of clothing that had lain there long enough to collect dust. "Let me assure you, I'm not Chase's current squeeze," she remarked as she shrugged off her coat.

Lucky looked chagrined, but only momentarily. "I'm sorry you overheard that, but what's going on? We've had his landlord here on the lookout for him. He was to notify us when and if Chase turned up. He called about half an hour ago and said he'd seen lights on in the apartment although

Chase's truck wasn't here. We rushed over and found Chase alone and dead to the world."

"And bandaged," Devon added. "Is he seriously hurt?"

"He's certainly uncomfortable, but the injury isn't serious. He got stamped on by a bull at the rodeo in Fort Worth last night."

Marcie told them about the accident and how she had happened to be there. She avoided telling them that she had spent the night in his hospital room. She had been away from him only long enough to return to the hotel where she was checked in, shower, change clothes, and pack, then drive to the coliseum to pick up his belongings.

"This morning, when I returned to the hospital, he was terrorizing the nursing staff. He refused to be shaved. A bed bath was out of the question. He insisted on leaving."

"He's crazy!"

Devon shot her husband a withering glance. "As if you'd be a more cooperative patient. I can see you submitting to a bed bath." Turning her attention back to Marcie, she asked, "Did he just walk out?"

"He would have, but I called the doctor. He got there in the nick of time. He examined Chase and recommended that he stay in the hospital for a few days. When he realized that he'd as well argue with a brick wall, he signed a release form.

"I volunteered to drive him here and promised the doctor that I would see to it he got into bed. He gave him a prescription for pain medication—the bottle of capsules on the night-stand," she said to Lucky. "He's taken only the prescribed amount."

Obviously relieved, Laurie lowered herself to the sofa.

"Thank God you happened to be there, Ms. Johns, and took it upon yourself to look after him for us."

"Please call me Marcie."

"Thank you very much."

"It was the least I could do."

They fell silent then. What had gone unsaid was that Marcie's assistance in this matter was nominal repayment for having been driving when Chase's wife had been killed.

Devon was the first to break the uneasy silence. "What's all that?" She pointed toward the sacks standing on the bar.

"Food. There was nothing but a can of spoiled sardines in the refrigerator. Nothing at all in the pantry. I also bought some cleaning supplies."

Laurie ran her finger over the coffee table, picking up a quarter inch of dust. "I don't think this place has been touched since Tanya died."

"That's right. It hasn't."

As one, they turned to find Chase standing in the doorway. He had pulled on a bathrobe, but sturdy, lean bare legs were sticking out of it. The white bandage showed up in the open wedge of the robe across his chest. His hair still looked like he had run through a wind tunnel, and his stubble had grown darker. It was no darker, however, than his glower.

"It hasn't had any visitors either," he added, "and that's the way I want it. So now that you've had your little discussion about me and my character flaws, you can all clear out and leave me the hell alone."

Laurie, still spry even in her mid-fifties, sprang to her feet. "Now listen here, Chase Nathaniel Tyler, I will not be spoken to in that tone of voice by any of my children, and that includes you. I don't care how big you are." She pushed up the sleeves of her sweater as though ready to engage him in a fistfight if necessary.

"You look so disreputable I'm almost ashamed to claim you as my eldest son. On top of that, you smell. This place is a pigsty, unfit for human habitation. All of that is subject to change. Starting now," she emphasized.

"I'm fed up with your self-pity and your whining and your perpetual frown. I'm tired of walking on thin ice around you. When you were a boy, I gave you what was good for you whether you liked it or not. Well, you're grown, and supposedly able to take care of yourself, but I think it's time for me to exercise some maternal prerogatives. Whether you like it or not, this is for your own good."

She drew herself up tall. "Go shave and take a bath while I start a pot of homemade chicken-noodle soup."

Chase stood there a moment, gnawing the inside of his jaw. He looked at his brother. "Go get me a bottle, will you?"

"Not bloody likely. I don't want her on my tail, too."

Chase lowered his head, muttering obscenities. When he lifted his head again, his angry eyes connected with Marcie's. "This is all your fault, you know." Having said that, he turned and lumbered down the hallway toward his bedroom. The door was slammed shut behind him.

Marcie had actually fallen back a step as though he had attacked her physically instead of verbally. Unknowingly she had raised a hand to her chest. Devon moved toward her and laid her arm across Marcie's shoulders.

"I'm sure he didn't mean that the way it sounded, Marcie."

"And I'm sure he did," she said shakily.

Lucky tried to reassure her. "He wasn't referring to the accident. He was talking about bringing Mother's wrath down on him."

"He's not himself, Marcie." Laurie's militancy had abated. She was smiling gently. "Deep down he's probably grateful to you for being there last night, forcing him to do something he really wanted to do—come home. You provided a way for him to do it and still save face. We owe you a real debt of gratitude and so does Chase."

Marcie gave them a tremulous smile, then gathered up her coat and purse. "Since you're here to take over, I'll say goodbye."

"I'll walk you to your car."

"There's no need to, Lucky," she said, hastily turning to open the door for herself. She didn't want them to see her tears. "I'll call later to check on him. Good-bye."

What had been falling as sleet a hundred miles west was a cold, miserable, wind-driven rain in East Texas. Marcie drove carefully, her vision impaired by the falling precipitation on her windshield . . . and her own tears.

Chase released a string of curses when someone knocked on his door late that evening. After having been dusted, mopped, scoured, vacuumed, and disinfected, his apartment was finally clean, empty, and silent. With only himself and the nagging pain in his ribs for company, he was finishing his dinner in blessed peace.

He thought of ignoring the knock. Whoever it was might think he was asleep and go away. However, on the outside chance it was Lucky sneaking him a bottle of something stronger than tea or coffee, he left his seat at the bar and padded to the door.

Marcie was standing on the threshold, holding a bouquet of flowers. He had never seen her in a pair of jeans that he could recall. They made her legs look long and slim—thighs that seemed to go on forever.

Beneath her short, quilted denim jacket, she was wearing a sweatshirt. It was decorated with splatters of metallic paint, but it was still a sweatshirt and a far cry from the business suits she was usually dressed in.

She'd left her hair down, too. Instead of the tailored bun she had worn that morning, the flame-colored curls were lying loose on her shoulders. They were beaded with rain-drops that glistened like diamond chips in the glow of the porch light. He didn't particularly like red hair, but he noticed that Marcie's looked soft and pretty tonight.

About the only thing that was familiar were her eye-glasses. All through school, Goosey Johns had worn glasses. It occurred to him now that she must have been wearing con-tacts, even two years ago when they had been reacquainted in his office just before she and Tanya left to look at a house to-gether—the afternoon Tanya died.

"It's a cold night out," she said.

"Oh, sorry." He shuffled out of her path and she slipped past him to come inside.

"Are you alone?"

"Thankfully."

He closed the door and turned to her. Her eyes moved over him in a nervous manner that made him want to smile.

To please his mother, he had bathed and shaved and shampooed. But he hadn't dressed and was still wearing only his bathrobe.

An old maid like Marcie probably wasn't used to talking to a barefooted, bare-legged, bare-chested man, although she had demonstrated aplomb when he had come out of his hospital bed wearing nothing more than his bandage.

A hospital room was a safe, uncompromising environment compared to a man's apartment, however. Chase sensed her uneasiness and decided that it served her right for butting in where she wasn't wanted.

"These are for you." She extended him the colorful bouquet.

"Flowers?"

"Is it unmacho for a man to accept flowers?" she asked testily.

"It's not that. They remind me of funerals." He laid the bouquet on the coffee table, which Devon had polished to a high gloss earlier that afternoon. "Thanks for thinking of flowers, but I'd rather have a bottle of whiskey. I'm not particular about brand names."

She shook her head. "Not as long as you're taking painkillers."

"Those pills don't kill the pain."

"If your ribs are hurting that badly, maybe you should go to the emergency room here and check in."

"I wasn't talking about that pain," he mumbled, swinging away and moving to the bar where he had left his dinner. "Want some?"

"Chili?" With distaste she stared down into the bowl of

greasy Texas red. "What happened to the chicken soup your mother made for you?"

"I ate it for lunch but couldn't stomach it for two meals in a row."

"I bought the canned chili today thinking it would make a convenient meal in a day or two. Spicy food like that probably isn't the best thing for you right now."

"Don't nag me about my food."

He plopped down on the stool and spooned a few more bites into his mouth. Raising his head, he signaled her toward another of the barstools. She slipped off her jacket and sat down.

After scraping the bowl clean, he pushed it away. Marcie got up and carried it to the sink. She conscientiously rinsed it and placed it in the dishwasher, along with the pan he'd heated it up in. Then she moved to the coffee table, got the flowers, placed them in a large iced-tea glass, and set them down on the bar in front of him.

"No sense in letting them die prematurely just because you're a jerk," she said as she returned to her stool.

He snorted a wiseass laugh. "You're going to waste, Marcie. You'd make some man a good little wife. You're so—" He broke off and peered at her more closely. "What's the matter with your eyes?"

"What do you mean?"

"They're red. Have you been crying?"

"Crying? Of course not. My contacts were bothering me. I had to take them out."

"Contacts. I didn't realize until I saw you in your glasses

that you usually wear contacts now. Your looks have improved since high school."

"That's a backhanded compliment, but thanks."

He looked down at her chest. "You're not flat-chested anymore."

"It's still nothing spectacular. Nothing like your ladylove."

The muscles in his face pulled taut. "Ladylove?"

"The woman last night."

He relaxed. "Oh. She had big boobs, huh?"

Marcie cupped her hands in front of her chest. "Out to here. Don't you remember?"

"No. I can't recall a single feature."

"You don't remember the silver hair and magenta fingernails?"

"Nope." Looking her straight in the eye, he added, "She was just an easy lay."

Marcie calmly folded her arms on the bar. Her eyes remained steady as she leaned toward him. "Look, Chase, let me spare you the trouble of trying to insult me. There isn't a single insult I haven't heard from being called Four Eyes and Bird Legs and Carrot-top and Goosey. So you can act like a bastard when I bring you flowers and it's not going to faze me.

"As for off-color comments, I've worked with and around men since I graduated from college. I could match every dirty joke you can think of with one even dirtier. I know all the locker-room phrases. Nothing you say can offend or shock me.

"I realize that your virility didn't die with your wife, though you might have wanted it to. You have physical needs, which you appease with whatever woman is available at the time. I neither commend nor criticize you for that. Sexuality is a human condition. Each of us deals with it in his own way. No, it's not *your* behavior that confounds me, but the women who let you use them.

"You have people who care about you, yet you continue to scorn and abuse their concern. Well, I won't allow you to do that to me any longer. I've got better, eminently more satisfying ways to spend my time."

She stood and reached for her jacket, pulled it on. "You're probably too stupid to realize that the best thing that ever happened to you was that damned bull named El Dorado. It's only unfortunate that he didn't give you a good, swift kick in the head. It might have knocked some sense into it."

She headed for the door, but got no farther than his arm's reach. He caught the hem of her jacket and drew her up short. "I'm sorry." For reasons he couldn't understand, he heard himself say, "Please stay awhile."

Turning around, she glared down at him. "So you can make more snide remarks about my single status? So you can try to shock me with vulgarities?"

"No. So I won't be so damn lonely."

Chase didn't know why he was being so baldly honest with her. Perhaps because she was so honest about herself. In everyone else's eyes, she was a successful, attractive woman. When she looked in the mirror, however, she saw the tall, skinny, carrot-headed bookworm in glasses and braces.

"Please, Marcie."

She put up token resistance when he gave her arm a tug, but eventually she relented and returned to her stool. Her chin was held high, but after their exchanged stare had stretched out for several moments, her lower lip began to quiver.

"You do blame me for Tanya's death, don't you?"

He took both her hands, pressing them between his. "No," he said with quiet insistence. "No. I never wanted to give you that impression. I'm sorry if I have."

"When you came to my hospital room the morning after the accident, I asked you if you blamed me. Remember?"

"No. I was saturated with grief. I don't remember much about those first few weeks after it happened. Lucky told me later that I acted like a nut case.

"But I do remember that I didn't harbor a grudge against you, Marcie. I blame the boy who ran the stop sign. I blame God. Not you. You were a victim, too. I saw that today when you were driving us home."

He stared at their clasped hands, but he didn't really see them. Nor did he feel them as he rubbed the pad of his thumb over the ridge of her knuckles.

"I loved Tanya so much, Marcie."

"I know that."

"But you can't understand . . . nobody can understand how much I loved her. She was kind and caring. She never wanted to make waves, couldn't abide anyone's being upset. She knew how to tease enough to make it fun but not enough to hurt. Never to hurt. We had terrific sex. She made bad days better and good days great."

He pulled in a deep breath and expelled it slowly. "Then

she was gone. So suddenly. So irretrievably. There was just this empty place, vapor, where she had been."

He felt an unmanly lump forming in his throat and swallowed it with difficulty. "I told her good-bye. Gave her a hug and a kiss. Waved to her as she left with you. The next time I saw her, she was stretched out on a slab in the morgue. It was cold. Her lips were blue."

"Chase."

"And the baby. My baby. It died inside her." Scalding tears filled his eyes. He withdrew his hands from Marcie's and crammed his fists into his eye sockets. "Christ."

"It's okay to cry."

He felt her hand on his shoulder, kneading gently. "If only I had gone with you like she wanted me to, maybe it wouldn't have happened."

"You don't know that."

"Why didn't I go? What was so damned important that I couldn't get away? If I had, maybe I would have been sitting where she was. Maybe she would have been spared to have our baby, and I would have died. I wish I had. I wanted to."

"No, you didn't." Marcie's harsh tone of voice brought his head up. He lowered his hands from his eyes. "If you say anything like that again, I'll slap you again."

"It's the truth, Marcie."

"It is not," she declared, shaking her head adamantly. "If you really wanted to die, why aren't you buried beside Tanya now? Why haven't you pulled the trigger or driven off the bridge or picked up the razor or swallowed a handful of pills?" She came to her feet, quaking with outrage as she bore down on him.

"There are dozens of ways one can do away with himself, Chase. Booze and easy women and bull riding are among them. But they sure as hell aren't the fastest means of self-destruction. So either you're lying about seriously desiring death or you're grossly inefficient. All you've done effectively is fall apart at the seams and make life miserable for everyone around you."

He came to his feet, too. Grief wasn't paining his injured chest now so much as anger. "Just where the hell do you get off talking to me like this? When you've lost the person you love, when you've lost a child, *then* you'll be at liberty to talk to me about falling apart. Until that time, get out of my life and leave me alone."

"Fine. But not before leaving you with one final thought. You're not honoring Tanya with this kind of bereavement. It's unintelligent and unhealthy. For the brief time I knew her, she impressed me as one of the most life-loving people I'd ever met. She positively idolized you, Chase. In her eyes you could do no wrong. I wonder if she would have the least bit of respect for you if she could see the mess you've made of your life since she's been gone. Would she be pleased to know that you've crumpled? I seriously doubt it."

He ground his teeth so hard it made his jaws ache. "I said to get out."

"I'm going." Hastily she fished in her purse and produced a folded sheet of pink paper. She spread it open on the bar. "That's the itemized receipt from the hospital bill that I paid for you. I'll collect it in full tomorrow."

"You already know I don't have any money."

"Then I suggest you get some. Good night."

She didn't even wait for him to go to the door with her, but crossed his living room, flung open the door, and marched out, seemingly impervious to the rain. She soundly pulled the door closed behind her.

"Bitch," he muttered, sweeping the receipt off the bar with one swipe of his hand. It fluttered to his feet. He gave it a vicious kick that sent a sharp pain through his ribs. Wincing, he hobbled toward the bedroom and the bottle of pills on his nightstand.

He uncapped the prescription bottle and shook out a capsule, then tossed it to the back of his throat and swallowed it without bothering to get a glass of water.

As he was returning the bottle of pills to the nightstand, he paused. Turning the amber plastic bottle end over end, he considered taking all the capsules at one time.

He couldn't even conceive of it.

He lowered himself to the edge of his bed. Was Marcie right then? If he had seriously wanted to end his life when Tanya's ended, why hadn't he? There had been many opportunities when he'd been away from home, on the road, in the company of temporary friends, lonely, broke, drunk, and depressed. Yet he had never even thought of actual suicide.

Somewhere deep inside, he must have felt that life was still worth living. But for what?

He lifted his gaze to the framed photograph of Tanya and him taken on their wedding day. God, she had been lovely. Her smile had come through her eyes straight from her heart. He had known unequivocally that she loved him. He believed to this day that she had died knowing that he loved her. How could she not know? He had dedicated his life to never letting her doubt it.

Marcie was right in another respect—he wasn't honoring Tanya's memory by living the way he presently was. Odd, that an outsider, and not one of his own family, had read him so right and had known just what strings to pull to make him sit up and take notice of his life.

Tanya had been proud of his ambition. Since her death he hadn't had any ambition beyond drinking enough to dull his senses and cloud his memory. At first he had put in token appearances at the office of Tyler Drilling, but one morning when he'd shown up drunk while Lucky was cultivating a potential client, his brother had blown up and told him he'd just as soon not have him around if he was going to jeopardize what little business they had.

That's when he'd gone on the road, following the rodeo circuit, riding bulls in as many rodeos as he could afford to enter. He won just enough prize money to keep him in gasoline and whiskey, and that was all that mattered. One kept him away from home and the other made him temporarily forget the heartache he had left there.

His life had become a nonproductive cycle of whoring, drinking, gambling, fighting, riding bulls. Winning money, spending it. Moving from place to place, roaming aimlessly, never stopping long enough to deal with what he was running from.

The smiling groom in the photograph on the nightstand didn't even resemble him now. In fact it mocked him. How naive he'd been then, to think that life came with a guarantee of unending happiness. He studied Tanya's blond prettiness, touched the corner of her smile, and felt remorse for the shame he'd brought to her memory.

According to his mother's speech, his family's patience with him was finally expended. He had alienated all his friends. He was flat broke. He was bedding women he couldn't even remember in the morning. Like the prodigal in the New Testament, he'd reached rock bottom.

It was time he pulled himself together. Life wasn't going to be fun no matter what he did, but it sure as hell couldn't get any worse than it had been.

Tomorrow he'd talk to Lucky and find out what was going on with their business or even if they still had a business. Tomorrow he'd go see his mother and thank her for the chicken soup. Tomorrow he'd scrape up enough money to repay Marcie. That would be a start. He would take it one day at a time.

But first, he thought, as he raised the picture to his lips and kissed her image, he would cry for Tanya one more time.

Chapter Four

"Damn, Sage!" Chase shouted at his younger sister as she drove straight over a chuckhole. "My ride on that bull was nothing compared to your driving." He tentatively touched his aching ribs.

"Sorry," she said cheekily, smiling at him across the console of her car. "That hole wasn't there the last time I was in town. Nor were you for that matter. The last we had heard, you were in Montana or someplace."

Chase had been glad to see her. She had knocked loudly on his door while he was brewing a pot of coffee after a surprisingly restful night.

"Chase!" she had cried, exuberantly throwing herself against him and hugging him hard before he yelped and set her away.

"Watch the ribs."

She had swiftly apologized and joined him for coffee and toast. Since he was still without transportation, he had asked her to drive him to the company headquarters as soon as he was showered and dressed.

"How often do you come home?" he asked her now.

"Hmm, every other month maybe. But when Mother called last night and said you were home, I dropped everything and drove in."

"In this weather?"

It was still cold and wet. The rain was expected to start freezing later in the day. Weathermen in the whole northern half of the state were warning people not to drive unless it was absolutely necessary.

"I was careful. By now I know the road between here and Austin better than I know the back of my hand."

He looked at her profile, which had matured since the last time he'd really taken notice of her. "You look good, Sage," he remarked truthfully.

"Thanks." She winked at him saucily. "I come from good stock." He harrumphed dismissively. "Don't pretend you don't know we're an unusually attractive family. All my girlfriends used to positively drool over you and Lucky. They begged to sleep over, hoping against hope they'd catch one or both of you in the hallways partially unclothed, like without your shirts. I think you two are the reason I had so many friends. Girlfriends that is. You scared the boys off."

"*You* scared the boys off," he said, chuckling. It had been a long time since he'd laughed, and for a moment it surprised him. "You never learned the art of flirting, Sage."

"If you mean that I never swooned over biceps, you're right. It just wasn't in me to make out like some dolt had invented the wheel. I couldn't gush and simper and keep a straight face. Thank God Travis doesn't expect that from me."

"Travis?"

"You don't know about Travis? Oh, yeah, you haven't been home when he's come with me."

"You're bringing him home? Sounds serious."

"We're not formally engaged, but it's understood that we'll get married."

"Understood by whom? You or him?"

She shot him a fulminating look. "Both. He's going through medical school now. We'll probably wait until he's in his year of residency before we get married. He wants to be a dermatologist and make tons of money."

"By squeezing zits?"

"Hey, somebody's got to do it. His dad is a bone surgeon. Does football knees and stuff. They live in Houston in this gorgeous house that one of the Oilers used to own. It has a pond with ducks and swans in the backyard. Everybody in the family has his own BMW."

"Good. Marry the guy so you'll no longer be a liability to us."

He was on the receiving end of another dirty look. "That's almost exactly what Lucky said."

"Great minds think alike."

Sage had accelerated her academic curriculum enough to graduate a semester ahead of schedule. Chase hadn't made it to her commencement. He apologized for that now.

"Forget it. You didn't miss anything. I looked terrible in a cap and gown. Anyway, I immediately enrolled in graduate school."

"Have you decided what you're going to do with your expensive degree? Or is being Mrs. Doctor Travis whatever going to be enough for you?"

"Heck no. Being Mrs. anybody wouldn't be enough for me. I'm never going to be totally dependent on any man. I want a career like Devon. She's managed to blend her work with a happy marriage. *Very* happy, if the silly grin on Lucky's face is any indication. Even after two years of marriage, our brother is still besotted with his wife."

"I can understand that," Chase said introspectively. Sage either didn't hear him or chose to let his remark pass without comment.

"Anyway, I haven't quite made up my mind yet what I want to do. I majored in business. I'm taking graduate courses that could apply to any field."

"Corn field? Cotton field?"

"Do you want another broken rib?" she threatened.

He chuckled. "Whatever field it is, I hope it makes you rich and self-supporting."

"Amen. I want to become independently wealthy like your friend Marcie Johns."

"Is she?"

"What, wealthy? She must be. She wins all kinds of awards. Realtor of the Year. Businesswoman of the Year. Things like that. Her picture is in the paper just about every month for selling the most houses even in this depression or recession or whatever it is that we're in."

"Business major. Right," he said sarcastically.

Sage ignored that crack. "Mother said Ms. Johns looked positively radiant yesterday."

"Radiant?"

"Which I think is remarkable considering that she had a difficult time recovering from the accident. I think she had to have some plastic surgery done to cover a scar on her forehead. I heard some women in the beauty parlor speculating on whether or not she had had an eye job and a chin tuck while she was at it.

"She's . . . what? Your age, right? Thirty-five? Isn't that about the time everything starts sliding downhill? For women, I mean. Damn you men. Your looks improve with age. That's one of many grievances I'm going to bring up with God when I get to heaven. It isn't fair that y'all get better looking while we go to pot.

"But I don't believe Ms. Johns had cosmetic surgery," Sage continued. "Her self-esteem appears to be well cemented. I doubt it would be shaken by a few character lines in her face. Anyway, why would she bother? She's already gorgeous."

"Gorgeous? Goosey?" Chase was stunned. He would never have attached that adjective to Goosey Johns, but then women had different criteria for beauty than men did.

"Her hair is to die for."

Chase barked an incredulous laugh. "It looks like a struck match."

"What do you know?" Sage said with scathing condescension. "Other women pay hundreds for hennas that color."

"For what?"

"Here we are. Lucky's here, so I'll just drop you off. I promised Mother I'd run errands for her so she wouldn't have to get out today. Pat called her this morning and advised her to stay indoors."

"How is Pat?"

Pat Bush was the county sheriff. Two years earlier he'd been instrumental in clearing Lucky of a false arson charge, which had eventually brought Lucky and Devon together. For as long as the Tyler siblings could remember, Sheriff Bush had been their family friend.

"Pat never changes," Sage said. "But ever since Tanya died in that car crash, he's skittish about traffic accidents and stays after Mother to be doubly careful when she drives."

Hearing Tanya's name sent a little dart of pain through Chase's heart, but he smiled at his sister and thanked her for the lift.

"Chase," Sage called to him as he ducked under the porch roof to get out of the rain. He looked back. She had rolled down her window and was smiling at him through the opening. "Welcome back."

His sister was more mature and insightful than he had given her credit for. Her words carried a double meaning. He formed a fake pistol with his hand and fired it at her. Laughing, she put her car in reverse and backed out to turn around. They waved to each other as she drove off.

His stomach roiled with the memory of standing on this same porch and watching Tanya and Marcie drive away that fateful afternoon. He had waved good-bye then, too.

Putting aside the unpleasant memory, he stepped into the office. Though he hadn't been there in months, nothing had changed. The company office hadn't been modernized since his grandfather had occupied it. It stayed untidy, cluttered, and unabashedly masculine. Even the smells were the same, from the mustiness of old maps and geological charts to the aroma of fresh coffee. The room's cozy warmth seemed to embrace him like a fond relative he hadn't seen in awhile.

Lucky was bent over the scarred wooden desk, the fingers of one hand buried up to the first knuckle in his dark-blond hair and the others drumming out a tattoo on top of the littered desk. He raised his head when Chase walked in, his surprise evident.

"Looks serious," Chase said.

"You don't know how serious." Lucky glanced beyond his brother as though expecting someone to follow him in. "How'd you get here?"

"Sage." Chase removed his shearling jacket and shook the rain off it. "She came by the apartment this morning."

"I nearly paddled her when she showed up last night. I hated to think of her driving all that way alone in this weather."

"I would have hated it, too, if I'd known about it. But I was glad to see her. She's . . ." he searched for the right word and came up short.

"Right," Lucky said. "She's a grown-up, not a kid any longer. But she's still a spoiled brat."

"Who's Travis? Seems I'm the only member of the family who hasn't had the pleasure."

Lucky winced. "Pleasure my ass. He's a preppie wimp. The only reason she likes him is because she can lead him around by the nose."

"If he marries her, he'll have his hands full."

"You can say that again. We played so many tricks on her when she was little, she learned to fight back. I'm about half scared of her myself."

The brothers laughed. Their laughter turned poignant, until both became uncomfortable with their rising emotions.

"God, it's good to have you back," Lucky said huskily. "I missed you, big brother."

"Thanks," Chase said, clearing his throat. "I only hope I can stay. If it gets to be too much . . . what I mean is, I can't promise . . ."

Lucky patted the air with his hand, indicating that he understood. "I don't expect you to jump in with both feet. Test the waters. Take your time." Chase nodded. After a short but awkward silence, Lucky offered him a cup of coffee.

"No thanks."

"How are you feeling this morning?"

He answered dourly, "Like a damn Brahman did the two-step on my chest."

"Which is no better than you deserve for getting on one in the first place." He gestured toward Chase's chest. "Think you're going to be okay?"

"Sure," Chase said dismissively. "They've got me bound up so tight those cracked ribs wouldn't move in an earthquake. I'll be fine." He nodded toward the paperwork scattered across the desk. "How's business?"

"What business?"

"That bad?"

"Worse."

Lucky got up and moved toward one of the windows. He rubbed a circle in the condensation and gazed out at the dripping eaves. Every so often a chip of sleet would land on the porch, then quickly dissolve. Hopefully the temperature would remain above freezing.

He turned back to face the room. "I'm not sure you're in any condition to hear this, Chase."

"Will I ever be?"

"No."

"Then give it to me straight."

Lucky returned to the desk and glumly dropped into the chair behind it. "We'll have to file for Chapter Eleven bankruptcy if a miracle doesn't happen. And I mean soon." Chase's shoulders slumped forward. He looked down at the floor. "I'm sorry, Chase. I just couldn't hold it together. The few projects we had going fell apart after you left."

"Hell, don't apologize. Even in my drunkest days, I kept abreast of the Texas economy. I knew it was bad."

"Our former clients are worse off than we are. Most independent oilmen have already gone belly up. The others are dead in the water, waiting for the lending institutions to pick clean their carcasses.

"I've tried my damnedest to cultivate new clients, people from out of state who still have working capital. No dice. Nobody's doing anything. Zilch."

"So all our equipment that was replaced after the fire . . ."

"Has stood idle most of that time. We might as well have left the price tags on it. That's not the worst of it." Lucky sighed with dread. "I couldn't keep the crew on a regular payroll when they were just standing around doing nothing, so I had to let them go. Hated it like hell, Chase. I know Granddad and Dad were rolling over in their graves. You know how loyal they were to the men who worked for them. But I had no choice but to lay them off."

"It becomes a vicious cycle because that places them in a bind."

"Right. They've got families. Kids to clothe, mouths to feed. It made me feel like hell to give them notice."

"What about our personal finances?"

"We've had to cash in some of Dad's savings. Mother and Devon are good money managers. A few months ago, I sold a colt. That helped. We can go another six months maybe before it becomes critical. Of course the longer Tyler Drilling is insolvent, the more vulnerable our personal situation becomes."

Chase drew a discouraged breath. When he made to leave his chair, Lucky said, "Wait. There's more. You might as well hear all of it." He met his brother's eyes squarely, grimly. "The bank is calling in our loan. George Young telephoned last week and said they couldn't settle for only the interest payments any longer. They need us to make a substantial reduction in the principal."

Lucky spread his hands wide over the desktop. "The funds simply aren't there, Chase. I don't even have enough cash to make the interest payment."

"I don't suppose you'd consider tumbling Susan."

Susan Young, the banker's spoiled daughter, had had designs on Lucky and had tried blackmailing him into marriage. Lucky, a natural con man, had outconned her. So Chase was teasing when he brought Susan's name into the conversation, but Lucky answered him seriously.

"If I thought it would make any headway with her old man, I'd be unbuttoning my jeans even as we speak." Then he laughed. "Like hell I would. Devon would kill me." He spread his arms wide, shrugged helplessly, and grinned like a Cheshire cat. "What can I say? The broad is crazy about me."

Chase wasn't fooled into thinking the love affair was one-sided. His brother had been a ladies' man from the time he discovered the difference between little girls and little boys. His reputation as a stud had been well-founded. However, when he met Devon Haines, she knocked him for a loop. He hadn't recovered from it yet.

"From what I hear and have seen for myself, the attraction is mutual."

Chagrined, Lucky ducked his head. "Yeah. As bad as things have been, I'm happier than I ever dreamed possible."

"Good," Chase said solemnly. "That's good." Another silence fell between them. By an act of will Chase threw off his melancholia again and got down to business.

"One reason I came over this morning was to see if there was any money in the till. I find myself indebted to a certain redhead."

"Devon? What for?"

"Another redhead. Marcie. She paid my hospital bill. God knows how I'll pay her back."

Lucky stood up and moved to a filing cabinet. From the drawer he took out a savings account passbook. "This is yours," he said, handing it to Chase, who looked at it curiously.

"What is it?"

"Chase, I sold that house you had me buy after Tanya was killed."

Everything inside Chase went very still. He had forgotten all about that. He had insisted his brother buy the house Tanya had been viewing the afternoon of the accident. In retrospect he realized it had been a knee-jerk reaction to her untimely death. He hadn't given it another thought. He had never seen the house, never wanted to. He certainly never planned to live in it.

He flipped open the vinyl cover of the passbook. There was only one entry—a deposit. The amount was staggering to a man who had believed himself penniless. "Jesus, where did all this come from?"

"Tanya's life insurance policy."

Chase dropped the passbook as though it had burned his fingers. It landed on the desktop. He shot out of his chair and moved to the same position in front of the window where Lucky had stood earlier. The scenery hadn't improved. It was still a dreary day.

"I didn't know what to do with the insurance check when it finally worked its way through all the red tape and was delivered. You were still around then, but you were drunk all the time and in no condition to discuss it or deal with it, so I endorsed it by forging your name, then used it to buy the house.

"About a year ago, Marcie came to see me. She had a client who was interested in buying the property. She thought you might want to sell the house since you had never occupied it and evidently never intended to.

"You were unavailable, Chase, so I had to make the decision on my own. I decided to unload it while I could, make you a couple of grand, and bank the money until you needed or wanted it."

Lucky paused, but Chase said nothing. Finally Lucky added uncertainly, "I hope I did the right thing."

Coming around, Chase rubbed the back of his neck.

"Yeah, you did the right thing. I never wanted the house after Tanya died. The only reason I had you buy it was because she wanted it so damn bad."

"I understand. Anyway," Lucky said, shifting moods, "you've got a little nest egg you didn't know you had."

"We'll use it to pay off our loan."

"Thanks, Chase, but it won't make a dent. It'll cover the interest, but we've got to take care of the principal, too. This time, they're getting nasty."

It was too much to deal with all at once. He felt like someone who had suffered a debilitating injury and had to learn to function all over again—walk, talk, cope.

"Let me see what I can do," Chase told his brother. "Maybe if I talk to George, assure him that I'm back and ready to get busy again, we can stave them off another few months."

"Good luck, but don't get your hopes up."

Chase took the keys to one of the company pickups. It hadn't been driven in months and was reluctant to start. The cold weather didn't help any. Finally, however, he got the engine to cooperate.

As he drove away from Tyler Drilling Company headquarters, he couldn't help but wonder if it would be there much longer. As the elder son, could he live with himself if it failed?

Chapter Five

From all appearances she was a kook. She had a pixie haircut that cupped her small head, eyeglasses that covered a large portion of her face, and earrings the size of saucers clipped to her earlobes. The name plate on her desk read ESME.

"I'm sorry, but Ms. Johns has left for the day," she told Chase. "Can I help you?"

"I need to see Marcie."

He supposed he could leave the check with Marcie's secretary, but he wanted the satisfaction of handing it to her in person. She had been so snippy about it last night, he wanted to place it in her greedy little hands and finish their business with each other. He was uncomfortable feeling indebted to her.

He was in a querulous mood. His ribs were aching because he hadn't taken any of the prescribed pain medication that day. His interview with George Young had been as unpleasant as Lucky had predicted. Not only was the banker trying to protect himself from the bank examiners, but Chase suspected him of holding a grudge against the Tylers because Lucky hadn't fallen head over heels in love with his devious daughter.

George had obviously taken Lucky's rejection of Susan as a personal affront. Or, Chase thought uncharitably, maybe he was simply disappointed that Lucky hadn't taken her off his hands. The girl was bad news, and for the time being, George was still stuck with her.

Chase was stuck with a check he wanted badly to get rid of. Finding that Marcie wasn't at her real estate office didn't improve his disposition. "Where does she live?"

"Can your business wait until tomorrow?" Esme asked. "Were you wanting to see Ms. Johns about listing your house or were you interested in seeing one? The weather isn't—"

"This isn't about a house. My business with Ms. Johns is personal."

The secretary's eyes were magnified even larger behind her lenses. "Oh, really?"

"Really. What's her address?"

She eyed him up and down. He obviously passed muster because she reached for a sheet of tasteful, gray stationery with Marcie's letterhead engraved across the top and wrote down an address. "The road is probably muddy," Esme said as she handed him the piece of paper.

"It doesn't matter." The company pickup had navigated creek beds, rocky inclines, thick forests, and cow pastures to reach drilling sites. No terrain was too rough for it.

He glanced at the address, but didn't recognize it, which was unusual since he'd grown up in Milton Point and had spent his youth cruising its streets. "Where is this?"

Esme gave him rudimentary directions and he set out. His windshield wipers had to work double time to keep the rain and sleet clear. There were patches of ice on the bridges, and after skidding a couple of times, he cursed Marcie for living in the boondocks. His family lived outside the city limits, too, but at least he was familiar with that road.

When he reached the turnoff, he almost missed it. The gravel road was narrow and marked only with a crude, hand-lettered sign. "Woodbine Lane," he muttered.

The name was appropriate, because honeysuckle vines grew thickly along the ditches on either side of the road. They were burdened with a glaze of ice now, but in the spring and summer when they bloomed, they would perfume the air.

The road was a cul-de-sac. There were no other houses on it. At the end of it stood an unpainted frame structure nestled in a forest of pine and various hardwoods. The entry was level with the ground, but the house sat on a bluff that dropped away drastically. The back of the house was suspended above the ground, supported on metal beams.

He pulled the pickup to a halt and got out. His boots crunched over the icy spots on the path as he carefully picked his way toward the front door. Slipping and falling on ice wouldn't do his cracked ribs any good.

The northwesterly wind was frigid; he flipped up the collar of his lambskin coat. When he reached the front door, he took off one glove and depressed the button of the doorbell. He heard it chime inside.

In a moment Marcie pulled open the door. She seemed surprised to see him. "Chase?"

"I thought the kook might have called you."

"How did you know about the kook?"

"Pardon?"

Shaking her head in confusion, she stepped aside and motioned him in. "It's gotten worse." She commented on the weather as she closed the door against the gusts of cold wind. "How did you know where I live? Come in by the fire. Would you like some tea?"

She led him into one of the most breathtaking rooms he'd ever seen. He hadn't known there was anything like its contemporary design in Milton Point. The ceiling was two stories high. One wall had a fireplace, in which a fire was burning brightly. Another wall, the one suspended above ground, was solid glass, from the hardwood floor to the ceiling twenty or more feet above it.

An island bar separated the large living area from the kitchen. It was utilitarian; it was also designed for casual dining. A gallery encircled the second story on three sides with what he guessed were bedrooms opening off it.

"There's another room behind the fireplace wall," Marcie explained, obviously noticing his interest. "I use it as an office, although it could be a guest room. There are two bedrooms and two baths upstairs."

"You sound like a realtor."

She smiled. "Habit, I guess."

"Have you lived here long?"

"Awhile."

"Aren't you afraid to live alone in a house this large, this far out?"

"Not really. It has a security system. I'm used to the solitude." Tilting her head to one side, she said reflectively, "I guess it's rather selfish for one person to occupy so much space, but I needed the tax shelter. The property is an investment, and with the mortgage that I—"

He held up both hands. "All that stuff is lost on me. I have never understood it. Suffice it to say you've got a nice place."

"Thank you. Let me take your coat."

He hesitated; he hadn't counted on staying that long. However, the fire did look inviting. After coming all this way, he might as well stay awhile and warm up.

He shrugged out of his coat, removed his other glove, and handed them to Marcie. While she was putting his things away, he moved to the fireplace, placed one foot on the low, stone hearth, and extended both hands toward the friendly flames.

"Feels good," he said when she moved up beside him.

"Hmm. I've been curled up in front of it most of the afternoon. Not too many people are house-shopping today, so I decided it was a perfect time to catch up on paperwork."

The cushions of a sprawling cream-colored leather chair were littered with contracts and property plats, as though she'd left them there when she got up to answer the door. There was a pencil stuck behind her right ear, almost buried in a mass of hair that his sister had said was to die for. She was dressed in a soft, purple suede skirt, a matching sweater, opaque stockings . . . and fuzzy, blue Smurf house shoes that enveloped her feet up to her slender ankles.

She followed his amused gaze down to her feet. "A gag gift from my office assistant."

"The kook."

Marcie laughed. "You met Esme?"

"I stopped by your office. She gave me directions here."

"Her zaniness is a pose, I assure you. She affects it so people won't know how smart she really is. Anyway, I'm always complaining about cold feet."

"Literally or figuratively?"

"Literally for myself, figuratively for buyers who back out at the last minute."

Chase suddenly realized that the conversations he and Marcie had engaged in were the longest conversations he had had with a woman since Tanya died. After asking a woman what she was drinking, few words were exchanged until he said a terse "Thanks" and left her on a tousled bed.

The thought made him wince. Marcie misinterpreted it. "Are your ribs hurting?"

"Some," he conceded. "I've been out and around today, so I haven't taken any painkillers."

"Would you like a drink?"

His eyes sprang up to connect with hers. They held for a moment before moving down to the cup and saucer sitting on the end table next to the leather chair. "Thanks anyway, but tea's not my bag."

"If you meant that as a pun, it's terrible."

"You were the word whiz."

"Instead of tea, what I had in mind was a bourbon and water."

"Thanks, Marcie." He spoke soulfully, thanking her for the vote of confidence she had placed in him, as much as for the drink.

She moved toward the island bar and opened the cabinet beneath it. Selecting a bottle from the modest stock, she splashed whiskey into two tumblers. "The bourbon can't be any more anesthetizing than one of your pain pills. Besides, you can't sip a pill in front of the fireplace," she added with a smile. "Ice?"

"Just water." He thanked her when she handed him the glass. She stacked together the paperwork she'd been working on and resumed her seat in the leather chair, curling her feet beneath her. Nodding toward the hearth, she suggested he sit there so they could face each other.

"And while you're at it, you can add a log to the fire. That's the price of your drink."

After adding to the logs in the grate, Chase sat down on the hearth, spreading his knees wide, and rolled the tumbler between his hands. "I have a check in my pocket for five hundred seventy-three dollars and sixty-two cents. That's why I came out. I wanted to repay you in person and say thanks for all you did."

She lowered her eyes to her own whiskey and water. "I behaved badly about that. I lost my temper. It made me angry to hear you say you wished you were dead. It was a stupid thing to say, Chase."

"I realize that now."

"So you didn't have to worry about paying me back so soon. Anytime would have been all right."

He laughed mirthlessly. "I might not have the money 'anytime.' If you hadn't sold that house, I wouldn't have a red cent."

"Then you know about that, and it's okay? Lucky was concerned."

He nodded. "I never intended to live there. I'd even

forgotten about it until today." He sat up straighter and attempted a smile. "So you can credit your salesmanship for your having a check today." He extracted it from the breast pocket of his shirt and handed it to her.

"Thank you." She didn't even look to see if the amount was correct before adding it to the stack of papers on the end table. "To your speedy recovery." She raised her glass. He tapped it with his. They each sipped from their drinks.

For several moments they were silent, listening to the crackling of the burning logs and the occasional tapping sound of sleet crystals hitting the windows that overlooked the woods. Even bare of foliage, the forest was dense. Tree trunks were lined up evenly, looking as straight and black as charred matchsticks, their edges slightly blurred by rainfall.

"Who told you about my phone calls?"

He turned his head away from his contemplation of the woods and looked at her inquiringly. "What phone calls?"

Then it was her turn to appear confused. "When you came in, you mentioned the kook. I thought you were talking about the kook who keeps calling me."

"I was talking about your secretary, that Esme."

"Oh."

"Somebody keeps calling you?"

"Uh-huh."

"Who?"

"I don't know. If I did, I'd confront him and demand that he stop it."

"What does he say?"

"Oh, he likes to talk dirty and breathe heavily."

"What do you do?"

"Hang up."

"How often does he call?"

"There's no pattern. I might not hear from him for weeks, then he'll call several times in one evening. Sometimes it gets really annoying, so I take the phone off the hook. If Esme tried to call and tell me you were coming over, she couldn't have gotten through."

He followed her gaze to the telephone on the entry-hall table. The receiver was lying next to the cradle. "He called today?"

"Twice," she replied negligently. "It became a nuisance because I was trying to concentrate."

"You're sure casual about this, Marcie. Have you reported it to Pat?"

"The sheriff? No," she exclaimed, as though the suggestion were ridiculous. "It's probably just a teenager who gets his kicks by saying dirty words into a faceless woman's ear. If he had any courage, he would be saying those things to her in person."

"What kind of things does he say?"

"Very unoriginal. He'd like to see me naked, et cetera. He tells me all that he'd like to do with his tongue and . . ." She made a vague gesture. "You get the idea."

When she demurely lowered her lashes over her eyes, Chase noticed that Goosey came close to being gorgeous, as Sage had described her. With the firelight flickering over it, her skin appeared translucent. From her hairline to the vee of her sweater it was as smooth and flawless as the porcelain figurines his grandma used to keep in her china cabinet. Her high cheekbones cast shadows into the hollows of her cheeks.

"Did you have an eye job and a chin tuck?"

"What?" The question took her so by surprise, she almost spilled her drink.

"Sage said the ladies in the beauty parlor were speculating over whether or not you had an eye job thrown in when you had plastic surgery."

"No!" she cried again, truly incredulous. "They must not have much else to gossip about if I'm the hottest topic."

"Well, Lucky got married."

She laughed in earnest then. "Yes, he did keep the gossip mill churning, didn't he?"

"So you didn't have the doctor take an extra tuck or two?"

"No, I did not," she said tartly. "He just had to smooth out one scar right here." She drew an invisible mark along her hairline. "A shard of glass got imbedded there."

The inadvertent reminder of the accident put a pall over their easy dialogue. Chase considered tossing back the entire contents of his highball glass, but remembering the resolution he'd made last night, he decided against it and set it on the hearth instead. He stood up.

"Well, I'd better let you get back to work. I didn't mean to interrupt."

"You don't have to go." Unfolding her long, slender legs, she stood also. "I'm not under any kind of deadline to finish."

He looked beyond her toward the glass wall. "It's getting pretty bad out there. Now that I've done what I came for, I should head back to town."

"Hmm. Oh, by the way, the clients I was entertaining the other night called today and inquired about you. They're still interested in buying property over here."

"So you didn't lose a sale on my account."

"Doesn't look that way."

"Good."

"Do you have plans for dinner?"

He had already turned toward the door when her question brought him back around. "Dinner?"

"Dinner. The evening meal. Had you made plans?"

"Not really."

"Chili or sardines?"

He gave a lopsided grin. "Something like that."

"How does a steak sound?" She made a circle with both hands. "About this big around. This thick." She held her index finger and thumb an inch and a half apart. "Grilled medium rare."

Dinner with Marcie. Dinner with a woman. Somehow that seemed like much more intimate coupling than having a few drinks followed by a roll in the sack, which had been his only interaction with women since he lost Tanya. No thinking was required. No commitment. No conversation.

Dinner, on the other hand, involved his head. Personalities entered in. And social graces, such as looking into her eyes when you said something to her, such as being expected to say something in the first place. He wasn't sure he was up to that yet.

But this was only Goosey, after all. Hell, he'd known her since he was five years old. She'd been a good friend to him the last couple of days. Apparently she had been looking after his interests for a while, because she had saved him the hassle of getting rid of that house he had bought for Tanya. And he couldn't dismiss how polite she'd been to Tanya, and how much Tanya had liked and respected her.

He could do her this one favor, couldn't he?

"Grill the steak blood rare and you've got yourself a deal."

She broke into a smile that made her face look—what was it his mother had said? Oh, yes. Radiant.

With no coyness whatsoever, Marcie excused herself to change into something more comfortable. She returned from one of the upstairs bedrooms dressed in a sweat suit and her Smurf shoes. The pencil had been removed from behind her ear, and she had swapped her contacts for her glasses.

Once the steaks were sizzling on the indoor grill, she put Chase to work making a green salad while she monitored the potatoes she was baking in the microwave oven.

She asked if he preferred formal or casual surroundings, and when he replied, "Casual," she spread place settings on the island bar instead of on the table in the separate dining room. In no time at all, they were seated, demolishing the simple but delicious food.

"I'm afraid there's no dessert," she said as she removed his empty plate, "but you'll find my stash of chocolate chip cookies in the canister on the counter."

The telephone rang—she had replaced the receiver when she returned downstairs. As she went to answer it she called over her shoulder, "You should feel privileged, Mr. Tyler. I don't share my chocolate chip cookies with just anybody. . . . Hello?"

She was smiling at Chase as she raised the receiver to her ear. He watched her smile collapse seconds after greeting her caller. She hastily turned her back to him. Tossing his napkin down onto the bar, he left his chair and in three long strides, crossed the room.

Before he could pluck the receiver away from her, she used both hands to cram it back onto the cradle of the phone, then braced herself against it as though wanting to hold down a lid over a garbage can full of something vile.

Her head remained lowered and averted, probably out of embarrassment. She wasn't as blasé about this as she wanted him to believe. She was visibly upset, her face leached of all color.

"Was that him?"

"Yes."

"Same kind of stuff?"

"Not quite." Her color returned, spreading over her cheeks like a rosy tide. "This time, instead of telling me what he wanted to do to me, he, uh, told me what he wanted me to, uh, do to myself . . . for his entertainment."

"Damn pervert."

Chase and his brother had been reared to respect women. Both their parents had drilled into them a sense of chivalry and sexual responsibility. Even during his drunkest binges, Chase had been careful to take the necessary precautions with the women he bedded. He had never taken advantage of a woman who didn't welcome him or even one who was reluctant to have him in her bed.

In their youthful, single days Lucky and he had enjoyed

plenty of women, but always with the women's consent. They had never had to be coercive, but wouldn't have been anyway. Their father had taught them that no meant no when a lady said it. A gentleman never imposed himself on a woman, no matter what.

In Chase's book, telephone pornography was imposition, and it made him furious that Marcie was being subjected to it. Pillow talk was one thing, when you were whispering naughtily into the ear of a lover whose sexual enjoyment you were heightening. Hearing the same words over the telephone from a faceless stranger was sinister and frightening. He didn't blame her for turning pale with anxiety and revulsion.

"Is that the kind of trash you've been having to listen to?" he demanded of Marcie. She nodded and turned away, returning to the kitchen. He caught her arm and brought her back around. "For how long?"

"A few months," she said quietly.

"You shouldn't put up with that. Have your number changed. Let Pat put a tracer on your line."

He was so caught up in his argument that he didn't initially realize he still had hold of her arm and that he'd drawn her so close their bodies were touching. When he did, he released her and quickly stepped back.

He cleared his throat loudly and tried to sound authoritarian. "I, uh, just think you should do something about this."

She returned to the bar and began clearing the dishes. "I thought that after a while, if I continued simply to hang up, he would get discouraged and stop calling."

"Apparently not."

"No, apparently not." She set a stack of dirty dishes on the countertop and turned on the hot-water faucet. "You never got your cookies. Help yourself."

"I don't want any cookies," he said irritably. For reasons he couldn't explain, he was angry with her for so blithely dismissing her obscene caller.

"Then why don't you make a pot of coffee while I'm putting these dishes in the dishwasher?" she suggested. "I keep the coffee in the freezer and the coffeemaker is right there."

She nodded toward the corner of the cabinetry. Chase recognized her suggestion for what it was—a conclusion to their discussion about her caller. Obviously she didn't want to talk about it anymore. Either she was too afraid to or too embarrassed to, or hell, maybe she got her kicks by listening to smut over the telephone.

She was, after all, a woman living alone, with no boyfriend on the scene. At least none he'd heard about or seen evidence of. The only man she had mentioned was the ex-fiancé in Houston. Maybe the caller was her no-hassle, nonbinding way of getting turned on. If so, why the hell was he worrying about it?

He started the coffee. It was ready by the time she had finished clearing the dishes. Loading a tray with fresh cups of coffee and a plate of chocolate chip cookies, she asked him to carry it into the living room. They resumed their original places near the fire, which Chase stoked before eating two cookies and washing them down with coffee.

"How are things at Tyler Drilling?"

He glanced across at her. "You're a savvy businesswoman, Marcie. You probably know more about the financial climate in this town than anybody else. Is that your tactful way of asking me how much longer we can hang on before declaring bankruptcy?"

"I wasn't prying. Honestly."

"It doesn't matter," he said with a philosophic shrug. "It's too late for pride. Before long, our financial status will be a matter of public record."

"It's that critical?"

"I'm afraid so." He gazed into the fire as he thoughtlessly poked another cookie into his mouth. "We're getting no new business. The bank has become impatient for us to pay back money we borrowed years ago when the market first started going sour. They've been generous to let it go this long, but our time has finally run out.

"Lucky has done the best he could, with no help from me," he added bitterly. "A couple of years ago we started trying to think of a way to diversify until the oil business picked up, but we never came up with any workable ideas. Then Tanya died and . . ." He shrugged again. The rest didn't need clarification.

"Chase." He raised his head and looked at her. She was running her fingertip around the rim of her coffee cup. When she felt his gaze, she looked up at him. "Let me put some money into your company."

He stared at her blankly for a moment, then gave a harsh, mirthless laugh. "I thought you were a shrewd businesswoman. Why would you want to do a damn fool thing like that?"

"Because I believe in you and Lucky. You're resourceful, bright, diligent. You'll eventually think of something to revive the business. When you do, I'll reap a tremendous profit on my investment."

Before she had finished, he was adamantly shaking his head. "I couldn't let you do it, Marcie. It would be like taking charity, and we haven't stooped that low yet. At this point we can retain a little pride.

"Besides, if we had wanted a partner, we would have considered that option a long time ago. We've even had offers, but always turned them down.

"My grandfather started this business during the thirties boom. My dad continued it. We're third generation. Tyler Drilling Company is a family operation, and we mean to keep it that way."

"I see," she said quietly.

"I appreciate your offer, but there's just no way I can accept it."

"There is one way." Her steady blue gaze locked with his. "You could marry me."

Chapter Six

Lucky replaced the telephone receiver and to his wife said, "He still doesn't answer."

From the doorway that connected their bedroom with the bath, Devon tried to reassure him. "That doesn't mean he's vanished again."

"But it might mean he's out getting blitzed."

"Not necessarily."

"Not *necessarily*, but probably."

"You're not showing much confidence in your older brother," she gently rebuked him.

"Well, in the past two years, name one thing he's done to inspire my confidence."

Devon turned on her bare heels and stamped into the bathroom, closing the door behind her so swiftly that it almost caught the hem of her peignoir.

Lucky went storming after her and threw open the door. Rather than finding her confrontational, she was seated at the dressing table, calmly pulling a hairbrush through her dark-auburn hair. Her loveliness squelched his anger.

She was an expert at igniting and defusing his temper and could do both instantly and effectively. Her reversals always came unexpectedly. That spontaneity made his life interesting and was one of the reasons he had fallen in love with her. Devon's unpredictability appealed to his own volatile nature.

He loved her madly, but hated when she was right. In this instance she was.

"That was a rotten thing for me to say, wasn't it?"

"Hmm," she replied. That was another thing he liked about her—she never rubbed it in when she'd been right. "He did come home, Lucky."

"Under duress."

"But it couldn't have been easy for him."

"He wasn't exactly dragging his tail between his legs."

"Wasn't he? I believe all his mumbling and grumbling was to cover up how embarrassed he was to show how glad he was to be home, surrounded by people who love him."

"Maybe," Lucky conceded.

"He went to the office today and showed an interest in the business."

"Which might be only a token interest."

"It might be. But I don't think so." She set her hairbrush aside and uncapped a jar of night cream. Extending her arm, she began spreading on the scented cream. "I think we should give Chase the benefit of the doubt. Maybe he's finally begin-ning to heal."

"I hope so."

Lucky took the jar of cream from her, scooped some out

with his fingers, and began smoothing it on where she had left off. He pushed her robe off her shoulders, slipped down the straps of her nightgown, and massaged the cream into skin so smooth it really didn't need extra emollients.

"Well, Laurie is encouraged by his coming home. That in itself makes me glad he's back." Devon bowed her head and moved aside her hair so he could rub her neck.

"But Mother doesn't know that he's out carousing tonight."

"Neither do you. He could be anywhere."

"It's not exactly a good night to take a drive."

"Even if he is out carousing, he's a grown man and accountable only to himself." She looked up at him through her lashes, speaking to his reflection in the mirror. "Just like you used to be."

"Humph," he grunted.

Lucky's attention had been diverted to his wife's alluring image in the mirror. The neckline of her nightgown had caught on the tips of her breasts. A single motion of his hand left the nightgown pooled in her lap, her breasts completely bare.

Both hands reached around to caress her. He watched his hands reshape, lift, stroke, and massage her breasts. When his touch began to have an effect, his own veins expanded with desire. "What did the doctor say today?" he asked in a soft voice.

"Baby and I are doing well," she told him, her lips curving into a madonna's sweet smile. "I'm a full five months."

"How long do you think we can keep it a secret?" His hands smoothed over the convex curve of her abdomen.

"Not much longer. If Laurie hadn't been so preoccupied with Chase, she probably would have noticed my thickening waistline."

"She and Sage are going to be mad as hell that we didn't tell them as soon as we found out."

"Probably. But I still think doing it this way was better. In case something happened."

"Thank God nothing has." He bent his head and kissed her shoulder.

"I don't believe Laurie could have withstood the loss of another grandchild. It was better that we not tell her we were expecting until I was out of the dangerous first trimester."

"But now you're into the second and the doctor doesn't expect any complications." He met her eyes in the mirror and smiled as he splayed his hand over her lower body. "I want to announce to the world that I'm going to be a daddy."

"But think of this, Lucky," she said, her smile gradually fading. "Now that Chase is home, maybe we should put off making an announcement for a while longer."

"Hmm." His eyebrows drew together. "I see what you mean. It's going to be tough on him to hear that we're going to have the first Tyler offspring."

Taking his hand, Devon kissed the palm. "You know how much I want our baby. But my happiness is clouded whenever I think of the child that died with Tanya."

"Don't think about it," Lucky whispered.

He drew her up, turned her around, and kissed her while he rid her of the peignoir. After stepping out of his briefs, he pulled her against him, letting her feel the strength of his erection. She sighed against his lips and suggested that he not waste any more time before taking her to bed.

Reclining together, he opened her thighs and kissed her there, testing her moisture with the tip of his tongue. Then he kissed his way up her body, pausing first to lay kisses across the slight mound of her abdomen, then lightly sucking the tips of her breasts, darkened and enlarged from pregnancy. At last he reached the welcome heat of her mouth and sent his tongue deep even as his sex delved into hers.

Marriage hadn't dimmed their physical passion for each other. It burned hotter than ever. Within minutes they both lay replete and satisfied.

Holding her close, Lucky gently stroked the area of her body where his child was nestled. He whispered, "In light of what he lost, how can I blame Chase for anything he does or doesn't do?"

"You can't," she answered, patting his hand. "You can only be patient until he finds a solution to his heartache."

"If there is a solution." He didn't sound too optimistic.

Devon stirred and said in that stubborn way of hers he found so endearing, "Oh, I have to believe there is."

Chase finally recovered his voice. His disbelieving stare was still fixed on his hostess. "What?"

"Are you going to make me repeat it?" Marcie asked. "All right. I said that you could save your business *and* keep it in the family if you married me. Because then, whatever I had would be yours."

He returned his unfinished cookie to the plate, dusted the crumbs off his fingers, and stood up. Quickly retrieving his coat, he pulled it on and started making his way toward the front door.

"Don't you think it warrants some discussion?" Marcie asked, following him.

"No."

She caught up with him before he could pull open the front door, placing her slim body between it and him. "Chase, please. If I had enough gumption to suggest it, the least you could do is have enough gumption to talk about it."

"Why waste my time and yours?"

"I don't feel like a discussion of my future is a waste of time."

He slapped the pair of chamois gloves against his other palm, trying to figure out how he was going to get away from there without hurting her feelings.

"Marcie, I don't know what prompted you to say such an outlandish thing. I can't imagine what was going through your mind. I'd like to think you were joking."

"I wasn't. I was serious."

"Then you leave me no choice but to say no thanks."

"Without even discussing it?"

"Without anything. It doesn't bear talking about."

"I disagree. I don't go around whimsically proposing marriage to eligible men. If I hadn't thought it was a workable idea, I would never have mentioned it."

"It *isn't* a workable idea."

"Why not?"

"Damn," he muttered with supreme exasperation. "You're forcing me to be unkind."

"If you have something to say, don't worry about sparing my feelings. I told you yesterday that I have a tough veneer when it comes to insults. They bounce right off me."

"Okay," he said, shifting from one foot to the other, but keeping his eyes on hers, "I'll be blunt. I don't want to get married again. Ever."

"Why?"

"Because I had a wife. I had a child. They're lost to me. No one can take Tanya's place. And besides all that, I don't love you."

"I couldn't possibly hope to take Tanya's place. In any event, I wouldn't want to. We are two entirely different individuals. And I certainly never imagined that you love me, Chase. People get married for a variety of reasons, the least of which, I believe, is love."

He stared at her, dumbfounded. "Why in hell would you want that, though? Knowing that I don't love you, that I'm still in love with my wife, why would you make such an offer?"

"Because, as you've pointed out numerous times just over the course of the last couple days, I'm an old maid. And even in this day and age, no matter how progressive our thinking, if you're a single person, you're odd man out. It's still a couples' world. People move through life in pairs. I'm tired of being a party of one."

"That argument doesn't wash, Marcie. You told me yesterday that you almost got married but backed out at the last minute because you didn't love the guy."

"That's true. But that was several years ago. I was still in my twenties."

"So?"

"So now I'm thirty-five. A thirty-five-year-old single who is either divorced or widowed isn't that much of a rarity. Even a thirty-five-year-old bachelor doesn't attract much attention. But a woman who is still unmarried at thirty-five is an old maid, especially if she lives alone and rarely goes out." She cast her eyes downward and added softly, "Especially if she's Goosey Johns."

Chase mumbled another curse. He regretted ever calling her that. He could argue now that the nickname no longer applied, but she would think he was just being kind.

"I know I'm not a raving beauty, Chase. My figure isn't the stuff fantasies and centerfolds are made of. But I can give you what you need most."

"Money?" he asked scathingly.

"Companionship."

"Get a dog."

"I'm allergic to them. Besides, we're talking about what you need, not what I need," she said. "We're friends, aren't we? We always got along. I believe we'd make a good team."

"If you want to be part of a team, join a bowling league."

His sarcasm didn't faze her. "You've had a year and a half of wandering, and though you haven't admitted it, I think you're sick of being a nomad. I can give you stability. I have a home," she said, spreading her arms to encompass the house. "I love it, but it would be so much nicer if I were sharing it with someone."

"Get a roommate."

"I'm trying."

"I meant another woman."

"I would hate living with another woman." She laughed without humor. "Besides, God only knows what the gossips of Milton Point would say about me if another woman moved in here."

He awarded her that point because she was right. Generally speaking, people were small-minded and always looking for scandal even where there wasn't any. But that was Marcie's problem and he wasn't the solution to it.

Still, chivalry required him to let her down easy. If nothing else, he respected her for having the courage to broach the subject of marriage with him. It couldn't have been an easy thing for her to do. She had had to swallow a hell of a lot of pride.

"Look, Marcie—"

"You're going to say no, aren't you?"

He blew out a gust of air. "Yeah. I'm going to say no."

She lowered her head, but raised it almost immediately. There was challenge in her eyes. "Think about it, Chase."

"There's nothing to think about."

"Tyler Drilling."

He placed his hands on his hips and leaned in close. "Don't you realize what you're doing? You're trying to buy a husband!"

"If I'm not worried about that, why should you be? I've got lots of money. More than I need. What am I going to do with it? Who am I going to leave it to? What good has it done me to work hard and achieve success if I can't share the dividends with someone who needs them?"

Jerking on his gloves, he said, "You won't have to look hard to find somebody. I'm sure there are plenty of men around who'd love a free ride."

She laid her hand on his arm. "Is that what you think this is about? Do you think I'd want you under my roof if you were content to be a kept man? Not on your life, Chase Tyler! I know you'll continue to work as hard as you ever have. I'm not trying to rob you of your masculinity or your pride. I don't want to be the man of the house. If I did, I would be satisfied to leave things as they are."

She softened her tone. "I don't want to grow old alone, Chase. I don't think you want to either. And since you can't marry for love, you'd just as well marry for money."

He contemplated her earnest face for a moment, then shook his head. "I'm not your man, Marcie."

"You are. You're exactly what I want."

"Me? A broken, beaten man? Bad tempered? Bereaved? What could you possibly want me for? I'd make your life miserable."

"You didn't make me miserable tonight. I liked having you here."

She just wasn't going to let him do this gracefully, was she? The only alternative she had left him was to say an abrupt no and get the hell out. "Sorry, Marcie. The answer is no."

He yanked open the door and went out into the storm. After hours of sitting idle, the truck was more reluctant than ever to start. It finally came to life and chugged home. The apartment was dark and cold.

Chase undressed, brushed his teeth, took a pain pill, and climbed between frigid sheets. "Marry Goosey Johns!" he muttered as he socked his pillow several times. It was the craziest notion he'd ever heard of, a ludicrous idea.

Then why wasn't he doubled over laughing?

His brother arrived at his apartment close on the heels of dawn. "Hi. You all right?"

"Why wouldn't I be?" Chase replied crossly.

"No reason. I just wondered how your ribs were feeling this morning."

"Better. Want to come in?"

"Thanks."

Lucky stepped inside. Chase shut the door. He could tell, though Lucky tried to pretend otherwise, that he was under close scrutiny. Stubbornly Chase refused to make it easy on his brother. After a lengthy silence Lucky finally got to the point of the early visit.

"I called here several times last night, but never got an answer."

"Checking up on me?"

Lucky looked chagrined.

"I was out."

"I gathered that much."

"I had dinner out."

"Oh, dinner."

Chase quickly lost patience with their beating around the bush. "Why don't you come right out and ask, Lucky?"

"Okay, where the hell were you?"

"Over at Marcie's."

"Marcie's?"

"I drove out to repay her for the hospital bill and she invited me to stay for supper."

"Well, if that's all it was, why didn't you just say so?"

"Because it wasn't any of your damn business."

"We were worried about your being out last night."

"I don't need a keeper!"

"Oh, yeah?"

By now they were shouting. Each brother's temper was as short as the other's. Yelling at each other was nothing new. Nor was it uncommon for them to reconcile just as quickly.

Chase shook his head, chuckling. "Maybe I do need a keeper."

"Maybe you *did*. Not any longer."

"Sit down."

Lucky plopped down in a living room easy chair across from his brother and immediately directed the conversation to their common worry. "How'd your meeting at the bank go yesterday?"

"George Young is a son of a bitch."

"Are you just now realizing that?" Lucky asked.

"I don't blame him or the bank for wanting their money. It's that sympathetic expression on his sanctimonious puss that I can't stomach. I think he's actually enjoying our situation."

"I know what you mean. He puts on this woeful, gee-I'm-sorry act, but he's laughing up his sleeve."

"Know what I'd like to do?" Chase said, leaning forward, bracing his forearms on his knees. "I'd like to take a big box of cash in the full amount we owe him and dump it on top of his desk."

"Hell, so would I." Ruefully Lucky smacked his lips. "When pigs fly, huh?"

Nervously, Chase's fingers did push-ups against each other. "You said yesterday it would take a miracle to get us out of this fix."

"Something straight from heaven."

"Well, uh . . ." He loudly cleared his throat. "What if, uh, the angel of mercy looked like, uh, Marcie Johns?" Lucky said nothing. Finally Chase lifted his wary gaze to his brother. "Did you hear me?"

"I heard you. What does it mean?"

"Say, do you want some coffee?" Chase came halfway out of his chair.

"No."

He sat back down.

"What has Marcie got to do with our predicament?" Lucky wanted to know.

"Nothing. Except . . ." Chase forced a laugh. "She offered to help us out."

"Christ, Chase, the last thing we need is another loan to repay."

"She, uh, didn't exactly offer to make us a loan. It was more like an investment."

"You mean she wants to buy an interest in the business? Become a partner?" Lucky left his chair and began to pace. "We don't want another partner, do we? You haven't changed your mind about that, have you?"

"No."

"Well, good, because I haven't either. Granddad and Dad wanted the business to be kept in the family. I'm surprised

Marcie even thought of it, and I appreciate her interest, but I hope you explained to her that we didn't want anyone outside the family in on our business."

"Yeah, I explained that, but—"

"Wait a minute," Lucky said, whipping around. "She's not thinking about a hostile takeover, is she? She wouldn't pay off the bank and expect to move in whether we liked it or not, would she? Jeez, I never even thought of that."

"Neither did Marcie. At least I don't think so," Chase said. "That wasn't what she proposed."

Hands on hips, Lucky faced his brother. "What exactly did she propose?"

There was no way around giving Lucky a straight answer now. He reasoned that if Marcie could be blunt, so could he. "She proposed marriage."

"Excuse me?"

"Marriage."

"To whom?"

"To me," he answered querulously. "Who the hell do you think?"

"I don't know what to think."

"Well, she proposed to me."

"Marcie Johns proposed marriage to you?"

"Isn't that what I just said?" Chase shouted.

"I don't believe this!"

"Believe it."

Lucky stared at his brother, aghast. Then his eyes narrowed suspiciously. "Wait a minute. Where were you at the time? What were y'all doing?"

"Not what you're thinking. We were having coffee and chocolate chip cookies."

"You weren't—"

"No!"

Lucky lowered himself into the chair again. A long moment of silence ensued while Lucky stared at Chase and Chase attempted to avoid the stare. Finally Lucky asked, "Was she serious?"

"Seemed to be."

"Son of a gun," Lucky mumbled, still obviously dismayed.

"She had her arguments all lined up. Friendship, stability, stuff like that. And of course, the, uh, money."

Lucky shook his head in amazement, then began to laugh. "I can't believe it. She actually said she would give you money in exchange for marrying her?"

"Well, sort of. Words to that effect."

"Can you beat that? I've heard when it comes to business, she's got brass balls, but who would have thought she'd do something like this? What did you say to her? I mean"—he paused and winked—"I assume you said no."

"That's what I said, yeah."

This time Chase was the one to stand and begin pacing. For some unnamed reason, Lucky's laughter irritated him. He suddenly felt the need to defend and justify Marcie's proposal.

"You shouldn't make fun of her," he said tetchily. "If she had stripped naked in front of me, it couldn't have taken more nerve than doing what she did."

Lucky caught his brother by the arm and drew himself up

even with him. "Chase, you can't be thinking what I think you're thinking."

Chase met his brother's disbelieving eyes and surprised himself by saying, "It's a way out of this mess we're in."

Lucky stared at him speechlessly for a moment, then reacted in his characteristic, short-tempered way. He shoved his face to within an inch of Chase's.

"Have you completely lost your mind? Has all that whiskey you've consumed over the last several months pickled your brain? Or did a kick from that bull jell your gray matter?"

"Is this a multiple-choice question?"

"I'm not joking!"

"Neither am I!" Chase slung off his brother's hand and spun away from him. "Think about it. Name one single, productive thing I've done since Tanya died. You can't. No one can. You've told me as much to my face. My lack of initiative has put the family business on the brink of bankruptcy."

"This slump has got nothing to do with your private life," Lucky cried. "Or your lack of initiative or anything else except a collapsed oil market."

"But I'm still the elder son," Chase argued, repeatedly stabbing his chest with his index finger. "I'm the one who's accountable, Lucky. And if Tyler Drilling goes down the tubes, it'll be on my conscience for the rest of my life. I've got to do whatever I can to prevent that from happening."

"Even going so far as to marry a woman you don't love?"

"Yes. Even going that far."

"You wouldn't have let me marry Susan Young two years

ago to save us from rack and ruin. Do you think I'd let you do something so foolhardy?"

"You won't have any say in the matter."

It suddenly occurred to him that he was arguing strenuously in favor of Marcie's plan. Since when? His subconscious must have dwelt on it all night. Sometime before he woke up, he had made up his mind that her idea wasn't so unworkable after all.

Lucky let loose a string of obscenities. "You're not over Tanya yet, Chase. How can you think of becoming involved with another woman?"

"I don't intend to become involved. Not emotionally anyway. Marcie knows that. She knows I'm still in love with Tanya, and she's willing to settle for companionship."

"Bull. No woman is willing to settle for companionship."

"Marcie is. She's not the romantic type."

"All right, and why is that? I'll tell you why. Because she's an old maid who—as a last resort—will buy herself a husband."

"She's not an old maid." It made Chase unreasonably furious to hear Lucky verbalize the very thoughts he had entertained twelve hours earlier. "It's not easy for a woman as successful as Marcie to find a man who isn't threatened by her success." That argument popped into his head and he was inordinately pleased with it.

"Okay, forget that for the time being," Lucky said, "and think of this. She's probably buying herself a clear conscience, too. Remember, she was driving when your beloved wife was killed."

Chase's face went white with fury. His gray eyes took on the cold sheen of slate. "The accident wasn't Marcie's fault."

"I know that, Chase," Lucky said patiently. "You know it. Everybody knows it. But does *she*? Has she reconciled that yet? Is she trying to do something charitable to ease her burden of guilt, even though it's self-imposed?"

Chase ruminated on that for a moment before speaking. "So what if she is? We'll still both benefit from the marriage. We'll each be getting what we want. Tyler Drilling will be in the black again and Marcie will have a husband and a clear conscience."

Lucky threw up his hands in a gesture of incredulity and let them fall back to his thighs with a loud slapping sound. "Do you even like this woman, Chase?"

"Yes, very much," he said truthfully. "We were always good pals."

"Good pals. Great." Lucky's disgust was apparent. "Do you want to sleep with her?"

"I haven't thought about it."

"You'd better think about it. I'm sure she has. I'm reasonably sure that sex is part of the bargain." Lucky used Chase's temporary silence to drive home his point. "Sleeping with a tramp one night and moving on the next day is different from sleeping with someone you have to face over the Cheerios."

"Thanks for the lesson on women, little brother," Chase sneered. "I'll make a note of it in case I ever need your words of advice."

"Dammit, Chase, I'm only trying to get you to think this through. You'll pay off the bank loan immediately, but you'll be committed to Marcie for life. Unless you plan to dump her once she's fulfilled her part of the bargain."

"I'd never do that!"

"But you've said you still love Tanya."

"I do."

"So every time you take Marcie to bed, it'll be out of obligation, or worse, pity. It'll be a charity—"

"If you finish that sentence, I'll knock the hell out of you." Chase's index finger was rigid and aimed directly at his brother's lips. "Don't talk about her that way."

Lucky fell back a step and gazed at his brother with disbelief. "You're defending her, Chase. That means you've already made up your mind, haven't you?"

In that moment Chase realized that he had.

Chapter Seven

"Thank you for coming, Pat."

Laurie Tyler ushered Sheriff Pat Bush into her kitchen. He was "back-door company." She would have been insulted if he'd gone to the front door and rung the bell. All her married life, Pat had been a good friend to Bud and her. Bud had died several years earlier of cancer, but Pat had remained a steadfast family friend. He could be relied on in times of need. As now.

"What's going on? You sounded upset when you called." He set his brown felt Stetson on the kitchen table and shrugged off his uniform jacket, draping it over the back of his chair before sitting down. Laurie set a mug of coffee in front of him. "Thanks. What's the matter, Laurie?"

"Chase is getting married."

The rim of the mug was already at Pat's lips. Her stunning announcement gave him a start. He burned his tongue with hot coffee. "Getting married!" he exclaimed.

"That's right. Pat, I'm so upset I don't know what to do."

"Who's he marrying? A gold digger claiming he gave her a kid or something like that?"

"No, no, nothing like that," Laurie told him, sadly shaking her head.

Her hair was pale. Formerly blond, it was now softened to beige by the addition of scattered white strands. It was cut short and fashionably styled. She could pass for ten years younger than she was. Her slim figure was the envy of her peers, and her blue eyes were animated and lively. Now, however, they were dulled by concern for her oldest child.

"He's marrying Marcie Johns."

The startling revelations were coming so quickly one after the other that drinking hot coffee proved hazardous. Pat lowered his mug to the table. "Marcie Johns," he whispered. "Son of a gun. Talk about irony."

"Yes, isn't it?"

"How'd that come about?"

Laurie told him what she knew, beginning with Marcie's driving Chase from Fort Worth after his injury and concluding with a verbatim account of a telephone call she'd had from Chase earlier that afternoon.

"He said they'd decided to get married the day after tomorrow in Judge Walker's chambers. He suggested that Sage stay in town if she wanted to be present and if she could afford to miss her classes. He said Marcie wanted her parents to come up from Houston for the ceremony. They were concerned about the roads being clear between here and there."

"Roads! He's fixin' to get married when he's just come off a two-year drinking binge brought on by the death of his wife, and he's worried about roads?"

"That's my point," she said, her voice cracking emotionally. "I don't think he knows what he's doing."

Pat pulled a large, calloused hand down his face. It was a full face, rather ruddy, but he was considered nice looking. He still had a full head of hair, though it was as much gray as brown.

Dozens of women in Milton Point had pined for him through the years. He had dated a few off and on, but the nature of his work and the commitment it demanded had kept him a bachelor. He had more or less adopted the Tyler kids as his own. That's why he shared Laurie's concern for Chase now. He remembered the extent of the young man's suffering when his wife had been killed.

"You want me to talk to him, Laurie?"

"It wouldn't do any good," she said sorrowfully. "Lucky tried talking sense to him this morning. Lucky said the more he argued the reasons against Chase's marrying right now, the more stubborn Chase became that it was the right thing for him to do.

"Naturally Sage had several firm opinions on the subject when I told her. I had to threaten her to within an inch of her life if she said anything to him. Lord only knows what she would spout off.

"Nobody is taken with the idea, but I don't want this to cause a rift in the family when we've just gotten Chase back. He might close doors on us that would never be opened again." Tears began to shimmer in her eyes.

Pat reached across the table and covered her hand with his. "I didn't realize Chase knew Ms. Johns that well."

Laurie dabbed at her eyes with a tissue. "They were class-mates. They didn't see each other after high school gradua-tion because her parents moved to Houston. She and Chase didn't become reacquainted until Tanya started house hunt-ing right before she was killed.

"Don't get me wrong, Pat. It's not Marcie I object to. I think she's perfectly charming. She's turned into a beautiful woman and she's always been smart as a whip." Her pretty face drew into a frown. "That's why I can't understand why she would let herself in for this."

"You lost me on that one."

"Well, according to Lucky, who called right after I spoke with Chase, Marcie asked him to marry her, not the other way around."

"You don't say."

Laurie recounted to Pat everything that Lucky had told her.

"He's marrying her for the money," Pat observed when she was done. "He's doing it to save Tyler Drilling."

"So it seems. That's why I'm so upset. Whether con-sciously or not, Bud and I instilled that sense of responsibility into Chase. He takes everything to heart, assumes every-body's burdens."

"That's usual for an oldest child, Laurie."

"I know, but Chase takes it to the extreme. After Tanya was killed, he blamed himself for not going with her that af-ternoon, believing that if he had been there, she wouldn't have died."

"That's crazy."

"Yes, but that's the way he is. He takes everyone's problems onto himself. He probably feels guilty for abdicating his business responsibilities over the last eighteen months. This is his way of making up for that. I had hoped his coming home would mark a new beginning. I didn't count on its taking this form.

"He's committing himself to years of unhappiness in order to save Tyler Drilling. And he's sentencing Marcie to misery, too. I can't imagine what her motivation is. But I know beyond a shadow of a doubt that Chase is still in love with Tanya. Just like with Bud and me. I didn't stop loving him when he died."

Unobtrusively, Pat withdrew his hand from hers. He sat quietly and let her cry for a moment before asking, "What do you want me to do, Laurie?"

She raised her head and gave him a watery smile. "What you're doing. Listening. I needed to talk to somebody. Devon hasn't been feeling well lately—something else that's worrying me. Lucky loses his temper, gets mad, and stamps around cursing under his breath and ramming his fist into his palm. Sage talks off the top of her head and says things that only cause me more distress. I needed someone solid like you to listen."

Smiling ruefully, Pat rubbed his hand over his slight paunch. "That's me. Solid. Glad to be of service though. You know I promised Bud before he died to look after his kids. I've a good mind to yank Chase up by the collar and after I've shaken some sense into him, give him a good thrashing. If for no other reason than for putting you through hell all these months."

"He'd probably thrash you back." She gave a shaky little sigh. "They're not children anymore, Pat. They're grown-ups. They make their own decisions, and there's little or nothing I can do about it, even when I think they're making a terrible mistake."

Her tenuous smile gradually receded as she gazed into her dear friend's face. "Oh, Pat, what can Chase possibly be thinking to do this?"

Waiting outside Judge Walker's chambers, Chase was wondering what he could possibly be thinking to do this.

The last two days had been so hectic he hadn't really had time to let the reality sink in. Perhaps he had subconsciously made things hectic so he wouldn't have to dwell on it.

Marcie had received his decision with more equanimity than he had anticipated. Shortly after his dispute with Lucky, he had gone to Marcie's real estate office. Esme, wearing a solid green dress with purple tights, announced him. Marcie was in her inner office, thumbing through the biweekly multiple-listings book.

As soon as Esme had withdrawn he said, "I think you had a good idea last night, Marcie. Let's get married."

He hadn't expected her to throw her arms around him, cover his face with ardent kisses, and blubber thank-yous through her streaming tears. He hadn't expected her to prostrate herself at his feet and pledge undying fealty.

But he had expected a little more enthusiasm than a handshake.

"Before we shake on it," he had said, "I have one stipulation." She seemed to catch her breath quickly and hold it, but he might have imagined that because her face remained calm. "I will pay back every cent you put into Tyler Drilling."

"That's not necessary."

"It is to me. And it is to this marriage's taking place. If you can't agree to that, the deal's off. It might take me years to do it, but you'll get your money back."

"It will be our money, Chase, but if that's the way you feel about it, that's how it will be."

They had sealed the agreement with a very unromantic, businesslike handshake. From there, things had snowballed. They notified their families and cleared the date on the judge's calendar.

Although it could have been postponed to a more convenient time, Chase vacated the apartment where he had lived with Tanya from the day they were married. A few weeks after her death, her family had come in and disposed of the things he hadn't wanted to keep, so he was spared having to deal with that.

It hadn't taken long for him to pack his belongings and move them to Marcie's house. In effect, moving had sealed off his escape hatch—the reason, perhaps, why he had done it. There was no backing out.

There was one awkward moment during the move.

"This is my bedroom," Marcie had told him as she opened the door to a large, cozy room. The wall behind the bed was covered with fabric that matched the bedspread and drapes. A chaise lounge in the corner was also upholstered in a complementary fabric. Her bedroom wasn't as starkly contemporary as the rest of the house's decor. It was feminine without being cloying and fussy, a pleasant mix of warmth and spaciousness.

His gaze moved to the bed, and he instantly felt uncomfortable. "Where's my bedroom?"

"There."

She had pointed toward a closed door on the opposite side of the gallery. It was into that room that Chase moved his belongings. Marcie hadn't extended him a specific invitation to share her room. He was relieved. He was spared having to tell her no.

Ever since Lucky had mentioned sleeping with her, Chase had given it a great deal of thought. She hadn't come right out and said it, but she obviously expected them to have a sexual relationship. At first he couldn't imagine writhing naked with Goosey Johns, but once he got used to the idea, he reasoned that it wouldn't be all that bad.

She was an attractive woman. He was a man with a healthy sex drive. Looking at it from a purely pragmatic standpoint, he figured he could have occasional sex with her without too much difficulty.

Sharing a bedroom, however, was an intimacy reserved for his wife. Even though he was about to take vows legally bestowing that title upon Marcie, in his heart Tanya would forever be his wife. He might periodically share a bed with Marcie, but he would sleep in another room.

In addition to moving from the apartment there had been

blood tests to take, a license to buy, his brother to argue with, his mother to reassure, his sister to keep from murdering if she shot off her smart mouth about his questionable sanity one more time, and a new dark suit to buy.

Because of a fortunate break in the weather, his in-laws had arrived the night before and taken Marcie, him, and his entire family to dinner at the Milton Point Country Club. The couple were almost giddy over their only child's finally getting married. They seemed so pathetically relieved that she wouldn't end up an old maid, Chase felt embarrassed for Marcie. Theirs were the only two happy faces at the table.

To her credit, Laurie had done her best to make the strained occasion convivial. Pat Bush had been there to lend moral support. Devon, too, had kept the conversation going when it flagged, but had displayed her nervousness with an enormous appetite, which became the butt of several jokes.

Under threat of death, Sage had kept her opinions to herself. At the end of the evening when she hugged her prospective sister-in-law good night, one would have thought Marcie was a woman doomed to the gallows rather than a bride on her way to the altar.

Lucky had kept a civil tongue, but his thoughts had been telegraphed by his perpetual glower. It was obvious that he believed his brother was making a dreadful mistake.

Chase wondered if that was true as he glanced at the woman standing beside him now. Marcie wasn't hard on the eyes at all. In fact, she looked beautiful. She was dressed in a white wool suit that somehow managed to look soft and bridal in spite of its tailored lines. Her hair was pulled up, and she was wearing a small hat with a veil that reached her nose. Behind it her blue eyes were sparkling and smiling.

"Nervous?" she asked him.

"Uncomfortable," he said. "I didn't have time to get the coat of this suit altered. It's snug."

She reached up and ran her hand across his shoulders. "That's the price you pay for having such broad shoulders."

Chase jumped reflexively, but he wasn't sure if it was because of Marcie's unexpected and very wifely touch or because the receptionist chose that moment to tell them the judge was ready for them.

They filed into the hushed, paneled chamber—the bride and groom, Marcie's parents, all the Tylers, and Pat Bush. It was an austere gathering.

Chase's thoughts were pulled back by tethers of memory to the lovely, candlelight church wedding Tanya and he had had. Her large family had filled up the first several pews. It had been a happy occasion, though both mothers had cried a little into dainty lace handkerchiefs that Tanya had embroidered and given to them as gifts.

No one in attendance could have doubted their love for each other. Tanya had looked breathtakingly beautiful as she glided down the aisle in her white gown. They had pledged each other love and faithfulness until death—

"Will you, Chase, take Marcia Elaine Johns to be your lawfully wedded wife? Will you love her, honor her, protect and keep her for as long as you both shall live?"

The question plucked Chase from his sweet reverie and cruelly thrust him into the present. He stared at the judge, who looked back at him with puzzlement. Then he looked down into Marcie's expectant face.

"I will."

The judge posed the same questions to Marcie. She responded in a soft, solemn voice. They exchanged the simple gold bands they had purchased together yesterday. The judge pronounced them man and wife, then said to Chase, "You may kiss your bride."

And Chase's heart stumbled over its next beat.

He had slept with countless women since Tanya's death, but he hadn't kissed a single one. Somehow that melding of the mouths seemed more intimate and personal than climaxing while inside a female body. Kissing was done face-to-face, eye-to-eye, and required some measure of participation from both parties.

He turned toward his bride and took her shoulders between his hands. He lowered his head a fraction. He paused. Their small congregation seemed collectively to hold its breath.

He couldn't look into Marcie's eyes because he didn't want to see her anxiety or censure. So he concentrated on her lips. Well-shaped lips. The color of peaches in the family orchard when they're ready to be picked. Soft looking and now, slightly tremulous.

He bent his head and touched them with his. They were pliant enough to make him curious and tempting enough to make him cautious. He yielded to the former and pressed against them a trifle more firmly. Then he quickly pulled back. She smiled. So did he. But his smile felt wooden.

Thankfully, he was hastily embraced by Marcie's mother. Mr. Johns enthusiastically pumped his hand, welcoming him into their small family. While saying something appropriate to his new mother-in-law, he reflexively whisked his tongue across his lips . . . and was shocked to taste Marcie there.

Chapter Eight

"When did your folks say they're going back to Houston?"

"In the morning."

Chase helped Marcie out of her fur jacket and hung it on the coat tree just inside her front door . . . *their* front door. "What's their hurry? Why don't they stick around for a few days?"

"Since they retired, all they do is play golf. They don't like to break golf dates. Besides, they felt as if being in town would put a damper on the honeymoon."

"Oh." He slipped out of his suit jacket. Glad to be rid of it, he flexed his arms, rolled his shoulders and loosened the knot of his necktie. "Should we open the champagne?"

"Why not?" Her gaiety sounded forced. She removed her hat and set it on an end table, then went for glasses. "It was thoughtful of Devon and Lucky to give it to us. Especially since he's so against our marriage."

"What makes you say that?" He popped the cork on the champagne and poured it into the stems she held out to him.

"Are you kidding? I'd have to be blind not to see his disapproval. He scowls every time he looks at me."

"It's not you he's scowling at. It's me. His reservations have nothing to do with you. He's afraid that I'm going to make us both very unhappy."

"Are you?"

Their eyes connected. Though her mouth was softly curved into a smile, he could tell that her question wasn't flirtatious or frivolous. "I'm going to try my best not to, Marcie."

"That's enough for me." She clinked her glass against his. Holding their stare, they sipped the cold, biting champagne. "Hungry?" she asked.

"Sort of."

Turning her back on him, she went into the kitchen. As she moved away from him, Chase noticed that the slender skirt of her suit fit her fanny very well. Good legs, too. He loosened his necktie even more and wondered why the heat was turned up so high.

To distract himself from his growing uneasiness he said, "Besides, Lucky has his nerve to criticize me when it comes to choosing a wife. Devon was married when they met."

"I remember. It was quite a scandal at the time. His alibi for the arson crime was a married woman he'd spent the night with."

"There were extenuating circumstances."

"Yes, I know. Seeing them together now, no one could doubt that they're made for each other." When she opened the refrigerator, she exclaimed, "Oh, my! Look, Chase!" She held up a large, cellophane-wrapped basket filled with cheeses, fresh fruit, a box of chocolates, and even a small canned ham.

"There's a card." Opening the white envelope, she read aloud, " 'With love and best wishes for your happiness.' It's from your mother and Sage. Wasn't that sweet?"

He joined her at the island bar where she was unwrapping the cellophane. "It certainly was."

He was feeling unusually benevolent toward his sister because she had saved him from making an unforgivable faux pas. Earlier that day, she had asked him what kind of bouquet he'd arranged for Marcie to have. Shamefaced, he had admitted that a bouquet hadn't even crossed his mind.

In a panic Sage had said she would take care of it. Two hours later, and in the nick of time, she had returned with the bridal bouquet of white roses, white lilacs, and baby's breath, which Marcie had gently laid on the island bar beside the gift basket.

Obviously, going to the florist hadn't been the only errand Sage had run for him. Seeing the pleasure on Marcie's face as she unwrapped the goodies made him grateful to his mother and sister for thinking of it.

"They must have delivered it while my parents were here. I'd gone to the hairdresser. Here, want some cheese?" She held a cube of baby Swiss up to him and he ate it from her fingers. His stomach took a nosedive when he felt her fleeting touch against his lips.

"Thanks."

"You're welcome. Newlyweds usually do this with wedding cake."

"We should have had a cake."

"It doesn't matter. I like doing things untraditionally." She was smiling, but he sensed a tinge of sadness in her voice. It disappeared quickly. She even gave a soft laugh. "You'll stay hungry if I feed you every bite. Why don't you build a fire and I'll fix us each a plate. I was too nervous to eat much lunch."

By the time he had a fire burning brightly, she joined him in the living room, carrying two plates filled with crackers, cheese, wedges of apple and pear, and sliced ham.

She stepped out of her shoes and took off the jacket to her suit, making herself comfy in the leather chair she'd been sitting in seventy-two hours ago just before proposing to him.

In what he hoped was a good omen, the sun had come out that afternoon for the first time in days. By now, however, it had already slipped beneath the horizon, and the sky beyond the wall of windows was a deep lavender. There was a generous moon, but the light it cast looked brittle and cold.

Inside, by contrast, enveloped in the fire's glow, they were warm. Marcie shone as bright as the firelight, Chase noticed as he methodically ate from the plate she had fixed him. Her skirt and blouse were almost the same ivory color as the leather she was cushioned by. The monochromatic background set off the vibrant color of her hair. Her blouse was silk, he guessed, and soft looking. It conformed to her shape in a tantalizing, yet modest, way.

"Chase?"

Her hesitant voice brought his eyes up from her breasts. "Hmm?"

"Are you wondering what I look like without my clothes on?"

His mouth dropped open and stayed that way for several seconds. Then he closed it and smiled with self-derision. "I guess I was, subconsciously. Consciously I was thinking how pretty you look in the firelight. Your coloring matches it. Even your eyes. They're the same color as the blue in the flames."

"I wasn't fishing for compliments."

"I know."

She set her plate aside and picked up her glass of champagne, which he had already refilled. She gazed into the bubbly wine as she asked, "Have you ever wondered what I look like without my clothes on?" Before he had a chance to reply, she hastily added, "Never mind. I know you haven't." She took a quick drink of champagne.

"Actually I have."

"You have?"

"Yep."

"When?"

"When we were in eleventh grade, I believe. It was the end of the year. Awards day. You walked across the stage to receive one of your many awards. As class president I was seated on the stage. You walked right in front of the spotlight, which was at the back of the auditorium. For several seconds you were cast in silhouette and I caught your profile. I remember thinking then, as a randy seventeen-year-old boy is wont to do, what you looked like naked."

She laughed a low, throaty laugh. "I wondered if you noticed." His baffled expression made her laugh again. "I knew exactly where you were sitting. As I passed you, I stuck out my chest on purpose."

"No fooling?" She nodded. "Why?"

"I guess I was trying to get your attention. Little good it did me," she remarked, brushing a nonexistent crumb from her skirt. "Your curiosity wasn't strong enough for you to try to find out what I looked like naked."

"Well, I was going steady with somebody else then. I think it was Linda—"

"No. Debbie Aldrich."

"Oh, right, Debbie. We broke up that summer right before our senior year."

"And then you started dating Lorna Fitzwilliams."

He shook his head. "How do you remember that?"

"I remember," she said softly. After draining her champagne, she left the leather chair. "Would you like some chocolates or should we leave them for tomorrow?"

"Tomorrow. I'm full."

She smiled girlishly. "Okay. It'll give us something to look forward to." Leaving her jacket and shoes where she had discarded them, she headed toward the stairs in her stocking feet. "I'll go on up."

"Okay."

"See you in a minute then." There was a trace of inquiry at the end of her sentence.

"Sure. I'll just, uh, bank the fire."

She continued upstairs. When she reached the door to her bedroom, she looked down at him from the gallery and smiled beguilingly before disappearing through the bedroom door and closing it behind her.

Chase rubbed his palms up and down the thighs of his dress slacks. Then he gathered their dishes and carried them into the kitchen. He conscientiously replaced the gift basket in the refrigerator. Dutifully, he checked the doors to make certain they were locked. He set the alarm system. He banked the fire.

When there was nothing left to do, he headed upstairs. About halfway up, he changed his mind. Retracing his steps, he returned to the island bar, took a bottle of whiskey from the cabinet beneath it, and only then went to his room.

In the connecting bath, he filled the toothbrush glass with whiskey and downed it in one swallow. The liquor brought tears to his eyes and stung his esophagus, but spread a welcome heat through his midsection. It did little to relieve his anxiety, however.

How the hell was he going to get through this?

Damn his brother! Lucky had either been dead-center correct or else had planted a self-fulfilling thought in Chase's head. Either way, a one-night stand was altogether different from a wedding night.

The woman waiting for him in the next bedroom wasn't just a warm body. She was a personality, a smile, a heart that didn't deserve to be broken. But he had only so much to give and he feared it wasn't going to be enough.

Dammit, she had known that.

She had asked for this.

She had said that she would take whatever he had to give and expect nothing more.

With that in mind he removed his shirt but left his slacks on. The bandage around his middle showed up very white against his tanned chest and dark trousers. He took off his shoes and socks. He raked a hairbrush through his hair. He brushed his teeth. He splashed on some cologne. For good measure he threw back another shot of whiskey.

Then he sat down on the edge of his bed and stared at the door. It was like when he was a kid, knowing he had to get a shot and waiting in the doctor's reception room. Dreading it was the worst part. That's when the stomach fluttered and the palms sweat. The longer he put it off, the worse it became. Best to get it over with. He got up, left his room, and marched down the gallery. He knocked on her closed door.

"Come in, Chase."

There were burning candles and vases of fresh flowers scattered throughout the room. The combination smelled wonderful, as intoxicating as the whiskey.

His eyes made a wide sweep of the room before stopping abruptly on Marcie. She was an angelic vision where she stood beside the king-size bed, which had already been turned down to reveal satin sheets the pastel color of the inside of a seashell.

Her peignoir was pale and silky. The shape of her body was outlined beneath it. Through it, he easily located the centers of her breasts and the delta of her thighs. She had taken down her hair. With candlelight shining through it, it looked like a halo surrounding her head. But the look in her eyes wasn't innocent. Not by a long shot.

Mentally Chase groaned. She was making this out to be something special, a typical wedding night made for lovers.

"I thought you might like more champagne." She indicated a silver ice bucket on the nightstand. In it was an unopened bottle that she must have brought up ahead of time. There were two tall tulip-shaped crystal glasses standing beside it.

"No thanks," he said gruffly.

"All right."

This was no doubt where the bridegroom was supposed to seize the initiative. Moving stiffly, he crossed the room until he reached her. He knew he was expected to say something nice. "I like your . . . your thing." He gestured down at the nightgown.

"Thank you. I hoped you would."

A kiss was called for. Okay. He could handle that. He'd been kissing girls for decades.

Placing his arms around her, he drew her forward—stopping short of bringing their bodies together—and kissed first her forehead, then her cheek, and finally laid his lips upon hers.

Hers parted invitingly. Her breath was sweet and clean. He experienced a flurry of curiosity. Should he acknowledge it, gratify it? Should he slip his tongue into her mouth? It would be the kind and considerate thing to do.

But no. No sense in taking this thing any further than it was required to go. He kept his lips resolutely closed and after a few seconds, raised his head. It had been about as dry, uninspired, and sterile a kiss as one could bestow. Yet his heart was knocking.

That erratic heartbeat forced him to admit that the emotion keeping him from intimately kissing her was fear—the cold, stark fear that once he started, he wouldn't be able to stop. He'd had one taste of her today, and the essence had lingered on his lips for hours. If he indulged that sudden craving now . . .

Another thought suddenly occurred to him, more terrifying than the previous one. What if he couldn't get an erection? Even at his drunkest he had never failed to perform sexually. Of all the women he had bedded, none could fault him when it came to physical preparedness. Knowing Marcie as a friend might make a difference.

Dear Lord, he hoped not. The fear of failure paralyzed him.

Marcie must have sensed that he was having difficulty of some sort. Smiling tentatively, she crossed her arms over her chest and slowly lowered the thin straps of her nightgown from her shoulders, pulling them down her arms until she was bare to her narrow waist.

Her breasts were high and round and pale. She had possibly the pinkest nipples he had ever seen. And the most sensitive. Because when she removed her nightgown and the air touched them, they shriveled and darkened to an even deeper shade of pink. They became very hard.

Chase's mouth began to water. He swallowed to keep from drowning. His body quickened behind the fly of his slacks and he felt a surge of relief.

Marcie let her nightgown slide to the floor. Gracefully, she stepped out of the circle of fabric and faced him naked. Her feet were high arched and slender. Her long legs were almost coltishly thin, but well shaped. There was a definite flaring curve to her hips, but they weren't voluptuous.

What drew his eyes like a magnet, however, was the cluster of ginger curls between her thighs. It was a lush, wanton, feminine sight. He touched it with the back of his fingers. Springy. Alive. Alluring.

His veins exploded with raw desire. A torrent of blood flowed into his groin. That's when he realized he needed to rush this. Otherwise he was apt to explore every inch of her porcelain skin, take her nipples into his mouth, nuzzle that fiery cloud between her thighs. He was liable to make a damn fool of himself over his good pal, Goosey Johns.

"Lie down, Marcie," he whispered thickly.

Hastily he went around the room blowing out the candles, because if he tried this with the lights on, it might not work—and at that moment he desperately wanted it to work.

He removed his own clothing, fumbling in the dark, and slipped on a condom. When he lay down beside her, she moved into his arms willingly. She felt incredibly dainty and crushable as he moved on top of her and opened her thighs.

His entry was so hard and swift, he thought he might have hurt her, but she made no sound except for a long, serrated sigh when he began to move inside her.

No, dammit, no. I'm not supposed to like it.

He couldn't like it. Couldn't enjoy. Couldn't luxuriate. Had to hurry. Had to get it over with before it became habit-forming. Before he wanted to do it all night. Before he wanted to do it every night for the rest of his life.

He pumped feverishly. Gasping for breath, he ducked his head. His cheek accidentally grazed one of her pointed nipples. Turning his head slightly—just to help him get it over with quickly—he flicked it with his tongue.

That did it. It was over.

As soon as his head had cleared and he had regained his

breath, he got up and groped for his clothing. Retrieving it, he headed for the door.

"Chase?" He heard the rustle of the satin sheets and knew she must have sat up.

"My ribs hurt. I'll be tossing and turning all night. Don't want to disturb you," he mumbled.

He ducked out, closing the door behind him, feeling as if he had escaped from the most deadly, most delicious torture a man could endure.

Chapter Nine

Raising her head from the sink after bathing her face in cold water, Marcie gazed at her reflection in the mirror. It was a disheartening sight. Having silently cried most of the night, her eyes were puffy and red. Without the enhancement of cosmetics her skin looked washed-out and sallow. She looked every day of her thirty-five years.

She asked her reflection how she could possibly have hoped to entice a handsome, virile man like Chase who could have any woman he wanted. Even the tramp who had come to see him in the hospital had had a better chance of pleasing him than skinny, freckled Goosey Johns.

Salty tears filled her eyes again, but she refused to submit to them. She lowered her body into the hot bath she had drawn. The soothing water eased the soreness between her thighs. His lovemaking had been quick, but it had also been hard and intense.

As she lathered her body she assessed it critically. Cupping her breasts in her hands, she lifted them, wishing they were heavier, fuller. She even considered surgery to enlarge them, but discarded the idea as rapidly as it formed. Big boobs were not going to make Chase Tyler love her.

She despaired that nothing ever would.

It was a bone-deep despair that she had lived with for almost as long as she could remember.

Leaving the tub, she dried herself and began to dress.

Ever since grade school Chase had been her ideal, to whom none other compared. Along with everybody else he had called her Goosey, but somehow, coming from him it had never sounded cruel. She had imagined that he used her nickname with a degree of affection.

Of course she was someone he would never have thought of dating. It was an unwritten law that class favorites never dated class geeks. That would have been taking friendliness and kindness too far.

Graduating from Milton Point High School with her love still unrequited, she had entered college with the hope of finding a boy among her classmates who would equal or surpass Chase Tyler. She had actively dated—college men didn't seem as bent on dating the beauty queens as high school boys—but she had entered graduate school without finding anyone to supplant Chase in her heart or mind.

It actually came as a relief when her parents left Milton Point and moved to a retirement community near Houston. No longer was she required to take trips home where she invariably heard about the romantic escapades of Chase and his brother or saw him in town, always squiring a beautiful woman.

When she heard that he had married, she cried for two whole days. Then, pulling herself together and pragmatically charting a course for the rest of her life, she decided that carrying a torch was one thing, but obsession was another. It was mentally unhealthy and emotionally demoralizing to pine for a man who didn't know or care that she was alive.

Soon after reaching that momentous decision, she launched her career in residential real estate. Within her first year she had the third-best sales record in the whole Houston metropolitan area. The following year she was number one and held that position for two more consecutive years.

She met the man to whom she would later become engaged. Following that debacle, she decided to begin her own agency, and to the dismay of her parents and friends, she decided to establish it in Milton Point where her only real competition was a nonaggressive, family-owned firm that had been in business for so long, they'd become complacent.

She had been back in Milton Point for two years before Chase's wife had sought her services. Tanya McDaniel Tyler had been lovely, inside and out. Marcie had been inordinately pleased to meet her. She felt better knowing that Chase was married to someone who so obviously adored him.

She had never seen them together, however. The hardest thing Marcie had ever had to do was go into the office of Tyler Drilling and shake hands with Chase as though he were nothing more than a classmate she hadn't seen in a long while.

He had pulled her into his arms and hugged her. She touched him, smelled him, and her heart had nearly burst. He seemed genuinely glad to see her. But he had kissed his wife and held her lovingly while Marcie's heart was breaking.

Then Tanya had died in the passenger seat of her car. While lying injured in the hospital, Marcie had prayed to God for an explanation. Why had he done that to her? Why had he laid on her conscience the death of the woman whose husband she lusted after and loved?

She had vowed then that she would make up his loss to him.

And now, as she descended the stairs, she made that same pledge. She would do anything to restore Chase to the vital man he'd been before the accident, even if it meant having him make love to her when she knew that only his sex organ was involved, not his mind, certainly not his heart.

He turned when she entered the kitchen. "Morning." His eyes didn't stay on her for more than a millisecond before flickering away.

"Good morning, Chase. Did you sleep well?"

"Fine."

"You're up early."

"Habit."

"If I'd known you were up, I'd have been down sooner."

"It's okay. I've got the coffee started. Shouldn't be more than a few more minutes and it'll be ready."

"How are your ribs?"

"My what?" He turned.

She nodded at the bandage swathing his bare chest. He was dressed only in a pair of old, faded, button-fly Levi's jeans. Looking at them made her knees weak. The soft cloth molded to his shape, defining his sex. "Your ribs. You said last night that they were hurting you."

"Oh, yeah, right." Turning his back, he opened several

cabinet doors until he located cups and saucers. "They're better this morning."

So his excuse for leaving her bed last night had been a fabricated one. He simply hadn't wanted to sleep with her. Even though he had moved his things into the extra bedroom, she had hoped that once they had made love . . .

Speaking above the ache in her throat, she asked, "What do you like for breakfast?"

"Coffee."

"I don't mind cooking you something. Just tell me what you want."

"Nothing, really. Only coffee."

"Sit down. I'll pour it."

He sat on a stool at the bar. Several moments later she joined him there. They sipped their coffee in silence. Their eyes connected once, briefly.

Was this how it was going to be? Would they occupy the same house, share rooms, breathe the same air, have periodic sex, but live the lives of quiet desperation that Thoreau had written about?

"The sun's coming out again today," she commented inanely.

"Maybe it'll warm up."

"Maybe." After another teeming silence she asked, "What are your plans today?"

"I told Lucky I'd meet him at the office midmorning. He told me I didn't have to feel obligated to come in on account of its being, well, you know, the day following my wedding, but I told him it didn't matter. . . . Does it?" he asked after a brief pause.

"No, no, of course not." She hoped he wouldn't notice how shaky her smile was. "I intended to go to my office, too."

"Well, then, guess I'd better go finish dressing and get on my way." He set down his cup and stood up.

"Maybe you should go see a doctor today about your ribs."

He touched the bandage. "I might. This thing is bugging me. About time it came off."

While he was upstairs, Marcie sat staring into her cooling coffee and trying not to weep with frustration and disappointment. She had hoped that they would spend the day together, not necessarily in bed, as was customary with newlyweds, but getting to know each other.

She had entertained fantasies of his being so taken with her that he couldn't tear himself away, of their lying in bed all day, exploring each other's nakedness with eyes and hands and mouths, going without food and water for long stretches of time in which they appeased another appetite that was scandalously voracious.

That was a fantasy all right. He was leaving for work. It was business as usual. Just another, ordinary day. To his mind, his part of the bargain had been fulfilled. Reminded of that, she left the bar and went into the room she used as an office.

By the time he returned downstairs, she was waiting for him at the foot of the staircase. She held his sheepskin coat for him as he slid his arms into the sleeves.

"What time will you be home this evening?" she asked as she patted the fleece collar into place.

"About five."

"Is dinner at six okay?"

"That's fine."

Reaching inside his coat, she slipped a white envelope into the breast pocket of his shirt. Leaving her hand lying against his chest, she came up on tiptoe and quickly kissed his lips. "See you then."

He bobbed his head once, abruptly. "Yeah, see you then." He rushed toward the door as though the house were on fire.

Because she never went to the office this early in the day, Marcie sank down onto the hearth, took the poker in hand, and dejectedly stirred the live coals beneath the cold ashes. After she carefully fed them kindling, they ignited.

Watching the new flames devour the logs, Marcie wished she could ignite her husband's passion as quickly and easily. Right now it seemed hopeless, but if there was a way, she was determined to find it. She had overcome the—mostly unintentional—cruelties of her childhood peers. Successfully, she had earned the respect of her colleagues and amassed a fortune. She was no longer looked upon as merely Goosey Johns.

All her other goals, however, paled in comparison to making Chase love her. The money she had bartered with was insignificant. She had gambled much more—her pride, her womanhood, her future happiness. With that much at stake she simply had to make it work.

Chase tapped the white envelope against his opposite palm several times before working his finger beneath the flap and opening it. The check was written on her personal account, made out to him personally. She'd had the sensitivity not to make it directly to the bank, thereby sparing his pride. Leave it to her to handle the transaction in a face-saving manner. The amount of her check was generous, more than he needed. The excess would provide operating capital for several months.

With a trace of irritation he tossed the check onto the desk and moved to the window. He sightlessly stared through the cloudy glass.

He felt like a heel. He *was* a heel.

She hadn't uttered a single word of censure or complaint, but he knew he must have hurt her last night, emotionally for sure, and perhaps even physically.

Unaware of it, she had grimaced slightly when she sat down on the barstool. He had left her tender if not in pain; that made him feel like a brute. It had been on the tip of his tongue to express his concern over her discomfort, but he hadn't wanted to broach the subject of their wedding night. Not in any context.

Because if they talked about her physical pain, they might touch upon her emotional battering, and that would have been too difficult for him to handle. He could promise never to hurt her again physically. But emotionally?

It had been readily apparent that she expected them to spend the day together at home. She had said she planned to go to her office, but since when did she wear silk lounging pajamas and ballet slippers to the office?

He couldn't spend the day alone with her and stay away from the bedroom. No way in hell. So, like a gutless coward, he had left her feeling badly about herself, little knowing that he had run not because last night had been so bad, but because it had been so damn good.

Yeah, Marcie probably thought he'd left her bed last night because he'd been repulsed, when, in fact, the opposite was true.

Shoving his hand through his hair, he cursed. Up to last night he hadn't felt guilty about this marriage. Now he felt guilty as hell. Guilt had made his stomach queasy. Guilt was eating at his entrails like an insidious bacteria.

"Face it," he hissed to himself, "last night you didn't want to leave her bed." That's why he hadn't trusted himself to stay. She'd been so tight, so . . . God, help him. He had wanted to make love to her a second time. A third. That hadn't happened to him since Tanya.

He pressed his forehead against the cold pane of window glass and squeezed his eyes shut, trying not to remember how Marcie had looked wearing nothing except the golden, wavering glow of candlelight. Porcelain and fire.

Inside his jeans he grew stiff, thinking of her impudent nipples. He had wanted to test them against the tip of his tongue, suck them into his mouth, tug . . .

He was so lost in the fantasy, he hadn't seen Lucky's Mustang as it rounded the bend in the road and pulled to a halt outside. Chase jumped when his brother bounded in, shedding his jacket before he was fully inside.

Lucky stared at him stupidly. "What are you doing here?"

"I work here."

"Don't play dumb. What are you doing here today? Where's your bride?"

"Probably at her office by now."

"Kind of a short honeymoon, wasn't it?"

Chase frowned at him in a way that he hoped would quell his curiosity. Lucky, however, had never been daunted by his brother's intimidating frowns. "How'd it go?"

"What?"

"Have you gone dense?" Lucky cried impatiently, resting his hands on his hips. "Last night. How was it?"

"Do you expect a blow-by-blow account?"

Lucky's face broke into a wide grin. "Is that particular choice of words significant?"

"None of your damn business."

Lucky barked a laugh, drawing his own conclusions. The check on the desk caught his eye. He picked it up, read the amount, whistled. "Well, you must have done something the lady liked. And done it real good."

"That's not funny." Chase snatched the check from his brother's hand. "Keep your filthy mind off my wife and out of my personal business."

Still chuckling, Lucky went to the hot plate and poured himself a cup of the coffee Chase had brewed. "Careful, big brother. I'm beginning to think all those rationalizations you piled up for marrying Marcie were just so much crap."

"Go to hell." Chase rounded the desk and sat down. "If you're done with being cute and cocky, read that."

He had previously circled an article in the business section of the morning newspaper. When Lucky had finished reading it, Chase asked, "What do you think?"

"I don't know," Lucky said, his brows steepling. "They're from out of state. They don't know us."

"They don't know any locals. That's why they're soliciting bids for drilling equipment and know-how."

"It says they're operating on a shoestring budget."

"A shoestring is better than nothing. Thanks to Marcie's, uh, loan, we can come in with a low bid. We might not clear much, but it would be something."

For the first time in two years, Chase felt a rising excitement about his work. There was a glimmer of optimism on the horizon. A contract, any contract, would do his tottering ego a world of good. Apparently his excitement was contagious.

Lucky grinned. "Hell, why not? We've got nothing better to do. Let's go for it."

Chapter Ten

Eager to discuss the business prospect with Marcie as soon as he got home, Chase rushed through the front door at five to five, loudly calling out her name.

"Oh, there you are," he said when he spotted her standing near the hall table. He hooked his jacket on the coat tree. "Guess what? Today I was reading about these—" Getting his first good look at her face, he drew up short. "What's the matter?"

"Nothing." Looking stricken, she turned away abruptly. "You sound enthusiastic about something. Come into the kitchen and tell me about it."

At first he was mystified by her strange behavior. Then he noticed the telephone on the table. The receiver was off the hook. "Did you get another call?" She ignored his question, so, as he repeated it, he caught her by the upper arm and pulled her around to face him. "Did he call again?" Swallowing visibly, she nodded yes. "What did he say?"

Lowering her eyes to the open collar of his shirt, she shrugged. "More of the same. Nasty propositions. Lewd scenarios."

"Why didn't you just hang up?"

"Because I thought if I listened, I might be able to place his voice among the men I know."

"Did you?"

"No."

"That's not all, is it?" He tipped his head down until he could read her eyes. "Come on, Marcie. What else?"

"He . . . he said that my being married won't make any difference. He plans to keep calling."

"You told him that you got married?" he asked incredulously.

"Of course not. He already knew."

"Christ." Chase realized now why this particular call had upset her so much. "That means the guy is keeping mighty close tabs on you. He knows what you do and when."

"It doesn't mean anything of the sort. It only means he reads the newspaper. Our wedding announcement was in this morning's issue." She gave him a faltering smile. "Now, let's not let him spoil the rest of our evening. I'll fix you a drink and you can tell me your news."

He followed her into the kitchen. "I'm going to call Pat and have him put a tap on our line."

"I'd rather you wouldn't, Chase."

"Why?"

"Because I don't want all our telephone conversations to be overheard. Clients often talk to me about their personal business and financial affairs. That's privileged information intended for my ears only. Sooner or later, the caller is bound to get discouraged and stop calling."

"In the meantime he scares you spitless every time he calls."

"I'm not scared. Just annoyed."

"Marcie, I saw your face. I know the difference between fright and annoyance. You were scared."

Acting on instinct, he pulled her into his arms. Once again he was impressed by how fragile she felt within his embrace. He rested his chin on the top of her head while his arms slid around her waist and linked at the small of her back.

"I hate to think of some sicko creep jacking off while he's whispering dirty words to you."

A shudder rippled through her. She turned her head so that her cheek was lying against his chest. Raising her hands, she lightly rested them on either side of his waist. "I appreciate your concern."

They stayed that way for several moments. Holding her began to feel so good that Chase warred with himself over whether or not to sweep her into his arms and carry her up to bed.

She needed comforting. Wasn't that the least a husband could do for his wife, comfort her when she needed to feel safe and protected?

The only thing that stopped him was the niggling suspicion that providing comfort might not be his only motivation for wanting to take her to bed. He seriously doubted that once they were lying down they would stay dressed for long or that his caresses would remain entirely noble.

Thankfully Marcie relieved him of having to make the

choice. She eased away from him, but left her hands at his waist. She tentatively flexed them, then relaxed them, repositioned them, flexed again.

"Your bandage is gone."

"I went to the doctor today. He stripped off the tape, examined me, and pronounced me well."

"Did it hurt?"

"It didn't feel good. But it didn't hurt as bad as it would have if they hadn't shaved me before they wrapped me."

She winced. "Ouch! I can imagine."

"Oh, yeah?" he asked teasingly. "I didn't notice any chest hair on you last night."

At the inadvertent reminder Chase lowered his gaze to her breasts. She was wearing a thick sweater, but his memory penetrated her clothing like X-ray vision.

In vivid color he envisioned the milky mounds of her breasts and their delicate pink centers, that shallow groove that bisected her rib cage into perfect halves, the smooth slope of her belly, and that beguiling, downy delta between her thighs.

He turned his groan into a loud, unnatural-sounding cough. Marcie moved to the bar and mixed them each a drink. Handing him a whiskey and water, she said, "You seemed excited when you came in. Sit down and tell me what's up."

He doubted she really wanted to know. Or maybe she already did. They had been standing very close. How could she not have felt his arousal pressing against her middle?

He observed her as she went about preparing dinner. Her cheeks looked abnormally rosy, but that might have been caused by the simmering pans on the cooktop. Steam was rising from one of them, causing the tendrils of hair on either side of her face to curl.

Willfully tamping down his misplaced desire, Chase told her about the prospect they had for a drilling contract. "Lucky and I spent all day working up a proposal. We submitted what we think is a rock-bottom bid. All we can do now is wait."

"I'll keep my fingers crossed." She drained the boiling pasta in a colander in the sink.

"Sell any houses today?"

"They don't sell just like that, you know," she said over her shoulder.

"Show any?"

"Unfortunately, yes."

"Unfortunately?"

"I've been working with this couple for months. The Harrisons. They still haven't made a decision. About the only thing they agree on is their penchant to argue. I doubt I'll ever get them to sign a contract on a house. Oh, and I talked with Sage. She called to say good-bye before she left for Austin."

"Good riddance."

"Chase! She adores her big brothers."

"She's a pain in the backside."

Her expression told him that she didn't take his invective seriously. "After Sage said good-bye, Laurie got on the phone. She invited us out to lunch Sunday. I accepted."

"Fine."

"She also said she would love for us to join her at church."

She had her back turned, ladling an aromatic sauce over the platter of pasta. When he didn't immediately respond, she swiveled her head around. "Chase?"

"I heard you," he said tersely. "I just don't like the idea of church. I haven't been inside one since Tan . . . since the funeral."

Marcie's posture improved to the point of rigidity. For a moment she was still. Then she set down the ladle, turned, and spoke to him directly.

"It's up to you how you resolve your anger with God, Chase. But I must say this. Your first wife's name was Tanya. She is a fact of our lives. We can't continue to dance around her name. I'm not going to feel sick and grow ghastly pale every time it's spoken out loud."

"But I might."

Marcie recoiled as though he had struck her. She did, in fact, grow ghastly pale. Even her lips lost their color. She spun around and braced herself against the countertop as though she might slide to the floor, unable to support herself.

Instantly regretting what he'd said, Chase left his seat and moved up behind her. "I'm sorry, Marcie," he said hoarsely.

He raised his hands and considered laying them on her shoulders, but he couldn't bring himself to. He thought of planting a conciliatory kiss on the nape of her neck where several curling strands of hair had escaped her ponytail. But he didn't dare do that either.

Lamely he said, "I shouldn't have said that."

She turned to face him. He expected her to be tearful. Instead, her eyes were bright with indignation. "I don't like having to walk on eggshells inside my own house. I don't like having to weigh everything I say before I say it, wondering how you're going to take it."

Her anger sparked his own temper. "You know how I feel about Tanya."

"Indeed, how could I not?"

"Okay, then, you know that the wound is still raw."

"Yes," she said, raising her chin a notch. "You made all that perfectly clear before we got married. If not then, certainly last night left no doubt in my mind."

She tried to step around him, but he blocked her path. "Last night? What about last night?"

"Nothing. Forget it. If you'll step aside, I'll get dinner on the table."

"Screw dinner!" He caught her beneath the chin with his fingers and forced her head up. Their eyes clashed. "What was wrong with last night?"

She lifted her chin off the perch of his fingers and retorted haughtily, "Nothing from your perspective. It was less than thrilling for me, however."

He fell back a step, his jaw going slack. "Huh? Oh, I get it. I hurt your feelings, so you retaliate by castrating me, is that it?"

She rolled her eyes. "Spare me the macho tripe. Believe whatever you want to." She stepped around him then, but instead of setting dinner on the table, she headed for the stairs. "Since you decided to 'screw dinner,' I'm going up to my room. When you want me, you know where to find me. Which shouldn't be too difficult for you," she added sweetly. "You managed to find me in the dark last night."

"Listen," he shouted up at her, "I didn't want to do it at all. I was only doing you a favor."

She halted abruptly, turned around, and glared down at him. One of her arched brows rose a fraction. "Well, Mr. Tyler, for your information, that kind of favor I can do without."

"Terrific. I won't have to go to the effort again. Unless, of course, you want to claim your rights as a wife."

"And get another slam-bam-thank-you-ma'am?" She laughed scoffingly. "I certainly won't be missing much, will I?"

His head felt so hot with rage, he thought steam was probably escaping his ears. He wanted to close the distance between them, strip her naked, crush her beneath him, and show her exactly what she was going to be missing.

But damned if he was going to make the first move, not after her scathing review of his lovemaking. Hell would freeze over first.

"Fine," he snarled. "We'll keep this a marriage in name only."

"Fine." She turned on her heel and marched up the stairs. After entering her bedroom, she slammed the door closed behind her.

Five hours later she knocked on Chase's bedroom door. He was lying in bed, but the lights were still on and he was awake. The sheets were tangled around his restless legs. His head was propped up on pillows. He was staring at the ceiling and gnashing his teeth.

At her unexpected knock his heart stopped for several seconds. His eyes eagerly swung toward the door. But his tone was hardly cordial when he growled, "What?"

She opened the door a crack and peered around it. "May I come in?"

"What for?"

"I think we should talk."

He made an assenting motion with his shoulders and she walked in. His fledgling smugness evaporated when he saw how she was dressed. It wasn't anywhere close to the bridal nightgown she had worn last night, but it was just as sexy in a different way.

The pajama set was pink-striped cotton knit. Boxerlike shorts and a T-shirt top. The wide legs of the boxers made her bare legs look even longer. Her hair was still pulled into a ponytail. She was wearing her eyeglasses. She was barefoot. She looked like a coed at a slumber party.

Except for her breasts. They were making pert, prominent impressions against her shirt, and they jiggled slightly as she moved from door to bed and sat down on the edge of it.

"Chase, I'm sorry I behaved so childishly earlier. I guess the pressure of the last several days built up until I had to blow or burst."

Since she had made the overture, he could be magnanimous. "I guess I've been on edge too," he grumbled.

"I took potshots at your male ego and that was uncalled for. Although, it would be dishonest of me to pretend that I was satisfied with last night."

She glanced at him shyly, then away. "You see, Chase, I expected a little more consideration. I don't think I got any more thought from you than the condom you slipped on. I barely got equal time."

His jaw tensed. He was guilty as charged. That made him that much angrier.

"I expected, wanted, more . . . more . . . I guess the word is involvement. I wanted more *involvement* from you."

"You wanted an orgasm," he said, being intentionally blunt. By God if she could tromp on his masculinity, why should he be skittish about calling a spade a spade?

"That's the least of it, yes," she admitted quietly. "I would have liked more attention and affection, too."

"Then you should have hired yourself a gigolo instead of buying a husband. You could have paid him by the hour, or by the orgasm, instead of making such a sizable investment."

It wouldn't have surprised him if she had hauled off and hit him, which he secretly felt he deserved. If a man had dared talk to Sage like that, she would have gone after him with the garden shears. Devon, too.

Instead, when Marcie spoke, her reply was calm and conceding. "After sulking all this time in my room, I reached the same conclusion."

Her unmitigated honesty disarmed him. Instead of getting any satisfaction from shocking her, he felt more rotten than he had before. She was a hell of a lot smarter than either his sister or Devon. Her method of disarmament was more poised, but just as effective.

She took a deep breath, drawing his attention to those damn taut nipples again. "If I had wanted hearts and flowers, I should have hired a gigolo. But I don't regret the decision I made," she told him. "You're legally and physically my husband now. I'll try to be a good wife to you." Raising her eyes to his, she added, "So if you want me tonight—"

"No thanks." It rankled that she didn't appear disappointed.

"Did I wound your ego too terribly?"

"I'll live."

"I suppose if you can survive years of bull riding, you can survive me. Does this itch?" Surprising him, she ran the back of her fingers up the center gully of his torso where the hair was beginning to grow back.

He sucked in a sharp breath and wheezed, "No. Not yet."

"It probably will before too long."

"I'll keep you posted."

"Listen, Chase, the thermostat for the whole upstairs is in this room. My room is cold. Do you mind if I turn the heater up several degrees?" She was already off the bed, moving toward the thermostat mounted on the opposite wall.

"Actually I do," he said contrarily. "I'm hot."

He shoved the sheet down another inch or two, until the thick hair on his lower abdomen was visible. He thrust one long, bare leg from beneath the covers. Only one corner of the sheet kept him decent. He was feeling ornery and wanted more than anything to get a rise out of her.

She didn't even flinch. "Oh, well, I certainly don't want you to be uncomfortable. So in that case, I'll just get another blanket for my bed. I store spares in this closet."

She pulled open the louvered door of the extra closet in his room, went up on tiptoe, and reached for the top shelf where several blankets were folded.

Her pose made Chase's mouth go dry. It emphasized every

lean muscle in her long legs. It raised her pajama top, baring a good three inches of midriff. The shorts were raised over twin crescents of derriere that he craved to cup in his palms while lifting her up and against him.

In danger of embarrassing himself, he reached for the covers and pulled them above his waist.

She dragged the blanket down from the shelf and hugged it against her with both arms. "There, that ought to do it."

He could swear that was a double entendre. Sure as hell, she was referring to making him rock hard and throbbing. Her statement had nothing to do with extra blankets. Then again, his warped imagination was probably reading more into her smile than was intended.

"Good night, Chase," she said innocently enough. "Sleep well."

He didn't trust himself to speak.

Chapter Eleven

Chase had very little to say for the entire month that followed.

Few had the courage to engage him in conversation. His sour disposition and perpetual scowl frightened off most who would otherwise have attempted it. Those who dared felt relieved if they escaped with their lives.

On a Friday night, sitting with his brother at the bar in the tavern known by locals merely as The Place, he didn't appear inclined to make conversation.

A half hour after his arrival, he was still nursing his first bourbon and water. He was hunched over it like a stingy dog with a bone who didn't really want the bone but didn't want another dog to have it. He was morosely staring into the drink, which melting ice had turned a light amber.

"Well, there's nothing we can do but wait them out."

Lucky's comment only deepened Chase's frown. "That's what we've been saying for a month."

"They've got to make a decision soon."

"When I called last week, they said they would award a contract by the end of this week. This week they said it will be next week. I think they're giving me the royal runaround."

"Well, if there's oil down there, it's not going anywhere," Lucky said philosophically. "All we can do is wait them out."

Chase banged his fist on the bar. "You sound like a damn broken record. Can't you think of something else to say?"

"Yeah, I can think of something else to say," Lucky replied testily, sliding off the barstool. "Go to hell."

"Wait a minute." Chase reached out and grabbed a handful of Lucky's jacket. "Come back. Have another drink."

Lucky threw off his brother's grip. "I don't want another drink."

"I'll buy."

"Doesn't matter. Your company stinks. I've got better things to do than sit around and take your abuse."

"Like what?"

"Like go home to my wife, that's what. Which is what you should be doing. This is the third time this week you've twisted my arm into coming here and having a drink with you after work."

"So? Now that you're married, you can't go out with the boys anymore?"

"I don't enjoy it as much as I used to."

"And one drink is your limit? Devon put a kink in your drinking habits, too, huh?"

"That's right. I'm so happy with her, I don't need any other kind of high."

"Oh, really? Does sex with her make you drunk?"

Lucky's hands balled into fists at his sides. His deep-blue eyes turned glacial and his nostrils flared. Two years ago he would have already charged his brother and been throwing bloodletting punches. Devon had taught him that discretion is the better part of valor. He no longer fought first and thought about it later. He had learned restraint, but Chase was testing the boundaries of it tonight.

Chase could all but see the numbers ticking across Lucky's forehead as he slowly counted to ten in an effort to control his short temper.

Chase set his elbows on the bar and plowed all ten fingers through his dark hair as he lowered his head. "You don't deserve that. Devon sure as hell doesn't." Holding his head between his hands, he rolled it from side to side. "I'm sorry. Try to forget I said that."

He fully expected his brother to leave. Surprisingly, Lucky returned to the stool beside him and sat down. "Why don't you tell me what's really bothering you?"

"We need that drilling contract."

"Uh-huh. Besides that. Something's eating at you, Chase. Mother and Devon have noticed it, too. Every Sunday when you and Marcie are at the house, you're as uptight as a man sitting on top of a keg of dynamite. The fuse is short and it's burning hot. What gives?"

Chase swirled the contents of his glass around several times. "Marcie," he mumbled.

"I figured as much."

His head snapped around, his eyes sharp and demanding. "Why'd you figure that?"

"Marcie's a lot like Devon. She had a life before you came

into it. She's been an independent lady for a long time." Lucky tossed back the handful of beer nuts he'd scooped out of the bowl on the bar. "I'm not surprised she found the role of wife uncomfortable. Like a new pair of shoes, it doesn't quite fit her yet."

"What, are you kidding?" Chase grunted scoffingly. "She's so bloody good at being a wife, it's enough to make you sick."

"Huh?"

"Dinner is on the table every night at six sharp. She bakes cookies. God knows when because she's always so busy with other stuff. The house is as neat as a damn palace. I lose something, she knows right where to find it."

"I'm relieved to hear it's working out so well," Lucky said cheerfully. "As you know, I had doubts that it would. Sounds like y'all are getting along great. What have you got to belly-ache about?"

Chase swiveled on his stool to face his brother. Now that the spillway had finally been opened, there was a lot he'd held back that needed to be released.

"She's too perfect." Lucky merely stared at him as though he'd gone daft. "I'll give you an example. She told me that she liked to go through the Sunday paper methodically. Last week I deliberately scattered it all over the living room, reading a section, then dropping it and letting it fall wherever."

"Why?"

"Just to be provoking."

Lucky shook his head with bafflement. "Why?"

Because I'm horny as hell! Unappeased horniness was a condition he couldn't admit, especially to a younger brother who had come by his nickname because of his uncanny success with women.

"I wanted to see if I could rile her," Chase said.

"Did you?"

"No. She didn't say a thing. Not even a dirty look. She just went around the living room, calmly collecting the newspaper and restacking it so she could go through it the way she liked to."

"I don't get it. You're complaining about a wife who obviously has the patience of a saint?"

"Have you ever tried living with a saint? With somebody so bloody perfect? I tell you she's just not normal. Why doesn't she get mad?" He blew out a gust of air. "It's nerve-racking. I'm always on guard."

"Look, Chase, if that's all—"

"It's not. She sneaks up on me."

Lucky laughed so hard he almost fell off his stool. "Sneaks up on you? You mean like we used to do with Sage? Does Marcie hide in your closet and then when you open the door, she jumps out and hollers boo?"

"Don't be ridiculous."

"Well, what do you mean?"

Chase felt foolish now. He couldn't tell Lucky about the morning he'd been standing at his bathroom sink shaving, when he happened to notice Marcie's reflection in the mirror. He spun around so quickly, he'd nicked his chin with the razor.

"I'm sorry I startled you, Chase. I knocked but I guess you didn't hear me." She had rushed forward and set the stack of fresh towels on the lid of the toilet. "You're bleeding. Here."

She ripped off a sheet of toilet tissue and pressed it against his bleeding chin . . . and held it there . . . for a long time . . . even though he was standing there buck naked and growing hard from the delicate touch of her fingertips against his face.

And just about the time the tip of his sex grazed her, she whispered, "How does that feel?"

For several seconds the blood had pounded through the veins in his head. He finally gathered enough wherewithal to mutter, "Better." He snatched up one of the towels she had carried in and wrapped it around his middle with the haste of Adam, who'd just been caught red-handed committing the original sin.

No, he couldn't tell Lucky that. Lucky would want to know why he hadn't just taken his wife to bed and made love to her until they were senseless. Chase wouldn't be able to provide an answer, because he wanted to know that himself.

Ignoring his brother's question, he said, "You wouldn't know it to look at her, but she hasn't got a smidgen of modesty. She's brazen. Remember how much stock Grandma used to place on a woman's modesty?" He laughed bitterly. "Good thing she never met Marcie."

"What the hell are you talking about?" Leaning in closer, Lucky peered into Chase's feverish eyes. "You haven't started smoking funny green cigarettes, have you?" Chase gave Lucky's shoulder a shove. Lucky only laughed again. "You're nuts. Marcie behaves like a lady."

"Not at home she doesn't. At home she parades around naked as a jaybird."

Lucky's interest was piqued. He cocked his head to one side. "Oh, yeah?"

Chase didn't notice that his brother's interest had a teasing quality. He was thinking back to a few days earlier when he had gone into Marcie's room with a shirt that needed a button replaced.

She had answered his decorous knock on her door, "Come in."

He had pushed the door open and walked in, but stumbled on his own two feet when he found himself face-to-face with her pretty, pink nakedness.

He had caught her arranging her hair. Her hands were raised above her head. She stood poised in front of her vanity table, the mirror over it offering him a view of her back so he could see her all over at once.

Her blue eyes challenged him to do something, say something. He wanted to pounce on her and feed on her beautiful flesh, but he wouldn't allow himself to. If she could act so blasé about her nudity, then, by all that was holy, so could he.

Pulse thundering, resolutely keeping his eyes on a spot just above her head, he asked, "Do you have a sewing kit?"

"I'll be glad to mend whatever needs it."

"It's just a button. I can do it. Have you got a needle and thread or not?"

"Sure. Right here."

She lowered her arms. Her hair drifted to her smooth, fair shoulders. The small chest where she kept her sewing kit was behind him. She could have gone around him. She could have excused herself and moved him aside. Instead, she practically walked through him, brushing herself against him. Every cell in his body had become a tongue of flame, licking him into a frenzy of sexual heat.

Just thinking about it now made him yearn to touch her impertinent breasts and stroke her translucent skin and explore the mystery at her beautifully decorated apex.

Lucky waved his hand in front of Chase's face. He drew himself back into the present and querulously growled, "I think she was an old maid for too long. It made her an exhibitionist. What does it sound like to you?"

"Sounds like a fantasy I read in *Playboy* once."

"Dammit, Lucky, I'm serious. She's like a nympho or something."

"Damned shame to be married to one, isn't it? I speak from experience you understand." He winked.

Both Lucky's sarcasm and his gesture escaped Chase, who was still deep in thought. "She brushes up against me all the time. Remember the cat we had that rubbed herself against our legs when a tom wasn't around? Marcie's like that. She can't walk past me without bumping into me. It's like she's in heat."

"Maybe she is."

Lucky's flippant comment goosed Chase out of his erotic trance. "What?"

Lucky vigorously chewed another handful of beer nuts and swallowed. "I said maybe she is. Devon believes that a woman gets pregnant when she wants to, when she has subconsciously made up her mind to."

"Pregnant?" Chase repeated, looking stunned. Then he shook his head adamantly. "She's not going to get pregnant. At least she had better not. I don't want anything to do with a baby. I don't even want to talk about one, think about one."

Lucky's grin gradually receded. Uneasily he glanced

beyond his brother's shoulder. Instantly his vision cleared. "Speaking of your lady, she's here."

"Huh?"

Chase followed the direction of Lucky's gaze until he sighted Marcie. She was standing just inside the door of the noisy, smoky tavern, surveying the rowdy Friday-night crowd. When her gaze connected with his, he saw relief break across her features.

As unobtrusively as possible, she wended her way through the largely male crowd until she reached the end of the bar where they were seated. "So you are here." She smiled at Chase breathlessly. "I thought I recognized your truck outside." To his brother she said, "Hi, Lucky."

"Hi. I don't suppose Devon is with you. The Place isn't one of her favorite nightspots."

Marcie laughed. "So I've heard. And with good reason. But don't worry. I understand some of the most lasting love affairs have inauspicious origins."

"At least in our case that's true. It started with a fistfight in this hellhole. Look where it got us. Into a marriage made in heaven." He grinned broadly. "Want a drink?"

"No, thank you."

"What are you doing here?"

Chase's abrupt question cut through their lighthearted exchange like a steel rapier. It sounded accusatory and instantly put Marcie on the defensive.

"Remember the couple from Massachusetts? They're in town today. I was showing them a lake house and had to come by here on my way back to town. As I said, I spotted your pickup outside."

"You were checking up on me," Chase said. "Can't I be a few minutes late coming home without you hunting me down?"

"Hey, Chase, relax."

He ignored his brother. "Or don't you trust me to stop with just one drink? Did you think I had run off and joined the rodeo circuit again?"

"What the hell are you doing?" Lucky asked through his teeth, intentionally keeping his voice low so that they wouldn't attract attention.

"He's trying to humiliate me," Marcie said candidly. "When all he's actually doing is making himself look foolish."

With that, she turned her back on them. Proudly, shoulders back, fiery head held high, she moved toward the door.

Before Lucky could speak the admonishment he had ready, Chase turned to him and warned, "Shut up. I don't need any advice from you." Digging in his jeans pocket for currency, he tossed down enough bills to cover the cost of their drinks and adequately tip the bartender.

He elbowed milling patrons aside as he followed Marcie's light-capturing hair toward the door. One grinning, boozy face blocked his path and stood his ground firmly even when Chase tried to set him aside.

"Better catch that one, Tyler. She's one classy piece."

"So then Chase snarls something to the effect of, 'That's my *wife*, you s.o.b.' Sorry, Deacon. Then his fist smashes into this guy's face and knocks his nose askew. Another punch landed square on his mouth. His partial plate flew right out. I could see it from where I was standing at the bar. Swear to God— pardon me, Deacon—it did. The teeth got crushed in the stampede. Everybody was trying their damnedest—sorry again, Deacon—to get out of Chase's way. He was like a madman."

After Lucky had finished his account of the fight that had occurred at The Place two nights earlier, everyone in the formal dining room of the Tyler's ranch house was held in speechless suspension for several seconds.

Marcie kept her eyes lowered to her plate, still mortified that she had unwittingly caused a brawl. She now shared Devon's aversion to The Place.

Apparently Chase was just as uncomfortable with the recounting of the one-sided fight. He had remained broodily silent, drawing little valleys through his uneaten mound of mashed potatoes with the tines of his fork.

Laurie, Marcie noticed, was nervously fiddling with the strand of pearls around her neck, possibly because Lucky hadn't censored his language in deference to their additional guest at the midday Sunday meal.

"I wish you boys would stay out of that tavern," Laurie said, finally breaking the awkward silence. "The only good thing that's ever happened there was when Lucky met Devon."

"Thank you, Laurie," Marcie's sister-in-law replied. "Would you like for me to clear the dishes for dessert?"

"That's sweet of you. Is everybody finished? Jess?"

Jess Sawyer blotted his mouth with the same meticulous precision as he had sweetened his tea, cut his meat, and buttered his roll one bite at a time. He was a small, neat man dressed in a stiff white shirt and a well-pressed brown suit. He had thin brown hair and dull brown eyes. If personalities had colors, his would be brown.

"Everything was delicious, Laurie," he said politely. "Thank you for inviting me."

With Lucky's help, Devon stood and began stacking empty dishes on a tray. When the table was cleared, Devon held the door for Lucky as he carried the tray into the kitchen. "We'll bring dessert and coffee in," she said, following her husband out.

"I'm glad I caught you as we left the sanctuary," Laurie was saying to Mr. Sawyer. "I hate to think of anyone's eating a meal alone, but I think eating Sunday dinner alone is a sacrilege. Feel welcome to come anytime," she said, smiling at him. "Pat, was the roast beef too well-done for you?"

Pat Bush, a perennial guest at Sunday dinner, shifted in his chair. "It was fine." Glancing across the table toward Mr. Sawyer, he added, "Just like always."

"You didn't eat but one helping."

"My lack of appetite has nothing to do with the food, Laurie. I'm still thinking about that ruckus out at The Place last Friday night." He cast a baleful glance toward Chase.

Devon and Lucky returned, bringing with them a three-layer chocolate cake and coffee with all the fixings. "I'll serve from the sideboard, if that's all right with you, Laurie."

"That will be fine, dear," Laurie told her daughter-in-law.

From her chair Marcie watched Devon slice the first piece of cake and put it on a plate. Some of the frosting stuck to her fingers. She raised her hand to her mouth to lick it off. Before she could, Lucky grabbed her hand, poked her finger into his mouth, and sucked it clean.

Marcie's stomach did a flip-flop.

She felt Chase go tense beside her.

Devon snatched her hand away from her playful husband and glanced quickly over her shoulder to see if their loveplay had been noticed. Marcie pretended she hadn't seen it. She didn't want to embarrass Devon or, more to the point, have Devon see her jealousy.

"Y'all seem to bust The Place up every time you go in it," the sheriff said to Chase.

"What was I supposed to do, Pat," Chase asked defensively, grumpily, "just stand there and let that guy insult my wife?"

"To my way of thinking, Chase had no choice but to deck the jerk," Lucky commented as he passed around dessert plates.

"Well, your opinion on fighting doesn't count for much, does it?" Pat asked crossly. "You fight at the drop of a hat."

"*Used* to fight at the drop of a hat. Now I'm a lover, not a fighter." He kissed Devon's cheek as she went past him.

Chase's knee reflexively bumped into Marcie's under the table.

"I'm certain that Chase did what he felt like he had to do," Laurie said in her son's defense. "He paid for all the damage done to the bar and took care of that man's medical bills. I just hate to think of his teeth being knocked out. Literally."

Lucky emitted a snicker. Before long, everyone around the table was laughing. All except Jess Sawyer, who was gaping at them with dismay.

"He may end up thanking me," Chase said when the laughter had abated. "Those were the god-awfulest-looking false teeth I've ever—"

"Devon!"

The alarm in Lucky's voice silenced Chase. Lucky shot from his chair and launched himself toward his wife, who was leaning over the sideboard. Her face was pale. She was taking quick, panting breaths. One of Lucky's arms went around her waist to help support her. The other hand cupped her cheek and lifted her bowed head.

"Devon? Honey?"

"I'm fine," she assured him with a feeble smile. "A little dizzy spell. I think I just got too warm. Maybe if we turn down the heat a little, hmm? Or maybe something I ate didn't set well with me."

"Oh, for heaven's sake!" Laurie laid her folded napkin beside her plate, left her chair, and joined the couple at the sideboard. "Why don't y'all stop this foolishness and announce to everybody else what I've known for months?" Taking the initiative, she turned toward the table. "Devon's going to have a baby."

"Oh!" Marcie never remembered giving that glad cry. She, along with everyone else, even Mr. Sawyer, converged on the beaming couple, who were alternately embracing each other and their well-wishers.

Marcie gave Devon an extended hug. Since her marriage to Chase, the two women had become good friends. Marcie admired Devon's intelligence and acerbic wit, which she put to good use in the columns she wrote for one of the Dallas newspapers. Recently she had told them she'd been approached by a syndicator.

"I'm so glad for you," Marcie said earnestly. "Are you feeling all right? Is there anything I can do?"

Devon clutched her hand. "Do you know anything about babies?"

"No!" Marcie laughed.

"Then a big help you'll be."

The two women smiled at each other with mutual admiration and growing affection. Then Marcie kissed the proud papa's cheek. "Congratulations, Lucky."

"Thanks. One of the little critters finally fought his way upstream."

"James Lawrence!" Laurie cried, aghast. "Remember that we have a guest. I won't stand for that naughty kind of talk. I don't want Jess thinking that I've reared a bunch of—"

The shrill, obnoxious scraping sound of chair legs against the hardwood floor brought them all around. Chase dropped his napkin beside his plate and stamped out.

Before he went through the archway, Marcie got a good look at his face. It looked like a man's shattered reflection in a broken mirror.

The ax arced through the air, making a whistling sound before it connected with the log. *Thwack!* The log, standing on its end, split down the middle. Chase bent at the waist and tossed the two pieces aside, then picked up another log and set it upright on the block.

"What are you doing?"

Thwack!

"Knitting a sweater. What does it look like?"

"That can't be good for your ribs."

"My ribs are fine."

Thwack!

Lucky put his back to the nearby fence. He leaned against it while hooking the heel of his boot on the lowest rail. He set both elbows on the top one.

"You know, Chase, you can be the most self-centered s.o.b. I've ever run across."

Thwack!

Chase glared at his brother before tossing aside the split log and getting another. "What did you expect me to do, pass out cigars?"

"That would have been a start."

"Sorry to disappoint you."

Thwack!

Lucky reached in and wrested the ax handle from his older brother while he was bent down. Chase sprung erect, his face fierce.

"I'm not disappointed," Lucky said, throwing the ax to the ground. "I'm mad. Our mother is disappointed. She was counting on your marriage to turn you around."

"Too bad."

"Damn right it's too bad. Because you've got a wonderful woman who is—for reasons I can't comprehend—in love with you. But you're too damn blind to see it. Or too plain stupid. Or self-pitying. I'm not real sure what your problem is."

"You're mad because I didn't make a big deal over your kid."

"And wasn't that small of you!"

"Why haven't you told me?" Chase shouted. "Why keep it a secret? Building anticipation?"

"No, trying to protect you."

"From what?"

"From the hurt that's tearing your guts out right now."

Chase assumed a combative stance. His breathing was labored, but not from the exertion of splitting firewood. He didn't strike his brother as he appeared ready to do. Instead, he turned his back on him and headed toward the house.

Lucky charged after him, grabbed him by the sleeve, and slung him against the toolshed beside the woodpile. He made a bar of his forearm across Chase's throat.

"I didn't tell you about my baby before now because I knew it was going to hurt you, Chase. I hate that. I hate it like hell. But that's the way the cards fell and there's not a damn thing I or you or anybody else can do about it.

"I didn't ask for my child to be the first Tyler grandbaby. I wish it had been yours, as it should have been. But is that supposed to make me less delighted about my own baby? It can't. I'm sorry. I'm thrilled. I'm bursting with happiness over this kid. I can't wait till it gets here.

"However," he enunciated, thrusting his face closer to his brother's, "that doesn't mean that Devon and I don't still grieve for yours that died with Tanya. We all do. We always will. But life goes on, Chase. At least for most of us it does.

"If you want to live the rest of your life from inside a grave, then do it. I think you're stupid, I think you're sick, but if your misery makes you happy, then by all means be miserable. Just don't expect the rest of us to crawl into that grave with you and pull the dirt over our heads. We're all damned sick and tired of catering to you."

With an abrupt little shove he let go of Chase and turned away. He had taken only a few steps when a heavy hand clamped down on his shoulder. Reflexively, he spun around, expecting a blow.

Instead, Chase extended him his right hand. Lucky saw the tears, which made Chase's gray eyes shimmery. His ordinarily firm lips were unsteady.

"Congratulations, little brother. I'm happy for you."

They shook hands. Then they embraced. Then they walked back to the house together.

Chapter Twelve

"You didn't have an inkling?"

"About what?"

"That Devon was pregnant."

"No."

"I thought Lucky might have told you."

"No."

Chase's mumbled replies were grating on Marcie's nerves. Her nerves were already raw. They always were after one of their Sunday dinners with her in-laws.

Not that she was shunned or made to feel unwelcome. The Tylers had graciously incorporated her into the family. Even Lucky, who had expressed the strongest reservations against her marriage to Chase, now teased and joked with her as if she'd been a member of the family for years. Along with Laurie and Devon, he included her in their warm camaraderie.

Chase's family wasn't at fault. Chase himself was the one who made her edgy and nervous. He was never verbally abusive. The one and only time that had happened was last Friday night in The Place. He had apologized later for it, and she had accepted his apology, knowing how worried he was about the future of Tyler Drilling and attributing his outrageous behavior to that.

No, she didn't have a quarrel with his deportment. While they were with his family, he was courteous to her. He didn't criticize her. He didn't embarrass her. He didn't ignore her by treating her as though she were invisible as she had heard wives complaining that their husbands did when they were in public.

In their case, quite the opposite was true.

"You hadn't guessed?"

She jumped, startled by his abrupt question. "What?"

He was driving her car, with his left wrist crooked over the steering wheel. His right hand was resting on his thigh, within easy reach of the gearshift . . . or her knee, which he'd found several occasions to cover and caress during the course of the afternoon.

"Women seem to have a sixth sense about that stuff," he said, referring to Devon's pregnancy. "I thought maybe you had suspected."

"No. Although I guess I should have read the signs. I remember somebody teasing her at our wedding dinner about eating two desserts."

"I just thought she was putting on a few extra pounds."

Marcie smiled. "I'm sure she is." Chase didn't smile. "She's already six months. I can't believe she hid it so well for so long. Of course, she's tall. And clothing can camouflage a lot. But my goodness, the baby will be here before we know it."

"Hmm."

"And when it gets here, are you going to continue acting like a jerk about it?" Chase's head came around. He opened his mouth to speak, thought better of it, and closed his mouth with an angry little click. "When you stamped out of the house like that, Chase, it broke your mother's heart."

"My heart's been broken, too."

"Oh, yes, we all know that. You wear it so well on your sleeve for all the world to see. Well, we've all seen it, and frankly, it's getting old."

"I apologized to Lucky, didn't I? I told him I was happy for him."

"I know, I know. I even saw you giving Devon an obligatory hug. That's the very least you could have done."

"If I had gushed and simpered, it would have been hypocritical."

" 'Hypocritical'? What an odd word for you to use."

"What's that supposed to mean?"

He stopped the car in their driveway. Marcie alighted and headed for the door. She was already inside shrugging off her coat when he caught up with her.

"What's that supposed to mean?" he repeated angrily, tossing his coat in the general direction of the coat tree and missing it by a mile.

Something inside Marcie snapped. For over a month she had been pampering him, humoring his dour disposition and overlooking his provocations, which she knew were deliberate. The harder she tried to make life pleasant, the harder he worked at being a jackass. Well, she had had it with him. Good wife be damned. It was time he got as good as he gave.

Her red hair was bristling. As she closed in on him her eyes narrowed. "What it means, Chase Tyler, is that you are a hypocrite every single Sunday we go out there. It means that your congratulations to them were no more genuine than your phony displays of affection for me."

He shook his head stubbornly. "That's not true. I'm very happy for my bro—Wait a minute. What phony displays of affection for you?"

"Come on, Chase," she cried. "You don't want me to spell it out."

"Like hell I don't. What are you talking about?"

She drew back her shoulders and glared up at him. There was heat radiating out of her cheeks. Every muscle in her body was pulled taut.

"I'm talking about the knee massages. I sit on the sofa, you sit on the sofa. I cross my legs, you cover my knee with your hand. I stand up, you place your arm across my shoulders. I shiver, you offer me your jacket. I look up at you, you touch my hair. I laugh. You laugh."

His jaw was working, the muscles in his face knotting. Marcie knew she was pushing, but she couldn't stop. For a month she had been living with a chameleon. For several hours each Sunday she had endured his sweet, husbandly caresses that she knew meant nothing. She would return home feverish and aroused to the point of agony. And there was never any relief. Because once they were away from his family, he reverted to being broody and remote.

"I'm only trying to be nice," he said defensively. "But if you don't like it, I'll dispense with these courtesies." He turned away and went to the fireplace in the living room, where he began stoking up the fire. All his motions were angry, jerky.

Marcie wasn't finished with him. She joined him at the hearth, catching his arm as he laid aside the poker. "Your family is carefully gauging us, watching to see how we relate to each other. Thanks to your Academy Award performance every Sunday, I'm sure they're convinced that everything is hunky-dory. Little do they know that we're celibates.

"Oh, no, because they're bound to have intercepted some of those smoldering looks you send my way when you know they're watching. I'm sure they saw you twining that strand of my hair around your fingertip while you talked NBA basketball with Lucky. How could they miss it when you nudged my breast with your elbow as you reached for your coffee cup?"

"Don't pretend now that you didn't like it, Marcie," he said in a low, vibrating voice. "Because even through my sleeve I felt your nipple get hard. I heard that little catch in your throat." He used her momentary speechlessness to launch his own attack. "While we're on the subject, I don't like your foreplay any—"

"Foreplay?"

"Foreplay. What else would you call it when you lay your hand on the inside of my thigh and rub it up and down? Oh, you're careful to make it look wifely and casual, but you know it's there and I know it's there and we both know what's going on about four inches up from there.

"And if you don't like having me place my arm across your shoulders, you shouldn't snuggle up against me. If you don't like my offering you my jacket, don't make sure I notice through your blouse that you're chilled. While I've got my hand on your knee, you've got your foot moving against my calf. Now if that's not an invitation, I don't know what is."

The building flames in the grate were reflected in his eyes, flashes of passion and anger that fed each other. "I didn't see you pulling your head back when I was fiddling with your hair. Oh, no. Instead, you nuzzled the palm of my hand. I felt your tongue. It left a damp spot.

"You laughed because I dripped coffee into my lap. And I dripped coffee into my lap because you jostled my elbow with your breast. And I laughed back because you blotted up the drips with your napkin, and then it was either laugh or moan. Now, which would you rather I do in my mother's dining room while you're mashing your hand against my crotch, laugh or moan?

"So don't preach to me about how to conduct myself. I'll be more than glad to put a stop to this sexual charade if you will. Because if this playacting we do every Sunday makes you crazy, you can imagine what it does to me!"

After his shouting, the quiet in the room was sudden and intense. Marcie took a step nearer to him and in a sultry voice asked, "What does it do to you, Chase?"

He reached for her hand, yanked it forward, and pressed it open against his distended fly. "That."

Her fingers closed around his steely erection. "Why do you stop with the foreplay, Chase? Why don't you do something with this?" With each slow, milking motion of her hand his breath grew louder, harsher. "Are you afraid you won't like it? Or are you afraid you will?"

She released him and raised both hands to his head, sinking her fingers into his hair and cupping his scalp. "Kiss me. Kiss me right." Stretching up so that her lips were just beneath his, she added in a seductive whisper, "I dare you."

The sound that issued from his throat was feral. The manner in which his lips swooped down on hers was savage. So brutal was his kiss that at first her lips were benumbed by it. Gradually, however, she was able to separate them. Then she felt the swift and sure thrust of his tongue. Madly, rampantly, rapaciously, it swept her mouth.

Like her, he buried his fingers in her abundance of hair and held her head in place for the plundering mastery of his kiss. He drew on her like a man starved, as though he wanted to suck her entire mouth into his. He pulled away to catch his breath. Even then, his tongue was flicking over her lips, tasting her. Unappeased, he came back for more. And more. And more.

Marcie reveled in the carnality of his kiss. She loved the texture of his tongue, the taste of his saliva, the firmness of his lips, the rasp of his beard against her chin and cheeks. Her senses wallowed in the pleasure of smelling his skin and feeling his hair—Chase's skin, Chase's hair, Chase's hardness gouging her middle.

As one, they dropped to their knees on the plush rug in front of the hearth. Their mouths went on feeding frenzies over each other's face, indiscriminately moving their lips over cheeks, chins, eyelids.

When their mouths fused again, he sent his tongue deep, penetrating her mouth and saturating her with desire. His hands smoothed over her back, moved to her sides, rubbed the crescents of her breasts with the heels of them. Then, exercising no subtlety, he covered her derriere and pulled her against him.

Marcie didn't even consider being coy. She allowed him to push suggestively against her cleft. She even gloried in the obvious strength of his desire and ground her middle against it.

Groaning, he wrapped his arms around her so tightly she could no longer move and whispered fiercely, "Stop or it'll be all over."

"Not yet. Not yet."

She put enough space between them to peel his sweater over his head. Next she attacked the buttons of his shirt. When it had been cast aside, her fingertips roved over him in an orgy of discovery, like a blind person who was seeing for the first time.

With a hungry whimper she leaned into his chest and pressed her open mouth upon it. He cupped her head, but allowed it to move freely from spot to spot. Her lips found his nipple in a spiral of dark, crinkly hair. Shyly at first, then more aggressively, she caressed it with her tongue.

Swearing in whispered agony, he set her away from him. "Take off your clothes."

"You take them off," she challenged huskily.

They stared at each other a moment. Marcie held her breath until he took the hem of her sweater in his hands. He removed it over her head. His eyes became fixated on her breasts. Reaching behind her, Marcie unhooked her bra and let it fall. Chase's chest rose and fell in one quick, tortured gasp. She saw his stomach muscles contract, but he didn't touch her. At least not intimately.

Pressing her shoulders, he guided her down to lie on her back on the rug. Without ceremony he unfastened her skirt and pushed it down her legs. He wasn't quite so detached when it came to removing her panties, because he had to reach beneath her garter belt to get hold of the waistband.

Once they were removed, he slid his hand between her thighs. They groaned in unison. The fingers that probed her were thorough, yet gentle. His thumb nimbly separated the folds and found that supersensitive tissue.

He only had to stroke it a few times before her blood began to bubble inside her veins and she saw lightning sparks in her peripheral vision.

"Chase!"

That was all the invitation he needed. He unfastened his fly and shoved his trousers past his hips. Marcie boldly assessed him, but for only a second before he mated their bodies.

She gave one sharp, glad cry. Chase murmured either a profanity or a prayer. They remained like that for several tense moments.

Then, bracing himself above her, he withdrew partially and looked down into her face. Eyes locked with hers, he slowly penetrated her again. She felt him deep, so deep that the immensity of his possession swept over, stealing her breath, seizing control of her senses. His dark hair hung over his forehead, mussed and wild. His eyes glowed with the firelight, adding to his animalistic attractiveness. The muscles of his arms and chest bulged with masculine power.

She wanted to concentrate on how gorgeous he was, but he withdrew and sank into her again. He held her breast in one hand, circled the stiff nipple with his thumb. She shuddered. Her eyes closed involuntarily. Her thighs gripped his hips. He slid his hand between their bodies, stroking her externally even as he pressed ever deeper inside.

And her love for him, which had remained unfulfilled for decades, finally culminated in a splintering, brilliant climax.

He let her savor it, experience all of it, even the shimmering afterglow, before he began moving inside her again. But Marcie surprised herself and Chase by clutching him and raising her hips to meet his thrusts.

By the time his crisis seized him, she had reached another. They clung to each other, gasping, grasping, dying together.

Marcie was grateful for the knock on her inner office door that came around eleven o'clock the following morning. The couple who had arrived at ten sharp for their appointment were about to drive her mad.

Of course, on this particular morning, her threshold of sanity had been lower than usual.

"Come in," she called.

"Pardon the interruption, Marcie," Esme said. "Mr. Tyler is here to see you."

Reflexively Marcie rose from her desk chair. "Mr. Tyler? Which one?"

"The one you're married to. The tall, dark, and handsome one."

Then Marcie saw his hand reach beyond her assistant's head and push open the door. "Can I see you for a minute?"

Chase was the last person she had expected to call on her this morning. Her knees almost buckled. Her mouth was so dry she could barely speak.

"Of . . . of course. I'm sure Mr. and Mrs. Harrison won't mind if I step out for a while. You may continue looking through the listings book," she suggested as she rounded her black lacquered desk.

The man sighed and came to his feet, hiking up his trousers importantly. "We're finished anyway. She's not ever going to find anything she's happy with."

"Me? I liked that four-bedroom on Sunshine Lane," his wife retorted. "You said we didn't need that much space. You said the yard was too big. You turned down a beautiful house because you're too lazy to mow the lawn. Which is just as well, I guess. You wouldn't do it right anyway."

"Chase, this is Mr. and Mrs. Harrison," Marcie said, interrupting. "Ralph, Gladys, meet my husband, Chase Tyler."

"Pleased to meet you." Ralph shook hands with him.

"The same."

"Well, come on, Ralph. Can't you see they want their privacy?" Gladys practically pushed her husband through the door.

Esme, rolling her eyes ceilingward, followed them out and closed the door as she went. Chase and Marcie were left alone. They faced each other awkwardly, but didn't meet each other's eyes.

"Are those the clients you told me about?"

"Real prizes, aren't they? I don't think they'll ever settle on a house. Looking is just a hobby with them. It gives them a break from fighting. Unfortunately it costs me valuable time and more patience than I've got."

"Hmm. Uh, these are for you."

He stuck out a bouquet of pink tulips, and confused by the gesture, Marcie took them. In effect, she caught them. Chase seemed anxious to get rid of the flowers once he had called her attention to them. If Marcie's reflexes had been any slower, the bouquet would have fallen to the floor.

"It's not my birthday."

"No special occasion," he said with a laconic shrug. "I had to go to the grocery store this morning to pick up some supplies for the office. I spotted them there in one of those little water buckets by the checkout. Thought you might like them."

She gazed at him with perplexity. "I . . . I do. Thank you."

"You're welcome." His eyes made a slow survey of the room. "Nice office. Fancy. Nothing like Tyler Drilling Company headquarters."

"Well, we have different needs."

"Right."

"Did you hear anything about your contract?"

"No."

"Oh. I thought maybe the flowers were part of a celebration."

"No."

"Oh."

He coughed. She tucked a strand of hair back into her bun.

He sniffed. She fiddled with the green cellophane cone around the tulips.

"Did you come here to talk about offices?" she asked after the lengthy silence.

"No." For the first time that morning his gray eyes connected with hers. He had left the house long before she'd gotten up. "We need to talk, Marcie."

A sharp pain went straight through her heart and she recognized it as fear. He looked and sounded so serious. He had never come to her office before. Unless it was absolutely necessary, he rarely even called her while she was there.

Only something extremely important and imperative would bring about this unprecedented visit. The only thing she could think of was that he wanted to back out of his commitment.

"Sit down, Chase."

She indicated the short sofa recently occupied by Ralph and Gladys Harrison. He dropped to the edge of the boldly striped cushions and sat with his knees spread wide, staring at the glossy white tiles between his boots.

Marcie returned to the chair behind the desk, feeling that she needed something between them to help blunt the blow he was about to deliver. She laid the tulips on the desktop. Getting them into a vase of water wasn't a priority just then.

"What do you want to talk about, Chase?"

"Last night."

"What about it?"

"I didn't say much afterward."

"No, but what little you said was very concise. You certainly got your point across. You said, 'Well, you came twice, so now you've got nothing to complain about.' "

"Yeah," he said, releasing a deep breath around the word. "That's exactly what I said."

He lowered his head again. Around the crown of his head his dark hair grew in swirls. She wanted to touch them, tease him about their boyish charm, play with them. But touching him seemed as remote a possibility now as casual conversation between them had been the night before.

Having delivered his hurtful line, he had gotten up, retrieved his shirt and sweater, and gone straight upstairs to his bedroom. More slowly, Marcie had collected her things, then retreated to her own room. She hadn't seen him again until now.

"Marcie, we can't go on like this anymore."

He raised his head and paused as though expecting her to respond. She remained silent and expressionless. If she tried to speak, she knew that both her control and her voice would crack.

"We're like two animals in a cage, continually competing, constantly tearing at each other. It's not good for me and it's not good for you."

"Don't presume to tell me what's good for me, Chase."

He swore. "Don't get your back up. I'm trying to approach this reasonably. I thought—hoped—we could talk this out without tempers flaring."

She clasped her pale, cold hands on her desktop. "What do you want to do? Just please say what you came to say."

"Sex shouldn't be treated like a contest." Her only response was a slight nod of assent. "Our wedding night, the first time we made love—"

"We didn't make love that night. It was impersonal. If you had rubber-stamped my forehead, it couldn't have felt more official."

"Well, thanks a lot."

"You know it's the truth."

He pushed his fingers through his hair. "I thought you promised not to get riled."

"I promised no such thing." If he was going to dump her, make her a laughingstock in front of a whole town that had always found Goosey Johns amusing, she wished he would stop pussyfooting around and do it.

"Would you just sit quiet and listen?" he said testily. "This isn't easy, you know."

He had his gall. He had come to weasel out of his marriage to her and expected her to make it easy for him. "Just tell me straight out, Chase."

"All right." He opened his mouth. Shut it. Stared hard at her. Looked away. Gnawed on his inner cheek. Moistened his lips. "For starters, I think we should start sleeping together."

If her chair had suddenly bitten her on the behind, she couldn't have been more stunned. Somehow she kept her astonishment from showing. But she held her breath so long that she became dizzy and covertly gripped the edge of her desk to keep from collapsing.

"And I don't mean just sleeping together in the usual sense. I mean, sharing a bedroom, living like a real husband and wife."

He sent her an uncertain glance, then left the sofa and began pacing along the edge of her desk. "I gave this a lot of thought last night, Marcie. Couldn't sleep. What I said after, you know, well, that was a spiteful thing to say. I felt like hell afterward.

"It occurred to me that we've been playing sexual one-upmanship. Driving each other crazy every Sunday afternoon. That's silly. On our wedding night, granted, I took you with no regard to what you were feeling. I think I even hurt you." He stopped pacing and looked down at her. "Did I?"

Lying, she shook her head no.

"Well, good. That's something. But anyway, where was I? Oh, yeah. Then last night when we got home, you seduced me. Pure and simple, I was seduced. You asked for it and . . . and you got it. When you, uh, touched me, I could hardly hide the fact that I wanted you. And Marcie, you were, well, uh, you were very wet, so I know you wanted me too."

He ran his palms up and down his thighs as though drying the nervous perspiration off them. "We've always gotten along. We were friends in school. Only since we've been married have we been at crossed swords with each other. Sometime last night in the wee hours, I figured out why."

Moving to the window, he slid his hands into the rear pockets of his snug-fitting jeans. "There's this chemistry between us. I feel it. You feel it." He glanced at her over his shoulder. "At least I think you do."

Her mouth was arid. Again she nodded.

He turned back to gaze out the window. "So I figured that

we're being dumb by fighting this chemistry. We're consent-ing adults, living in the same house, legally married, and denying ourselves the main bonus of marriage. I think we should stop that nonsense and give in to it. I mean, why not?

"Okay, so we agreed weeks ago to keep this a chaste, in-name-only marriage. I know that. But hell, it's driving me friggin' nuts, and if last night is any indication, you haven't enjoyed doing without either. I mean, you were as hungry for me as I was for you. I've got the claw marks on my back to prove it."

When he came around, she dodged his incisive gaze. She was glad that she wasn't required to speak because she still wasn't able to. Apparently Chase had memorized what he was going to say, and he intended to say it all before he stopped to get her response.

"You know why I married you, Marcie. I know why you married me. We're both intelligent. I like and respect you. I think you like and respect me. We had some pretty good sex last night."

She raised her eyes to his. This time, he averted his head.

"Okay, some *very* good sex," he amended. "I've been sex-ually active for a long time. Even since Tanya died. Some-times that was the only way I could forget . . ."

He paused, rested his hands on his hips, hung his head as though reorganizing his thoughts, and then began again. "Anyway, I don't want to dishonor you by going to another woman. Besides, I was taught that being unfaithful to your wife is about the worst sin you can commit." He looked at her soulfully. "But I can't go for months at a time without it."

She indicated her sympathetic understanding with another nod.

"I don't want it to be a competition, either, where we score points against each other. Our sex life can be an extension of our friendship, can't it? If we work on being compatible in bed, I think we'll be more compatible in other areas. We know it doesn't work the way it's been going. Maybe we should give this other way a try."

He waited a moment, then turned to face her. "Well, what do you say?"

Chapter Thirteen

"Hi."

"Hi."

With shining eyes and a shy smile Marcie greeted Chase at the front door of their house. She still couldn't believe the turn of events that had taken place in her office earlier that day. Her arms bore bruises where she had pinched herself throughout the day to make sure she hadn't been dreaming.

Apparently she hadn't been because now Chase bent down and kissed her cheek. It was an awkward kiss, more like a bumping of faces together.

After his lengthy speech they had agreed to erase the angst of their first month of marriage and start again, not only as friends, but lovers. There was only one thing he had wanted assurance of, and that was that she was taking contraceptives. Without equivocation she had assured him she was.

"How long have you been home?" he asked as she helped him out of his jacket.

"Awhile. Is it still raining?" She dusted drops of water off the sheepskin as she hung it on the coat tree.

"Sprinkling. Something smells delicious."

"Chicken enchiladas."

"Yum. Did you get another phone call from the kook?"

"No."

"Then why'd you take the phone off the hook?"

Her blue eyes sent him a silent but eloquent message.

He swallowed hard. "Oh."

"Would you like a drink?"

"Sure."

Neither of them moved.

"Are you hungry?" she asked.

"Very."

"Are you ready for dinner?"

"No."

Upstairs—they never remembered getting there—he kissed her repeatedly, with passion and heat. His tongue was questing. He used it to explore. Like a gourmand, he sampled and savored her mouth, as though unable to decide which texture and flavor he liked best.

Articles of clothing seemed to melt away from their bodies. When they were both naked, they embraced long and tightly for the sheer animal pleasure of touching skin to skin, body to body, male to female. She was soft where he was hard and smooth where he was hairy, and the differences enthralled them.

He sat down on the edge of the bed and drew her between his knees. His stare alone aroused her breasts. They crested. They ached to be touched. He didn't.

But with his fingertip he traced the shadows they cast on her belly. Like a child who would be chastised for coloring outside the lines, he carefully followed the curving outline of the silhouette and paid close attention to the projecting shadows the flushed nipples made.

Watching his fingertip move with such precision over her flesh, Marcie moaned. She drew his head forward and pressed her nipple against his lips, which opened to enfold it. The heat, the wetness, the sucking action he applied, was so piercingly sweet it was almost painful.

Parting her thighs with his hand, he gently massaged the swollen, pouting lips of her sex. Marcie gasped in ecstasy as his fingers tunneled into her moist center. Her tummy quickened. An electric tingle shot through the tip of his tongue into her nipple and from there into her womb. She softly cried his name.

He lay back on the bed, pulling her over him, and she managed to impale herself upon him in time for him to feel the gentle contractions that seized her. They rippled through her endlessly it seemed before she realized that some of the surges belonged to him.

Moments later, sated, she lay upon his chest. The upper half of it was hairy. The lower half of his torso was still prickly where the hair hadn't completely grown back. She loved it all.

Her thumb idly fanned his nipple while she listened to the strong beats of his heart as they gradually returned to normal. Then another sound caught her attention—a low grumble from his abdomen.

She raised her head and looked inquiringly into his face.

"*Now* I'm ready for dinner," he said.

Chase did something then that he hadn't done in bed with a woman for over two years. He smiled.

During the weeks that followed, Chase was frequently caught smiling. Some days he completely forgot to be sad, miserable, and bereaved. He still thought of Tanya several times every day, but the memories no longer came at him in stunting, debilitating blows. They were cushioned by his general contentment. If life wasn't as sweet and idyllic and rosy as it had once been, it was at least livable.

A little more than just *livable—pleasantly* livable.

The pleasantness was sometimes hampered by feelings of guilt, because the source of that pleasantness was his second wife. Each time his memory conjured up an image of Tanya's sweet face, he felt constrained to reassure it that she still had his love. Nothing would ever change that.

In his own defense he reminded himself that Tanya was dead and he was alive, and because she had loved him so unselfishly, she wouldn't want or expect him to deprive himself of life's pleasures.

Marcie made his life a pleasure.

She was funny and fun, intelligent and interesting, always thinking up innovative places to go and things to do. They even went to a rodeo together in a neighboring town. It surprised him how much she enjoyed it, although during the bull-riding event she laid her hand on his thigh and told him how glad she was that he was a spectator and not a participant.

"It would be a crying shame if you damaged your beautiful body."

He had taken inordinate pleasure in her simple compliment. She was always saying things like that to him, things that took him by surprise and delighted him. Sometimes she was sweet, sometimes playful, sometimes downright bawdy.

She became a bona fide member of his family. They were considered a unit. It was now "Chase 'n' Marcie" in one breath, not just Chase. Sage had started phoning long distance from Austin to ask Marcie's advice on this or that. Marcie hosted a baby shower for Devon. She went shopping with Laurie and helped her pick out a new dress. Lucky frequently remarked on how wrong he'd been about their marriage.

"I'm glad you didn't listen to me, Chase," Lucky had recently said. "You were right to marry Marcie. She's a prize. Smart. Good-looking. Ambitious. Sexy." The last word had an implied question mark following it.

"Sexy." Chase tried to stop the grin he felt forming. He wasn't quite successful. His brother laughed out loud.

"That sexy, huh?"

"That sexy."

"I thought so. These redheads . . . ," Lucky had said, shaking his head musingly. "There's something about 'em, isn't there? Like they've got fires smoldering inside them or something."

Chase was prone to agree, but discussing Marcie's internal fires made him uncomfortable for a multitude of reasons. He punched his brother in the gut. "You're a pervert, talking about your pregnant wife like that." He no longer winced when Lucky's coming child was mentioned. He could even talk about it freely, with only a remnant of a pang affecting his heart. "Poor Devon. Are you still going at her hot and heavy?"

Lucky bobbed his eyebrows. "There are more ways than one to do it, big brother. Or don't you know?"

He knew.

Because he and Marcie had tried just about all of them and then had made up a few of their own.

One evening she had brought him a bowl of popcorn while he was lounging in the large leather chair in front of the fireplace, mindlessly watching a detective show on television. Within minutes there was popcorn all over the place, and he and Marcie were tangled up in the chair recovering their breath.

Both had remained dressed. Chase had thought that finding her erogenous zones inside her clothing was about the sexiest time he'd ever had. Until a few mornings later when they'd showered together. Propped against the tile walls, they had made love, as slippery, sleek, and playful as otters.

But whether he was ducking his head beneath her sweater to take her breasts into his mouth or squeezing a soapy sponge down the center of her body and tracking the foamy trail with his eyes, he always had one hell of a good time.

So did she. She never demurred from openly expressing her enjoyment of all they did together. The lady was hot. From her cool, professional mannerisms and clipped practicality, no one would suspect the depth of Marcie's sensuality.

They hadn't reached the bottom of it yet. Just last evening

she had turned their hello kiss at the front door into one of the most erotic experiences of his life.

"I just can't wait," she had whispered against his lips as she undid his pants and slid her hand inside.

"Be my guest."

That was the last thing he had expected her to do when he came home from a routine day at work . . . until she knelt in front of him and replaced her caressing hand with her mouth. Before it was over, they were both left on the living room sofa feeling weak and wicked.

And when she smiled up at him, he had said, "God, you're gorgeous."

However, he had lived with her long enough to realize that she still considered herself the same Goosey Johns she had been as an awkward adolescent. She had a good self-image professionally. When it came to her appearance, she still nursed fundamental insecurities.

"I wish I were pretty."

They were lying close together in the king-size bed they now shared. Unlike their wedding night, the lights now remained on until they were exhausted and ready for sleep.

"You are pretty, Marcie."

She shook her head. "No. But I wish I were."

"You're pretty," he had insisted, kissing her soft, pliant lips.

And later when his hands moved to her breasts, she sighed despairingly, "I wish they were larger."

"It doesn't matter. They're so sensitive." The damp brushstrokes of his tongue proved him right.

"But not large."

Chase laid his finger across her lips, stilling them. "If they were any larger, it would be excessive. For that matter, I wish I had twelve inches."

Her eyes had grown huge and round and she exclaimed, "You mean you don't?"

He had hugged her hard and they had laughed. When they made love, neither noticed any deficiency in the other.

Chase's life had been so sensually enriched, he no longer invited Lucky to The Place for drinks after work. He never postponed going home unless it was absolutely necessary. If Marcie wasn't there because of an evening appointment to show a house, he paced impatiently until she arrived.

He always had so many things to tell her, it seemed. It took them a full hour to fill each other in on how their days had gone. She was a surprisingly good cook, an excellent conversationalist on an endless variety of subjects, and an adventurous and imaginative lover. Every evening he looked forward to going home to her.

That's why as he approached the house this evening he was dreading an upcoming business trip to Houston. Maybe he could persuade Marcie to leave her agency in Esme's capable hands and come with him. They could incorporate a visit to her folks. Do some shopping. Yeah, maybe she would come along.

He let himself into the house and called her name, although her car wasn't in the driveway and he assumed she wasn't at home. He disengaged the alarm, sorted through the mail, and brought in the newspapers. He got himself a beer from the refrigerator and checked for a note. She was good about leaving him notes, informing him where she had gone and when he could expect her to return. Tonight there was no note.

He was on his way upstairs to change clothes when the telephone rang. He retraced his steps back to the entry table and answered it.

"Hello?"

"Who is this?"

"Who did you want?"

Marcie's caller hadn't phoned in several weeks. Only a few days ago she had remarked on it. "I told you so," she had said in a singsong voice. "He's given up on me and moved on to another victim. One who doesn't have a sexy husband around to fend off unwelcome suitors."

Chase wondered now if this was the man. Had hearing a masculine voice surprised him into blurting out his question?

"I'm calling for Mrs. Tyler," the caller said.

"This is Mr. Tyler. Can I help you?"

"Uh, well, I'm not sure. I spoke with Mrs. Tyler before."

"Regarding what?"

"Painting."

"Painting?"

"I'm a house painter. She called and asked me for an estimate on doing some interior painting."

Chase relaxed. This wasn't Marcie's caller. "I'm sorry. She hasn't mentioned anything to me about it."

"Well, it was a long time ago. Couple of years in fact. I didn't even think about it till I was out your way today. Drove past Woodbine Lane and remembered talking to her. She never called me back, but I remembered her name 'cause she said you were the Tyler Drilling people. I checked my cross directory and got your phone number. I reckon she got somebody else to do the painting before, but if you ever need—"

"Just a minute, Mr., uh—"

"Jackson."

"Mr. Jackson, you said you heard from my wife a couple of years ago?"

"That's right. It was around the time your building burned down."

"And she was calling about *this* house?"

"Yeah, she said it was the only house on Woodbine Lane. Said y'all hadn't bought it yet, but were thinking about it. Said she needed a room painted for a nursery and wanted to know how much I would charge." After several moments of silence he said, "Mr. Tyler? You still there?"

"We don't need any painting done."

Chase slowly replaced the telephone receiver. For a while he merely stood there, staring into near space. Then he pivoted on his heels and gazed at the large living room with its appealing view of the forest beyond, now tinged with the green promise of spring. He tried looking at the room through different eyes, eyes now dead, forever closed.

The front door flew open behind him and he spun around, almost expecting Tanya's spirit to be hovering in the opening. Instead it was Marcie, gathering her windblown hair in her fist.

"Hi," she said breathlessly. "I thought I might beat you home, but I can see I didn't. I stopped and bought carryout Chinese food for dinner. I hope you don't mind. Everybody wanted to look at houses today," she told him with an excited little laugh.

Setting the aromatic sack of carryout food on the table beside the telephone, she shrugged off the jacket of her suit and stepped out of gray high-heeled pumps.

"In the spring the housing market always picks up. I think some people would rather move than do spring housecleaning. Anyway—"

She ceased her happy chatter abruptly when she noticed that he was standing woodenly beside the hall table and hadn't spoken a word. He was looking at her as though he'd never seen her before, rather like an oddity he couldn't figure out and was therefore highly suspicious of.

"Chase?" When he didn't immediately respond, she touched his arm. "What is it? Is something wrong?"

Using his free hand, he pushed hers off his arm. His eyes were dark, implacable. "Chase, what?" she cried, her voice underlain with panic.

"How long have you lived in this house, Marcie?"

"How . . . how long?"

"How long?"

"I, uh, I don't remember specifically." She picked up the sack of food and headed for the kitchen.

"That's bull." He yanked the sack out of her hand and returned it to the table. Gripping her by both shoulders, his fingers dug into her.

"You remember everything, Marcie. You've got a photographic memory. You were the only kid in Miss Hodges's history class who could remember all the state capitals and the presidents in order." His voice increased in volume and intensity. He shook her slightly. "When did you buy this house?"

"Last summer."

"Why?"

"Because I like it."

"Why?"

"Because I like it."

"Who owned it before you bought it?"

"Chase," she said plaintively, almost inaudibly.

He, on the other hand, roared, "Who did you buy it from, Marcie?"

She struggled with tears. She wet her lips. She was in obvious distress. Her lips were so rubbery she could barely form the words. "From you."

"Jesus!" Turning, he slammed his fist into the nearest wall. Then he leaned into the wall and banged his fist against it several times. He kept his head averted.

Extending her hand imploringly, she touched his shoulder. "Chase, please let me explain."

He flinched at her touch, but whirled around to confront her. His features were congested with outrage. "What's to explain? I get the picture. This is Tanya's house."

"It's my house," she protested. "I bought it—"

"From me. Because you think of me as some freaking charity case."

"That's not true. I bought it because I wanted to make a home for you here. This is where you were supposed to live."

"With another wife," he shouted. "The wife I loved. Doesn't that matter to you? Don't you have any more pride than to settle for second place? Are you so willing to settle for second place that you'd resort to tricks?"

"I never tricked you."

"Oh, really? Then why didn't you ever mention that this was the house Tanya was so crazy about? The house that you and she looked at right before she was killed. The house that she wanted me to see with her."

Her gaze fell beneath his accusing stare. He raised her head so that she had to look into his face. "Never mind answering. I know why. Because you knew I'd feel just this way about it."

"Maybe I went about it the wrong way. But I only wanted to make you happy."

"Happy?" he cried. "Happy? I've been balling you in Tanya's house!"

"And liking it very much!" she shouted back.

They glared at each other for the span of several seconds. Then, muttering a litany of vulgarities, Chase started upstairs. By the time Marcie caught up with him, his suitcase was lying open on the bed and he was pitching articles of clothing into it.

"Chase," she cried, her voice tearing, "where are you going?"

"Houston." He didn't deign to look at her, but stamped into the bathroom and began tossing his toiletries into a suede kit.

"Why?"

"I was scheduled to leave tomorrow anyway." He gave her a fulminating glare. "I believe I'll go tonight instead."

"When will you be back?"

Brushing past her where she stood in the connecting door, he placed the kit in the suitcase and slammed it closed, latching it with an angry thrust of his fingers against the metal locks.

"I don't know."

"Chase, wait!"

He stormed downstairs. She clambered after him. At the front door she intercepted him and tenaciously hung on to his sleeve.

"Please don't go."

"I've got to. It's business."

"Don't go like this. Not when you're so angry. Give me a chance to explain. Wait until morning."

"Why? So you can give me another night of sex to dull my memories of Tanya?"

Her whole body went rigid with affront. "How dare you talk to me like that. I'm your wife."

He merely snorted, an uncomplimentary sound. "On paper, Marcie. Only on paper. But never where it really counts."

He yanked his jacket off the coat tree and within seconds was gone.

"Lucky? It's Marcie."

"Hey, my favorite sister-in-law! How are you?"

"I'm fine," she lied.

Chase had been gone for three days. She hadn't heard a word from him. She didn't know where he was staying in

Houston or why exactly he had made the trip, so there was no way she could track him there. Unable to bear it any longer, she had swallowed her pride and called his brother to fish for information.

"What's up? Getting lonesome for that brother of mine?"

"A little."

A lot. Loneliness ate at her like a vicious rat. Its sharp, pointed teeth gnawed at her. When awake, she replayed the horrid departure scene in her mind, willing it to be only a nightmare. In her sleep, she yearned for him, reached for him, and awoke startled and bereft when she realized he wasn't lying beside her and that he might never again.

"Devon and I discussed taking you out to dinner one night while Chase is gone," Lucky was saying, "but she hasn't been feeling very well."

"I'm sorry to hear that. Has she told her o.b.?"

"Yes, and he tells her to stay off her feet, rest more, and try to be patient for another seven or eight weeks."

"If there's anything I can do . . ."

"Give her a call. It might improve her disposition. She's a regular bitch these days."

Marcie laughed, as she knew she was expected to. Lucky's criticism of his wife wasn't intended to be taken seriously. "I'll call her later this evening."

"I would appreciate that."

The conversation lagged. He was waiting for her to get to the point of her call. "Uh, Lucky, have you spoken with Chase today?"

"Sure. He called right after the interview."

"The interview?"

"With the oil company execs. That's why he went, you know."

"Yes, I know. I just didn't realize the interview was today." She hoped that her bluff sounded convincing.

"Yeah, they interviewed the three finalists, so to speak. Chase wants that contract so damn bad, Marcie. It's more than the money. It's a pride thing with him. I guess because you, well, you know, you bailed us out. He wants to prove to you and to himself that you didn't make a bad investment."

"Did using my money shatter his pride?"

"No," Lucky said, obviously pondering the response even as he gave it. "But he needs to feel as if he's in charge again."

"He is."

"*We* know that. I'm not sure he's convinced of it."

"Well, if you speak to him—"

"I'm sure he'll call you. He's probably just been busy. He had another appointment this afternoon."

Probably with a divorce lawyer, she thought miserably. "Yes, he'll probably call me tonight. Unless he's already on his way home," she suggested tentatively.

"I wouldn't look for him this soon. He said he wouldn't come home until they announced their decision and awarded the contract."

"Yes, that's what he told me before he left." Since when had she become a liar?

"Course if he gets so hot for your bod he can't stand it, he might hop in his pickup and make the trip in record time," he teased.

Unfortunately, she couldn't tease back. Lamely she said,

"Well, give Devon and Laurie my love when you get home. I'll try to call Devon tonight. Have patience with her."

"I'll grin and bear it till the baby gets here. Bye-bye."

Marcie hung up. Without interest she padded into the kitchen and poured herself a glass of milk. Ever since Chase left, she had had very little appetite. She would certainly never want Chinese food again.

Hours later, while lying in bed reviewing the latest property tax laws, the telephone on the nightstand rang. She stared at it suspiciously and decided at first not to answer. But what if it was Chase?

"Hello?"

"I'm coming to you," the whispery voice said. "I want you to see how hard I am for you."

Disobeying all the rules of common sense, she asked, "Who is this? Why don't you stop calling me?"

"I want you to touch me where I'm hard."

"Please stop."

"I know your husband isn't there. You're not getting any, are you, Marcie? You must be real horny. You'll be glad to see me when I get there."

Sobbing, she slammed down the receiver. It rang again immediately. This time she didn't pick it up. She reasoned that if he were calling, he couldn't be trying to break into her house. Nevertheless, she shoved her arms into the sleeves of her robe and ran downstairs.

Frantically she checked all the doors and windows. She monitored the alarm system to see if it was set. She considered calling Lucky, but he had enough to deal with. He didn't need a hysterical sister-in-law on his hands in addition to a cantankerous, pregnant wife.

She had insisted in her conversations with Chase that telephone creeps never actually did anything. They got their kicks by scaring their victims because they were usually terrified of or traumatized by women. So why was she placing any credence in this last call?

Because he had called her the night Chase left and every night since. He was knowledgeable about her comings and goings and seemingly everything else about her. And for the first time, he had started warning her that he was coming after her. He intended to take it a step further than telephone terrorism.

Leaving all the downstairs lights on, inside and out, she returned to her bedroom. She didn't fall asleep for a long time. Every sound in the house was magnified by her fright.

She scolded herself for being so afraid over something as ridiculous as telephone calls. It wasn't like her to cower in fear and tolerate something like this. She always tackled her problems head-on.

Tomorrow, she vowed, she would do something to put a stop to this.

Chapter Fourteen

It wasn't quite dark when Chase arrived at the house on Woodbine Lane six days after leaving it, but the sun had already set and the yard was deeply shadowed beneath the trees.

Marcie's car wasn't there. He was glad. He wasn't sure what he was going to say to her when he saw her. During his absence his anger had abated, but he was still distraught over living in Tanya's house with another woman . . . and liking it so much. Unable to deal with that aspect of it, he dwelt on Marcie's clever maneuvering and how unconscionably she had manipulated him.

He slid his key into the notched slot of the front door lock and tried to turn it. To his annoyance and puzzlement, it wouldn't unlock. After several attempts, he stood back, placed his hands on his hips, cursed impatiently, and tried to figure out another way into the house. All the other exterior doors locked from the inside.

The only immediate solution he saw was to break one of the frosted panes of glass beside the front door, reach in, and unlock it from the inside and then get to the digital alarm pad before it went off.

He scouted around the yard for a stout stick, and finding one, carried it back to the door. The window shattered after his first hard rap. He reached in, groped for the lock and un-latched it, then opened the door. His boots crunched on broken glass as he made for the alarm transmitter. He punched out the required code, but the forty-five-second interim beeping didn't stop.

"Damn!"

Wasn't anything working right tonight? He tried the code again, meticulously depressing the correct digits. The beeping continued. Knowing that the central control box was in the utility-room closet, he started across the living room at a run, hoping to get there and disconnect it before the actual alarm went off.

"Stop right there!"

Chase came to a jarring halt and turned toward the imperative voice. He was struck in the face by a brilliant beam of light and threw up both hands to ward it off.

"Chase!"

"What the hell is going on here? Get that light out of my face."

The light was switched off, but the glare had temporarily blinded him. Several seconds elapsed before he could focus. When he finally located Marcie, she had moved to the alarm pad. After she punched in the correct sequence of numbers, the beeping stopped, making the resultant silence even more pronounced.

It was as shocking as the sight of his wife, who, in one hand, was holding a high-powered flashlight, and in the other, a high-powered pistol.

"Is that loaded?" he asked temperately.

"Yes."

"Do you intend to use it on me?"

"No."

"Then I suggest you lower it."

Marcie seemed unaware that she was still aiming the handgun at his midsection. Her arm came unhinged at the elbow; she dropped the gun to her side. Chase realized the pistol would be extraordinarily heavy in her feminine hand. It would have been hard for many men to tote.

He moved to a lamp, switched on the light, and received his third shock. Marcie's face was ghostly pale, in stark contrast to the black, knit turtleneck pullover she was wearing. Her hair was pulled back sleekly away from her face and wound into a mercilessly tight bun on her nape.

Apprehensively he approached her and lifted the handgun out of her hand. She was staring at him fixedly, drawing his attention to her eyes. They were ringed with violet smudges, looking as though they had both been socked very hard. He remembered seeing them badly bruised when she lay in the hospital bed following her auto accident. She had been pale then, too, but nothing like now.

He clicked on the safety of the pistol and set it on an end table. Then he took the flashlight from her and set it aside also. "Want to tell me what's going on? Have you always had that gun?"

She shook her head no. "I bought it Tuesday."

"Do you know how to use it?"

"The man showed me."

"What man?"

"The pawnbroker."

"Jesus," he muttered. "Have you ever fired the thing?"

Again she shook her head no.

"Good. Because if you had, your shoulder would have probably knocked your ear off when you recoiled. Not that you would have needed an ear any longer because the blast would have deafened you. Who did you intend to shoot?"

She wilted like a starched petticoat on a humid day. One second she was standing, the next she was crumpled into a little heap on the sofa. She buried her face in her hands.

It wasn't like Marcie to have fainting spells or crying fits. Alarmed, Chase sat down beside her. "Marcie, what is happening here? What were you doing with that gun?"

"I wasn't going to shoot anybody. I was only going to frighten him with it."

"Frighten who?"

"The caller." She raised her head then and looked up at him. Her eyes were filled with tears, seeming larger and bleaker than ever. "He's called every night since you've been gone. Sometimes two or three times a night."

Chase's jaw turned to granite. "Go on."

"He knew I was here alone. He kept talking about your being away. He also knows where we live. And . . . and he said he was going to come after me. Chase," she said, her teeth beginning to chatter, "I couldn't stand it anymore. I had to do something. So I had a locksmith change all the locks. I set another code on the alarm. Tonight when I heard you on the porch, and you broke the glass and—"

He put his arms around her and drew her against his chest. "It's okay. I understand now. Shh. Everything's fine."

"Everything is not fine. He's still out there."

"Not for long. We're going to put a stop to this once and for all."

"How?"

"By doing what you should have done in the first place. We're going to see Pat."

"Oh, no, please. I'd feel so foolish making this a police matter."

"You'd feel even more foolish if you had accidentally put a hole through me."

She trembled. "I don't think I could ever bring myself to pull the trigger on that thing," she said, nodding down at the pistol.

"I don't think you could either," he said soberly. "So in effect, that still leaves you defenseless when you're here alone." He picked up the pistol and crammed the barrel of it into his waistband. "Come on, let's go."

"Right now?" She resisted when he tried to pull her to her feet.

"Right now. I've had it with this creep."

They reset the alarm. There wasn't much they could do about the broken window, so they just left it. "Where's your car?" he asked as they went down the front path.

"I started parking it in back."

Chase assisted her into the cab of his pickup and climbed behind the wheel. He'd just spent four hours driving from Houston and had been looking forward to getting out of the truck. Lately, things rarely turned out the way he expected or wanted them to.

"I spoke to Lucky," Marcie said quietly once they were under way. "He told me you'd gone to Houston to see about the contract."

"The decision makers had narrowed it down to three drilling companies that had bid on the job. They wanted to talk with us personally. After costing me five nights in a hotel and a week of eating out, they picked an outfit from Victoria."

It had been a crushing disappointment, which a four-hour drive and two hundred miles hadn't ameliorated. He had invested almost two months' time and a lot of worry and planning in getting this contract and had ended up with nothing to show for it except an exorbitant credit-card bill.

What was worse, he had no other prospects to pursue. Thanks to Marcie's loan, he didn't have to worry from a financial standpoint, but his pride and sense of professional worthiness were still on the critical list.

"I'm sorry, Chase. I know you were counting on that job."

He gave her a brusque nod, glad that they had reached the courthouse and that he wouldn't be required to talk about it any more.

They caught Pat Bush in the corridor on his way out. "Where are you going?" Chase asked him.

"To get a cheeseburger. I haven't had dinner."

"Can we talk to you?"

"Sure. Why don't y'all come with me?"

"It's official."

One look at Marcie apparently convinced the sheriff that the matter was urgent. That and the pistol tucked into Chase's waistband. He retraced his steps to his office and held open the door. "Come in."

Chase ushered Marcie inside. Pat's office hadn't changed since Bud Tyler used to bring his boys in for quick visits. While the two men discussed politics, the ten-point bucks that always got away, all levels of sports, and local happenings, Chase and Lucky would strut around twirling fake pistols and wearing badges Pat had pinned to their shirts.

One time they'd gotten in trouble for drawing mustaches and silly eyeglasses on all the wanted posters while their father and the sheriff weren't looking. Another time they'd gotten whippings for dropping a lighted firecracker into a brass spittoon in the squad room.

Now, Chase laid the pistol on the edge of Pat's desk. Pat regarded it closely, but didn't comment. He waited until they were seated across the desk from him in straight wooden chairs before removing the matchstick from his mouth and asking, "What are y'all up to?"

"Marcie's been getting phone calls."

"Phone calls? You mean obscene?"

"And threatening."

"He hasn't actually threatened my life," she interjected softly. "He just says that he's coming after me to . . . to—"

"To do all the things he's been talking about over the phone?" Pat prompted.

"That's right." After nodding, she left her head bowed.

"So it's definitely a man?"

"Definitely."

"And you don't recognize the voice?"

"No. He always whispers as though he's deliberately trying to disguise it."

"You think you might know him?"

"I have no idea. He might just want to make his voice sound scarier."

"When did this start?"

She raised her pale hand to her temples and massaged them. "Several months ago, I think."

"Before we were married," Chase said.

"Hmm. Does he always say the same thing?"

"No." The question made her curious. She raised her head. "Why?"

"Could be we're not dealing with an individual, but a group of kids. They try to see who can say the nastiest stuff, get the best response, that kind of thing."

With a small shake of her head Marcie said, "I don't think so."

"Neither do I." Chase leaned forward. "When Marcie first told me about this, she passed it off as a prankster who got his jollies by talking dirty. She figured he would eventually grow tired of her and move on to someone else. But he hasn't, Pat. He scares her spitless every time he calls. I think it's more than your average heavy breather."

Pat picked a fresh wooden match from a box on his desk and put it in his mouth. He'd traded cigarettes for matchsticks years ago. He maneuvered it from one side of his mouth to the other.

"What do you do when he calls, Marcie?"

"At first I just hung up as soon as I realized what it was. But he began calling repeatedly, sometimes several times a night. It got to be such a nuisance, I started listening, hoping I'd recognize his voice. I thought it might be someone I run into frequently—the man who sacks my groceries, the man who pumps my gas, the teller at the bank who always flirts. I wanted to embarrass him by calling him by name, you see. But I never could identify him."

"Any heartbroken lovers in your past?"

"No."

"What about the fiancé in Houston?"

She looked at Chase with incredulity. "He wouldn't do anything like this!"

"How do you know?"

"There's an ex-lover?" Pat asked, showing interest.

"I assure you, Sheriff Bush, it's not him."

"How can you be so sure?"

"Because he doesn't have the sexual imagination for one thing. I'd suspect Chase before I would suspect him."

When she realized the conclusion that could be drawn from what she had said, her eyes collided with Chase's. His were full of expression. Pat coughed behind his hand. Marcie wet her lips and tried to cover the blunder.

"It's not my ex-fiancé," she said staunchly. "Besides, they sound like local calls. Not long distance."

"Better give me his name anyway."

"Is it really necessary?"

"We'll check his long-distance bill through the phone company. Unless he's our man, he'll never even know about it."

"But the thought of invading his privacy—"

"Do you want to find this creep or not?" Chase asked impatiently.

Marcie glared at her husband defiantly, then reluctantly provided the sheriff with her former fiancé's name. "I promise we'll be discreet," Pat told her. He leaned back in his chair. "Why didn't y'all come tell me about this before now?"

"I wanted to," Chase said. "Marcie insisted that we wait."

"Why?" Pat wanted to know.

"I thought he would eventually stop calling."

"But when he didn't, why didn't you tell me about it?"

She wrung her hands. "I'm not sure. I guess I wanted to solve the problem on my own. In the scheme of things it seemed like such a piddling problem. It really didn't get so bad until this week. He called more frequently, and his voice was different."

"Different? How?"

"It wasn't just sleazy. It was sinister. He kept saying he was coming to fulfill my . . . my . . ." Again she rested her forehead in her hand.

"I know this isn't easy, Marcie," Pat said kindly.

"No, I assure you it's not." In a manner that Chase admired, she pulled herself together. In one long breath she told them, "He said he was prepared to fulfill my sexual appetites while my husband was away. Not in those exact words. But that was the gist of it."

Chase growled, "If I ever get my hands on the slimy sonofabitch—"

Pat pointed a stern finger at him as he interrupted. "You'll stay out of it, is what you'll do. I mean it, Chase. You just had to finance a new set of false teeth for that feller you bashed out at The Place. Don't you boys ever learn?"

"Nobody talks smut to my wife and gets by with it."

"If we catch him, he won't get by with it. This is a police matter."

Chase muttered a blue opinion. Pat ignored his muttering. "Which one of you is going to tell me about that?" He pointed at the pistol.

"I bought it for protection," Marcie told him, her cheeks turning slightly pink with embarrassment.

"Foolish thing to do," Pat said bluntly.

"Oh, I wouldn't actually shoot it at anybody. You didn't think that, did you?"

He looked at her for a moment, then dryly replied, "When somebody packs a .357 magnum, that's the conclusion I have to draw, yes, ma'am."

"She almost shot me." Chase told Pat about his hapless homecoming.

"Well, that kind of craziness is gonna stop," Pat said, coming to his feet. "These callers rarely do anything. They're cowards. Don't get me wrong, Marcie. You should exercise caution. Keep all your doors and windows locked and your alarm set even when you're there. But let's not get paranoid over this thing."

"What are you going to do?"

"Put a tap on your phone first thing tomorrow morning. And a tracer. Probably won't do much good. He probably calls from pay phones and knows just how long to talk before hanging up."

Pat opened the office door and called for a female deputy.

"In the meantime, I want Marcie to go with Deputy Davis here and give her some quotes of things he says. Key words are important. Try to remember words that he repeats. We'll send the report to Dallas and have them run it through their computer. If he's got a prior, we'll find him that way."

Chase assisted Marcie to her feet, placing his arm around her waist. He moved with her to the door, passed her off to the buxom woman in uniform, and was about to follow them across the squad room when Pat detained him.

"She might be less self-conscious talking about it if you're not there."

"I'm her husband, for crissake."

"Indulge me. Besides, I want to talk to you."

Chase reentered Pat's office. The sheriff closed the door again and returned to his chair behind the desk. "How'd it go in Houston?"

"The Rockets lost and I came home without a contract."

"Sorry, Chase. But don't worry. You'll eventually pull out of this slump."

"I'm beginning to wonder." He stared into near space for a moment. "Met an interesting guy while I was there, though. Named Harlan Boyd. He works as a troubleshooter in oil-related businesses. Or maybe he's just a con artist with a string of b.s. that sounds convincing. Anyway, he said he might have some ideas for us. Hell, I'd be open to anything."

"Chase?"

"Yeah?" Chase raised his head. The older man's tone of voice had changed. It was hesitant. He got the distinct impression that Pat had something except the suffering oil business on his mind.

"Have you ever answered the phone to this obscene caller?"

"He would hang up, wouldn't he?"

"That ever happen?"

"No. Why?"

Sidestepping that question, Pat posed another. "When did Marcie first tell you about him?"

"Let's see." He thought back. "I believe it was the night I went to her place to repay her for bailing me out of the hospital."

"How soon after that did y'all talk about getting married?"

"What the hell difference does that make?" Chase's eyes sharpened. "What are you leading up to, Pat? These aren't random questions, are they? What are you getting at?"

"How are you and Marcie getting along?"

"None of your damn business."

"When you walked through that door and laid a loaded pistol on my desk, you made it my business."

"Okay, then, get to your point," Chase said crisply. "What does our marital situation have to do with an obscene phone caller?"

"Maybe nothing. Maybe everything." Pat leaned forward and placed his forearms on the edge of his desk. "Doesn't it strike you funny that he's never called when you're there?"

Suddenly, Chase had the complete picture, as though Pat had colored in the last numbered space. Angrily, he threw himself out of his chair and made several pacing tours of the office before glaring down at the sheriff. "You think she's making him up?"

"Is it possible?"

"No! Hell, no! That's laughable."

"But *possible?*"

"Wait!" Chase exclaimed. "I was there once when he called."

"You heard him?"

"No. He hung up before I could get to the phone."

"He hung up? Or did Marcie?"

"Look, Pat, what you're suggesting is way off base. It's nuts. Why would she play out such an elaborate act?"

"To win your sympathy. Get attention, affection."

"Some women have PMS and some have obscene phone calls, is that your theory?"

"It's happened before."

Chase barked a laugh. "Don't ever let my sister-in-law, Devon, hear you say something like that. Not if you value your life."

"All I'm saying is that some women—"

"Some women, maybe. But not Marcie," Chase said with an adamant shake of his head. "Not her. She's the most self-sufficient, well-adjusted, both-feet-on-the-ground, pragmatic person I know."

"*Now,* " Pat said, emphasizing the word. "But I remember her when she was that carrot-topped, skinny kid in braces who the rest of you made fun of. Maybe Marcie remembers those times, too."

Pat stood up and rounded his desk. He sat down on a corner of it and pointed Chase back into his chair. Reluctantly he returned to his seat.

"I haven't said much about this hasty marriage of yours," Pat said. "Figured it was none of my business."

"You figured right."

Pat ignored the interruption. "Figured a grown man like you could make his own decisions and be held accountable if he screwed up. But Laurie's filled me in on the facts."

"She told you about the money?"

"Uh-huh." His expression softened. "Chase, everybody knows how you felt about Tanya. Marcie is no exception. And even well-adjusted, pragmatic women want to be loved. They want to be loved exclusively. A woman wants to be the only one her man can see."

"Since when have you, a bachelor, become such an expert on women?"

Pat chuckled, conceding the point. "Maybe I'm not an expert on women per se, but on cases like this I know what I'm talking about. I'm not saying it's a foregone conclusion. All I'm saying is that it's a possibility we've got to consider."

Chase met him eye to eye and firmly stated, "You're wrong, Pat. You're dead wrong."

"I hope so. But if I'm not, why did Marcie refuse to come see me sooner?"

"She's self-reliant. She likes to take care of things on her own. And she's good at it."

"Maybe that self-reliance comes across so strongly, she needs something that makes her look feminine and vulnerable in your eyes."

"Don't quit your day job to become a psychiatrist, Pat."

"I'm only playing devil's advocate. It's my job."

"Well, it's a pain in the backside."

"To me, too." Undaunted, he proceeded. "Why hasn't she changed her phone number?"

"That's easy. Clients might make a sudden decision on a house and need to get in touch with her. For that same reason she can't have an unlisted number."

Pat glanced beyond Chase's shoulder. "How's Devon?"

Sensing the reason for Pat's sudden shift in topic, Chase picked up his cue. "The last time I spoke with Lucky from Houston, he said she was giving him fits. Nothing he does or says pleases her."

The door opened behind him. He turned his head. Marcie was alone. "We're finished."

"I know that was tough, Marcie," Pat said. "Thanks for being such a trooper. I'll get that file off to Dallas first thing in the morning. There'll be a man out to install a tap on your phone, too." He grinned at them, but Chase had known him long enough to realize that it was forced. "Be careful what you say into the telephone from now on. Others will be listening."

Chapter Fifteen

"He didn't believe me, did he? He thinks I'm making it up."

In her peripheral vision Marcie saw Chase glance at her before returning his attention to the road. Since leaving the courthouse they'd driven in silence and were now almost home. Treetops merged over the two-lane highway, forming a tunnel lit only by their headlights. It gave her a claustrophobic sensation, like being caught in a grotesque chamber in a fun house.

"Sure Pat believed you."

"Give me some credit, Chase." Wearily she rested her head on the back of the seat. "You're always saying how smart I am. I'm smart enough to see through your friend, the sheriff."

"He's your friend, too."

"Until tonight. Tonight he thinks I'm a hysterical female who invents boogers in the vain hope of holding a husband who married her for money and not for love." She rolled her head to one side so she could see his profile. "Doesn't he?"

Chase fidgeted in his seat. "It's Pat's job to look at every angle. It's uncomfortable for him sometimes, especially if the role of sheriff interferes with the role of friend. He didn't like arresting Lucky for arson, but he did it because it was his sworn duty."

"Then while I was with the deputy, he did express some doubts about my mysterious caller."

"Not doubts exactly."

"Doubts," she countered. "Exactly."

They were silent for the remainder of the trip. When they reached the house, Chase went in ahead of her, switching on lights.

"You look ready to drop," he said.

"I am. As soon as I bathe, I'm going to bed." She was halfway up the staircase when she turned around and said, "Your mail is there on the bar."

"Thanks."

She hadn't known what to expect from Chase when he got home. She'd had no guarantee that he would return at all. When he did, she wouldn't have been surprised if he had told her he was moving out permanently and seeking a divorce.

She couldn't allow herself to feel relieved that he hadn't mentioned a separation. It might be that he simply hadn't had the time or opportunity to discuss it with her yet.

She took a long bath. The hot water helped relax her tight muscles. Just knowing that Chase was in the house soothed her nerves like a balm.

But when the phone rang as she was drying off, the living

nightmare began again. On the one hand she resented her caller's ability to shatter her peace of mind every time the telephone rang. On the other, she prayed it was he.

Hastily she finished drying off and pulled on a nightgown. She rushed into the bedroom to find Chase turning down the bed. "Who called?"

"Mother. Pat had called her."

"About me?"

"No. He's more professional than that. He just mentioned to her in passing that I was home. She called to say hello."

"Oh." Her disappointment was keen. "I thought it might be . . . him."

"No. Come on. Get in." Chase was holding back the covers for her. She slid between them and laid her head on the pillow. The nightstand lamp was bright on her face. She reached up and switched it off.

She didn't want Chase to see her looking so unattractive. Without makeup, her hair a mess, pale and fatigued from nights of sleeplessness, she looked a wreck. These days she resembled a redheaded scarecrow.

"It would make sense, wouldn't it?" she asked musingly.

"What?"

"For me to dream up a mystery man. You're too chivalrous to desert a woman when she's in trouble."

"Look, Marcie, if Pat wants to entertain some off-the-wall theories, that's fine. That's his job. But don't foist them on me."

"For all you know, I could be lying."

"You're not."

"We had a fight last week. You walked out without a word

about where you would be or when you were coming back. And while you were away, the caller got more aggressive and threatening." She laughed, but its foundation was desperation. "No wonder Pat thinks I'm making him up. It's almost a classic case. Pathetically classic."

"You're about the least pathetic individual I've ever met."

"I'm falling apart. Look at me. I'm trembling." She held her shaking hand parallel to the counterpane. "Hardly a pillar of strength and stability."

"Something like this would be nerve-racking to the best of us. In any case, I'm not going to argue with you about it tonight. You need to go to sleep. I don't think you've slept since I left."

"Not much," she admitted.

"Here, take this." He extended her a capsule and a glass of water to wash it down with.

"What is it?"

"One of the sedatives they gave me when my ribs were cracked. I was supposed to take two at a time to help me rest. Surely taking one won't hurt you."

"No, thanks. I'd better not."

"It'll help you sleep."

She shook her head no. "I'll sleep without it."

"Sure?"

"Sure."

With a small conceding motion of his shoulders he set the tablet and glass on the nightstand. "Good night."

He had almost reached the door before she blurted out, "I bought it for you."

Chase stopped, turned. "What?"

"The house."

"This isn't a good time to go into that, Marcie. You're exhausted."

"But I won't rest until I've made you understand why I did it."

"I understand perfectly. You tricked me into living with you in Tanya's house."

"It's my house!"

"Only because you paid for it. In spirit it belonged to Tanya."

"I discovered this house. I saw it before Tanya ever did." She sat up. The covers slid to her lap. "Tanya wouldn't have even known about it if I hadn't brought her to see it."

"Which brings up a pertinent question. If you wanted it, why did you show it to Tanya? Why not just buy it for yourself then?"

"Because I wanted you to live here."

He gaped at her incredulously and lifted his hands away from his sides. *"Why?"*

Because she had loved the house so much, and because Chase had needed a house then, she had wanted to give it to him. The only way she could do that at the time was through his wife.

After the fatal accident she had wanted him to have it more than ever, as recompense for what he'd lost. When it became apparent that he wasn't going to occupy the house he had bought only days after Tanya's demise, a germ of an idea had begun to form in Marcie's mind.

She had purposefully let Lucky believe that the buyer of the house was someone other than herself. From the day she became the owner, she had moved toward one goal—making this a home for Chase and living here with him. She wanted to give it to him like a gift, but without his ever knowing about it.

She had selected furniture and decor she thought he would like. She had planned everything, except attending the rodeo that night in Fort Worth. That had been a coincidence, one that she viewed as a sanction.

Fate approved of her intentions. The gods smiled upon her plan. Her years of unrequited love were finally going to be rewarded. She had been granted permission to do this. She was being allowed to make up for the accident that had robbed him of his wife.

He, however, didn't see it that way.

Now, while he stood searching her face for a plausible explanation, she considered telling him the simple truth—that everything she'd done, she'd done because she loved him, always had, always would. But it was difficult, if not impossible, to declare undying and unconditional love to someone who looked so patently angry.

"I guess I was trying to make up for your other loss, Chase," she said, her voice faltering. "I wanted to give you back a part of it. Obviously I badly bungled it."

Some of the tension ebbed from him. He bent his head down and rubbed the back of his neck. "I don't believe you did it maliciously."

"Thank you for that." She toyed with the hem of the bedsheets, unable to look at him without nakedly revealing her love. The last thing she wanted to be to him was an object of pity. Garnering all her courage, she asked, "Where do we go from here?"

"Damned if I know, Marcie. The only thing I'm sure of right now is that we're both too tired and upset to think beyond tonight." He went to the door and pulled it open. "I'll be in the next room if you need me."

I need you, her heart cried out. "You won't disturb me if you want to sleep here."

He looked at the empty pillow beside hers, but shook his head. "I think we should sort out the rest of this first, don't you?"

"I suppose," she said, trying valiantly to keep her disappointment from showing. "Good night."

"Good night."

After he left her, Marcie rolled to her side and drew her knees up to her chest. Tears streamed from her eyes, down her cheeks, and into her pillowcase. He would never trust her again. He felt she had duped him, and if she were being painfully honest with herself, she would admit that's exactly what she had done.

But only because she loved him so much.

He had denied believing in Pat Bush's speculations that her obscene calls were only a ploy to get attention, an old maid's last, desperate attempt to keep her man. But could she really blame Chase if he had his doubts?

The calls *were* real. The threats were real. She could sense that they were. And as soon as the man called back and Chase heard a replay of his voice, he would know she was telling him the truth. This time, she wasn't trying to trick him.

*   *   *

"Hello?"

"Hello, Marcie."

At last! It was he! Her heart began to pound. "You've got to stop calling me," she said, trying to keep the elation out of her voice. Finally he had called. Chase would believe her now.

"I won't stop calling till I get what I want. You know what I want," he said in the raspy tone of voice that sent chills up her spine. "I want you under me. Wet and wiggling."

"You're disgusting."

"Are your nipples hard? Touch them for me, Marcie. Hmm, Marcie, that's good. That's good." He moaned.

"They ought to lock you up and throw away the key. You're sick. You're a menace to society."

He laughed, sounding superior and condescending. "I know the sheriff has tapped your phone, but I know how to get around that."

Was he bluffing? How could he know the sheriff's office was now apprised of her calls? He couldn't. It was only a lucky guess.

"I know just how long to talk before hanging up so they can't trace the call."

"I don't know what you're talking about."

"They don't believe you, do they, Marcie? Not the sheriff. And not your husband. They think you're making me up, a figment of your imagination."

"No." Her mouth had gone dry. She gripped the receiver

harder, until her knuckles turned white. She tried to swallow, but had no saliva. "Chase believes me."

Again that nasty laugh. "I'm coming for you, Marcie. Soon."

"Leave me alone. I'm warning you—"

"You'll like me, Marcie. I'm a better man than your husband." He cackled. "And he doesn't even believe you. He won't be there to save you when I've got you naked and spread open."

"Stop." She whimpered.

"Good-bye, Marcie. Be seeing you."

"No," she said, suddenly panicked. "Wait! Don't hang up. Please, not yet."

"Good-bye."

His voice was singsong. He was playing with her. She knew better than to cry. Her intellect told her that was what he wanted, but she couldn't stop her tears or hiccupping sobs.

"My husband will kill you when they catch you."

He laughed, with more malice than before. "He doesn't love you."

"He does. He will."

"Never, Marcie. You tricked him," he taunted. "Good-bye. See you soon. Soon, Marcie. Marcie. Marcie . . . Marcie . . ."

The voice changed; it became Chase's voice. Her eyes flew open and she sprang erect. Chase was there, sitting on the edge of the bed, rubbing her shoulders gently and speaking her name, drawing her out of her nightmare.

With a harsh cry she flung herself against his bare chest,

despising the feminine weakness that caused her to clutch at him. She had always been contemptuous of women who weakly clung to men and used tears to get attention. But when Chase's strong, warm arms enfolded her, she forgot to be resentful of her own frailty. She nuzzled her face in his chest hair.

"You were having a nightmare," he whispered. "I could hear you crying all the way into the other room. But you're awake now and I'm here."

"Hold me, Chase. Please."

He lay down with her, drawing her even closer against him and pulling the covers over them. He stroked her back, cupped her head, and tucked it beneath his chin.

"He was on the phone."

"Shh. He's not there now."

"But I want him to be," she cried frantically. "It's been two weeks since we went to the sheriff. I want you to hear him. I want you to know. Then you'll believe me."

"I believe you."

"He reads my mind, Chase. It's like he knows that I want him to call. He's not calling on purpose."

"Shh. Just relax. Go back to sleep."

"When he calls, you'll know I'm telling the truth." She was babbling, but she couldn't help it. She was desperate to regain his trust. "When he calls, you'll believe me, Chase."

"I believe you."

"He's got to call."

But another week went by and he didn't call.

*   *   *

Lucky came into the office, stamping the mud off his boots. He inspected the bottom of them, decided they were reasonably clean, then glanced up to find his brother slumped in the chair behind the desk, his feet resting on the corner of it, staring into space.

"I thought you would be on your way home by now."

Chase roused himself and lowered his feet to the floor. "No, not yet."

"It's still coming down in buckets out there."

"Hmm."

Chase had regressed into the strong, silent type again, Lucky thought. For a while there, he'd actually acted like a human being. For the past several weeks, though, he'd been morose, uncommunicative, surly.

"That guy from Houston called again while you were at lunch," Lucky told him. "Harlan Boyd. Did you get the message?"

"Yes."

"Did you return his call?"

"No."

It was on the tip of Lucky's tongue to ask why the hell not, but that would no doubt provoke a quarrel, which would serve no purpose. Or maybe it would. Maybe it would clear the air. He knew, however, that his brother's problem wasn't with him. It wasn't even directly related to Tyler Drilling.

"I take it that Marcie hasn't heard from the creep." Chase's head came around quickly, his expression dark and suspicious. Lucky gave a helpless shrug. "Pat told Mother about it."

"That was nice of him." Chase bolted from his chair. "Dammit! Now I'm sure all of you think she's a nut case."

"No, we're relieved to know what the problem is. We all thought she was sick and dying or something too dreadful for y'all even to tell us about."

Again Lucky was on the receiving end of a glower that demanded explanation. "Do you think we're blind, Chase? She's lost weight. She's pale as a spook. She's as jumpy as a turkey the day before Thanksgiving. None of that characterizes the Marcie we've come to know and love. She's usually in control, unruffled and well balanced. Didn't you think we would notice this personality change?"

"Why go to Pat? Why didn't you ask me?"

"Mother didn't go to Pat specifically. They were just talking, and she expressed her concern over Marcie, and to lay her mind at rest that Marcie didn't have cancer or something, Pat told her about the pond scum that's calling Marcie."

"While he was giving away privileged information, did he also mention that he thinks the caller is a product of Marcie's imagination?"

Lucky looked away guiltily.

"I can see that he did."

"Well, I for one think that's crap. And the strength of my opinion can't even compare to Devon's. She went positively berserk when it was even suggested. To his face she called Pat a redneck conservative and a chauvinistic dinosaur. I'll tell you something, Chase," he said, shaking his head, "if our two ladies ever team up against us, we've had it."

Chase's stern lips cracked a smile, but Lucky could tell his heart wasn't behind it. "How're things otherwise?"

Chase asked testily, "What things?"

"You know, things."

"You mean like our sex life? That kind of *things*? You want to know how many times a week I make love to my wife, is that it?"

Lucky refused to get angry. One man with a rigid stance, balled fists, and red face was about all the small office could accommodate. "For starters. How many?"

"Why, are you keeping score?"

"Something like that."

"None of your damn business."

"Come on, Chase, have a heart," he wheedled. "Devon and I have had to taper off these last few weeks. I've had to re-sort to voyeurism."

"Are you sure you haven't been making those phone calls to Marcie?"

Lucky laughed, not the least bit offended. But within seconds he grew serious. "I hit it, didn't I? Y'all aren't, uh, sleeping together."

Chase flung himself back into the chair, frustration incarnate, a man whose skin had suddenly shrunk too small to fit him.

"I recognize the symptoms, big brother," Lucky said sympathetically. "Remember how much I wanted Devon but couldn't have her because she was married? I nearly went out of my freaking mind. If being horny was a terminal illness, I wouldn't be here to tell about it."

He dragged a stool across the floor and set it a few feet in front of Chase. "Abstinence was forced on me. What I can't figure," he said, leaning forward from his seat, "is why you're not availing yourself of your very lovely, very sexy wife, who is very much in love with you."

"She's not in love with me," Chase grumbled.

"Bull. And I'm not the only one who thinks so. Mother and Devon agree. So does Sage."

"Oh, well, hell, if Sage thinks so . . ." He let the sarcastic response trail off. "What are we, the constant topic of conversation out there?"

"Actually, y'all are about on equal par with the baby."

Chase muttered a series of curses. Not to be so easily dismissed, Lucky reminded him that he hadn't answered his question.

"No, I haven't," Chase said, "because it's none of your business."

"You're not put off by this pervert who's calling her, are you?" He got a dirty look for an answer. "You don't think Marcie's turned on by it, do you? Or that it's somehow her fault?"

"What do you take me for, an idiot?"

"Well, what else could it be? Did you do something to make her mad?"

"No."

"Did she lock you out?"

"No!"

"So if it's not Marcie, then you're the one whose holding out. Why, Chase?"

Chase made to get up. Lucky shoved him back into the chair. The brothers stared one another down. Finally Chase shrugged indifferently. "Okay, you might as well know.

You'll probably find out sooner or later. By accident. Just like I did."

"Find out what?"

Chase told him about the telephone call from the house painter. "It made no sense until I figured out that he wasn't talking about the current Mrs. Tyler, but the late Mrs. Tyler. He was talking about Tanya. The house we're living in now was the house Tanya had picked out, the one I was supposed to be looking at with her the day she died, the one I subsequently had you buy. Marcie told you she had a buyer for it. She was that buyer."

This time when Chase left the chair, Lucky made no attempt to stop him. He was preoccupied by this astounding piece of information. He swore softly. "I had no idea."

"No. Neither did I."

"She told me she would handle everything, the closing and all that. I never would have guessed."

"Startling, isn't it? You can imagine how I felt when I found out."

"To think that she loved you that much, all that time."

Chase caught Lucky by the shoulder and spun him around. "What did you say? What are you talking about? Love? She tricked me. She played the dirtiest, rottenest trick—"

"Man, are you muleheaded!" Lucky shouted, surging to his feet. "You're too stupid to be my brother. They must have mixed up the babies at the hospital."

"Make your point," Chase ground out.

Lucky roughly poked him in the chest with his index finger. "You can't see past Marcie's deception to the reason behind it." Then he peered shrewdly into Chase's gray eyes, which were as turbulent as the low clouds that scuttled across the twilight sky.

"Or maybe you can. Maybe that's what's eating at you. It's not the house that bothers you so much. What you can't accept is that you have been loved so well. Twice."

He placed a hand on each of Chase's shoulders. "What's the single worst thing that could happen to you, Chase? The worst possible thing?"

The following silence was broken by the shrill ringing of the telephone. Chase, grateful for the interruption, snatched up the receiver and growled a hello.

"Chase, is Lucky there?"

Lucky saw the expression on his brother's face change as he passed him the telephone receiver. "It's Devon. It sounds urgent."

Lucky grabbed the phone. "Devon? Is this—"

"Yes. My water just broke. I called the doctor. He said to come to the hospital right away. The pains are coming hard."

"Christ." He pulled his hand down his face. He was a good five miles from home. "Okay, okay. Everything's fine. I'll meet you at the hospital. Hurry. But tell Mother to drive carefully. It's raining and the roads—"

"She's not here."

"What?"

"She went out."

"Out? Out where? When?"

"A while ago. I think she was taking some food to a sick friend. Anyway she left with a jar of homemade soup and a pecan pie. Or maybe it was an apple pie."

"Devon, who gives a damn about a pie!" he roared. "Sit down. No, lie down. Yeah, lie down. Stay calm. I'll be right there."

"I am calm. And I'm perfectly capable of driving myself to the hospital."

Every blood vessel in Lucky's head seemed to explode. "Don't pull that feminist crap on me now, Devon!"

"Stop yelling at me! As soon as I shave my legs I'll drive myself."

"*Shave your legs?* If you even attempt to drive, I'll murder you. I mean it, Devon. I'm on my way. Five minutes. Lie down, for crissake!"

He hung up before she had time to respond and raced for the door. Chase followed closely on his brother's heels. He had a fair grasp of the situation even hearing but one side of the conversation.

"We can call an ambulance to go get her," he suggested.

"I'll beat their time."

"That's what I'm afraid of."

Chase jumped into the passenger seat of the Mustang because Lucky took the wheel. They sped off into the rain.

Chapter Sixteen

"Lighten up, Pat, or I'm liable to think you're arresting me."

Sheriff Pat Bush, his hand wrapped firmly around Laurie Tyler's elbow, was almost dragging her down the sidewalk toward his squad car parked at the curb. The twirling emergency lights were painting an electric rainbow across the gloomy dusk.

"Maybe I should."

His mouth was grimly clamped around a matchstick. He pulled open the passenger door of the squad car and practically stuffed her inside, then jogged around the hood and slid behind the steering wheel. He engaged the gears and peeled away from the curb with a screech of tires.

"I don't know why you're so angry with me, Pat. I'm not clairvoyant," she said in her own defense. "How could I know Devon would go into labor today? She's four weeks early."

"Nobody knew where you were. Somebody should always

know how to contact you, Laurie, for your own safety. If some pervert had snatched you, we wouldn't know where to start looking. As it is, I've been running all over town trying to find you."

Pat had been in his office when Chase called him from the ranch house. "Lucky's carrying Devon to the car now," he had told him. "We're on our way to the hospital, but we don't know where Mother is."

"I'll find her."

"Thanks, Pat, I was hoping you'd say that. I'd look for her myself except Lucky is demented. We barely made it from the office to here in one piece. I can't let him drive."

"I guess an ambulance is out of the question."

"Totally."

"Okay." Pat sighed. "Soon as I locate Laurie, I'll bring her to the hospital."

For the better part of an hour Pat had been driving the streets of town in search of Laurie's car—on the grocery store parking lot, at the dry cleaners, anyplace he could think of that she patronized routinely. In the meantime he'd kept his mobile telephone busy trying to track her through friends. The fourth call he made proved productive.

"I think she was planning to take some supper over to a sick friend," he was told by one of Laurie's bridge club friends. "When I spoke with her this morning about next week's meeting, she was baking a pie."

"A sick friend? Do you know who?"

"That man she's been seeing. Mr. Sawyer, I believe his name is."

Now Pat took the splintered matchstick out of his mouth

and dropped it on the wet floorboard of his car. "How's Mr. Sawyer feeling?"

"Much better," Laurie said stiffly.

"I'll bet."

"I'll tell him you inquired."

"Don't bother."

"Poor man."

"What's the matter with him?"

"He's got a cold."

"Humph."

She turned her head, one brow eloquently arched. "What's that supposed to mean?"

"What?"

"That sound."

"It doesn't mean anything."

"Well, I didn't like it. It sounded derisive."

"The guy's a wimp," Pat declared crossly. "Why would you want to play nursemaid to a puny, skinny little wimp like that?"

"I brought you soup when you had the flu last year. Does that make you a wimp, too?"

Pat hunched over the steering wheel, gripping it tighter. "That was different."

"How so?"

"For one thing Sage was with you when you came to my place." Angrily he addressed her across the interior of the squad car. "For godsake, Laurie, have you stopped to consider what people will think about you going to Sawyer's place alone? In the middle of the afternoon? While he's in bed? Jeez! Heaven only knows what people will think was going on in there between you two."

"What do you think was going on?" She tilted her head to one side and fixed a quelling stare on him through slitted eyes.

Matching her stare, he said, "Frankly, I don't know what to think. He's a milquetoast, but obviously you're smitten. Though why in hell, I can't imagine."

" 'Smitten' is such an antiquated word."

Pat was too caught up in his own argument to notice her gibe. "He's a regular at Sunday dinner now. One night last week I drove out to see you. You were with him at a party at his lodge. The weekend before that, you spent all day Saturday in Canton together at the flea market. Tuesday night it was the spaghetti supper at church."

"I invited you to go to the spaghetti supper."

"I was working!"

"That's not my fault. Nor Jess's."

Pat brought the squad car to a halt at the hospital's emergency room entrance, got out, and came around to assist her out. Taking her arm, he hustled her through the rain toward the door that was reserved for official personnel.

"I'm only thinking of your reputation, Laurie. I don't want your name dragged through the muck, that's all."

"I doubt Jess and I are a hot item."

"Oh, yeah? Everybody already knows you're seeing him."

"What's wrong with that?"

"What's wrong with that?" Pat repeated, coming to a sudden halt in the deserted hospital hallway. He turned her to face him. "What's wrong with that? Okay, I'll tell you what's wrong with that." He raised his index finger and pointed it toward her face. He opened his mouth. Nothing came out.

Laurie gazed at him inquisitively. "Well? I'm waiting."

He drew her face beneath the dripping brim of his hat and kissed her.

When he finally lifted his lips off hers, she wrapped her arms around his waist and whispered, "Took you long enough, Pat."

With a low, hungry groan he kissed her again.

Chase came barreling through a swinging door at the end of the hallway but pulled up abruptly. Pat jumped as if he'd been shot and instantly released Laurie, who was looking blushingly young and more beautiful than he'd ever seen her, and that was covering four decades.

Chase looked as if he'd just walked into an invisible glass wall and hadn't yet recovered from the shock. "Uh, somebody, uh, noticed the squad car pulling in and said you'd be coming in through this entrance."

Pat could only stand there embarrassed and tongue-tied. Laurie handled the awkward situation with grace. "How's Devon?"

"Doing fine. But you'd better rush upstairs if you don't want to miss the main event."

"It's a girl!" Lucky, grinning from ear to ear, emerged from the delivery room. Draped in a surgical gown, with a green cap on his head, he looked sappy and jubilant. "Hey, Mother, you made it in time after all."

"Thanks to Pat." Chase sidled a glance at them and smiled devilishly.

"God, she's gorgeous! Gorgeous!" Lucky shouted, smacking his fist into his opposite palm.

"How's Devon?" Laurie asked anxiously.

"Came through like a pro. I suggested we start making another one right away. She socked me in the nose."

"How much did the baby weigh?"

"They're doing all that now. She's exactly two and a half minutes old. The doctor let me cut the cord. Then he handed her to me. Squishy, squalling, little red-faced thing. And I handed her to Devon. Made a fool of myself. Started crying. Jeez, it was great!"

Chase smiled, but he couldn't help thinking about the child of his who would have been a toddler by now. Considering that, he applauded himself for holding up very well.

"A girl," Chase said ruefully. Then he boomed a laugh. "A girl! If that's not poetic justice, I don't know what is. A girl! God has a terrific sense of humor."

Pat, catching his drift, began to chuckle. Laurie looked between them, perplexed. Lucky's face turned red.

"The fastest zipper in East Texas now has a daughter," Chase said, laughing and clapping his hands together. "Oh, that's rich."

"That's not funny," Lucky grumbled.

"I don't think so either," Laurie said primly.

"It's hilarious," Chase cried. Throwing back his head, he hooted. "Wait till Sage hears about it. She'll give you grief."

"Sage! Oh, my goodness." Laurie began fishing in her

handbag for coins. "She made me promise to call her the instant the baby was born. Pat, do you have some quarters?"

"I need to try Marcie again too," Chase said.

"Y'all excuse me," Lucky said. "I'm going back in to be with Devon. Stick around. They'll bring baby girl Tyler out in a few minutes."

"No name?"

"Not yet."

"We'll be right here." Laurie kissed her younger son on the cheek and gave him a bear hug. "I'm so happy for you, Lucky."

"Be happy for Devon. She did all the work."

He disappeared through doors marked DELIVERY. The three of them moved toward the bank of pay telephones. "Where is Marcie anyway?" Laurie asked Chase.

"I tried calling her when we first got here. Her secretary was about to leave for the day. She said Marcie was showing a house, but was expected to return to the office before heading for home. She promised to leave her a message. On the outside chance they missed connections, I'm going to try calling Marcie at the house. She'll want to be here."

"Speaking of her . . ." From his breast pocket Pat extracted a sheet of computer-generated data. "I just received this list of phone freaks from Dallas this morning. The technicians were thorough. The list covers the whole state and even includes suspects who were never convicted. Course her nut might be a new one who's never been caught at it. Anyway, tell her to look it over and see if she recognizes any of the names."

Marcie's ex-fiancé in Houston had been eliminated as a viable suspect. His telephone bills over the last few months showed only long-distance calls to his mother in Detroit and one to a mail order house in Pittsburgh. He had ordered a pocket calculator. He sounded like a singularly dull nerd, and that had secretly pleased Chase.

He, like any other, could be using a pay phone to make the calls, but Chase tended to agree with Marcie that this guy lacked the imagination.

It had taken longer than they had anticipated to receive the information from Dallas. Chase was pessimistic that it would do any good, but he was heartened to know that Pat was continuing the investigation even though the caller hadn't been heard from since the night they had involved the sheriff's office.

He hoped that something would break soon, and that it wouldn't be Marcie. The more time that passed, the more distraught she became. She was determined to prove to him the calls were real. He had never doubted it for a moment.

He'd seen her fear; he'd held her trembling body after she'd suffered through a nightmare. He hoped to God he never got his hands on the bastard who was putting her through this hell. He couldn't be held responsible for what he might do to him.

"Thanks, Pat." Chase took the paper from him and set it on the shelf beneath the pay phone. He dialed his home number. The tapping sound he now knew to listen for signaled that Pat hadn't stopped monitoring their telephone either.

It rang several times before he hung up and tried Marcie's office telephone. He got a recording saying that the office was closed and asking the caller to try again between nine and six the following day.

At the tone he said, "Marcie, it's me. Are you there?" He waited, but she didn't pick up the receiver as he had hoped.

"Sage is thrilled!" Laurie exclaimed as she hung up after speaking to her daughter. "She's leaving Austin now."

"That won't put her here until midnight," Pat said, consulting his wristwatch.

"I know. I tried talking her into waiting till morning, but she insisted on coming tonight."

Mentioning the time had reminded Chase just how late it was. So much had happened since Lucky had received the call from Devon, he hadn't realized the hour had grown so late. "Who's looking at houses at this time of day?"

"Pardon?" Laurie asked him.

"Nothing. Go on back. Don't miss your granddaughter's debut. I'm going to try again to reach Marcie."

Laurie headed toward the newborns' nursery. Pat hung back. "Chase, anything wrong?"

"No. At least I don't think so." Then he finally shook his head. "No, I'm sure there's not."

"Let me know."

"Sure. Hey, Pat." Pat had taken a few steps when Chase called his name. The sheriff turned around. "That was some kiss."

The older man opened his mouth as though to deny all knowledge of what Chase was referring to. Then he ducked his head with chagrin. "It sure as hell was." He and Chase smiled at each other, then Pat turned and moved down the hallway to rejoin Laurie.

Chase dialed his home number again. No answer. He called the office again. He got the recording. Taking the telephone directory from its slot, he looked up Esme's home phone number.

"Oh, hi. You still haven't talked to Marcie?"

"No. Did you speak with her before you left the office?"

"No. But I left your message on the telephone recorder and a note on her desk just in case there was a glitch with the tape. Whether she calls in or goes back to the office, she can't miss it. Was it a boy or girl?"

"What? Oh, it was a girl," he replied absently. Where the hell could Marcie be? Shopping? Running errands? Still showing a house? "Esme, what time did she leave?"

"Just before six. You only missed her by a few minutes. She'd just walked out when you called the first time."

"Hmm. Who was she with? Buyers or sellers? Was it someone she knew?"

"She wasn't with anybody. She had an appointment to meet Mr. and Mrs. Harrison at a house they're interested in."

"The infamous Harrisons?"

"The very same. Frankly, I think she's wasting her time on them, but she said you never know when clients are going to make up their minds and take the plunge."

Chase muttered his exasperation and shoved his fingers through his hair. "God only knows how long she'll be with them."

"As far as I know, they only asked to see one house tonight. It's a new listing on Sassafras Street."

"Well, thanks, Esme. Good-bye."

"I'm sure she'll be in touch soon."

He hung up. For a moment he stared at the phone, weighing his options. Marcie usually checked in with her office before going home. Surely, one way or the other, she would get his message to come to the hospital. In the meantime he would try at intervals to reach her at home. She would never forgive herself for missing the birth of Devon's baby.

He redialed their home number. After getting no answer, he hung up impatiently, retrieved his quarter, and turned away. When he did, the computer printout Pat had given him drifted to the floor. He bent down and picked it up.

As he made his way toward the nursery, where Pat and Laurie were waiting at the large window for a first glimpse of Lucky's daughter, he scanned the sheet.

It was printed in dot matrix. The fluorescent tubes overhead almost bled the letters out. The names were in alphabetical order. He had almost reached the midway point when his feet came to a standstill.

He gripped both sides of the sheet and raised it closer to his face so that there would be no mistaking the name. Then he crushed the paper between his hands and roared. The feral cry came up through his soul. "No!"

Laurie and Pat whirled around, their faces registering astonishment. The bloodcurdling noise stopped a rushing intern in his tracks. All up and down the corridor, heads turned, sensing disaster.

"Chase?" his mother asked worriedly.

Pat said, "What the hell, boy?"

Chase didn't acknowledge them. He was already tearing down the corridor, knocking aside a metal cart and a nurse's aide who was dispensing fruit juice and Jell-O to the maternity patients.

He didn't even consider taking the elevator. It would be

too slow. When he reached the door to the stairwell, he shoved it open with the heels of his hands and clambered down two flights at a run, taking several stairs at a time, hurdling the banister at every landing, his heart racing, his mind refusing to consider that, in spite of his haste, he might already be too late.

Chapter Seventeen

The house on Sassafras Street set well away from the street. Marcie commented on that amenity as she and her client approached the front door via a stone walkway.

"You'll notice some lichen on these stones, but plain laundry bleach kills it. Personally, I like it. Maybe Mrs. Harrison will too," she said hopefully.

"Yeah, maybe."

Because this house had a large yard, Marcie hadn't suggested it to the Harrisons. A few weeks earlier the expansive lawn of another house for sale had prompted a dispute between the couple. When Ralph Harrison had called and asked to see this house, Marcie had cited the yard as a possible drawback. To her surprise he had reversed his previous opinion on taking care of a large yard.

"The yard would be no problem," he had told her.

Now Marcie pointed out that even though the yard was generous, it would require minimal care. "As you can see, there's very little grass to mow. Most of it is ground cover, front and back."

"That's why I noticed the house as I passed it today. I liked it and wanted to see it right away."

"It's a shame Mrs. Harrison couldn't join us."

"She wasn't feeling well. But she was real excited about the house when I described it to her. She told me to go ahead and preview it. If I like it, she'll come see it tomorrow."

Things were looking up, Marcie thought. This was the most cooperative the Harrisons had ever been with each other.

It was dark inside the entry alcove, but it was dry. Marcie shook out her umbrella and propped it against the exterior brick wall. The gloom was so pervasive, she had to try the key several times before successfully opening the lock.

As soon as she cleared the front door she reached for a light switch. The chandelier in the front foyer had a bubbled, amber glass globe that she found distinctly offensive. It cast weird shadows on the walls.

She didn't like showing houses at night. Only rarely did a house show to its best advantage after the sun went down. For the Harrisons, however, she had made this exception. So much time had already been invested in them, she was in so deep, she couldn't afford to stop accommodating them now. The law of averages was bound to catch up with her soon. She *would* sell them a house.

"The living room is spacious," she said. "Nice fireplace. Lots of windows. Lots of natural light. Of course, you can't tell that now. But tomorrow when Gladys comes with you, you'll see." She opened the drapes.

"I liked it better the other way," he said.

You would, she thought. She drew the heavy drapes together again and led him through a narrow dining room into the kitchen. "The garage is through that door," she told him. "It has a built-in workbench I know you'll enjoy."

"I'm not much of a handyman."

"Hmm." She searched for something that would pique his interest. So far, he'd walked through the rooms, following closely on her heels as though he were afraid of the shadows in the vacant house, and displaying little reaction either positive or negative.

Not wanting this to take any longer than necessary, she seized the initiative and asked him point-blank, "What do you think of the house so far, Mr. Harrison?"

"I'd like to see the rest of it."

She nodded pleasantly, but she was secretly gritting her teeth. "This way."

It was the kind of house that Marcie personally abhorred, with long, dark hallways and small enclosed rooms. But because she had wisely realized years ago that tastes were as varied as people, and because Sassafras Street was treelined, gracious, and underpopulated, she had aggressively gone after this listing for her agency. Maybe for the very reasons she disliked the house so much, the Harrisons would admire it.

She switched on the overhead light in the master bedroom suite. The carpeting was covered with canvas drop cloths, which, in Marcie's opinion, were a vast improvement over the maroon carpeting. In the center of the room were a sawhorse, a bucket to mix plaster in, a sack of plaster mix, another bucket of white ceiling paint, and a pile of rags.

"There was a bad water spot on this ceiling. I've already taken care of the roof repair. As you can see, the inside repair isn't quite finished."

He didn't even glance up to see if the work was being done satisfactorily. He didn't ask a question about it. In fact, he showed no interest in the project at all, which was odd since he was usually such a stickler for detail and always found something wrong with every house.

"There are two closets."

Marcie went about her business, refusing to acknowledge her growing sense of uneasiness. For several months she had been showing houses to Ralph Harrison. His nagging wife had never failed to accompany him. They'd always viewed houses in the daytime. He was a nitpicker. Tonight he was keeping his opinions to himself. Marcie preferred his whining complaints to his unnerving silence.

"One closet is a walk-in. Gladys will like that, I'm sure. The other—" At the small clicking sound, she spun away from the open closet. Harrison was locking the bedroom door. "What in the world are you doing?" Marcie demanded.

He turned around to face her, grinning eerily. In a new, yet alarmingly familiar, voice, he said, "Locking the door. So that you and I can be alone at last."

She fell back a step, her spine coming up hard against the doorjamb of the closet. She didn't notice the pain. Nothing registered except his menacing smile and raspy voice. She wasn't so much afraid as profoundly astonished.

Ralph Harrison was her caller.

*   *   *

"What was that all about?" Laurie put the question to Pat, who was frowning at the exit through which Chase had just disappeared.

"Damned if I know." He walked to the spot where Chase had previously been standing and bent down to pick up the computer printout he'd wadded into a ball then dropped. "Must have something to do with this." Sheriff Bush spread open the sheet again and scanned it. "He must have recognized a name on here himself. Someone that Marcie knows."

"Pat, go after him," Laurie urged, giving his shoulder a push. "Catch him before he has a chance to do something crazy."

"My thoughts exactly. Will you be okay?"

"Of course. Go. Go!" Pat jogged down the hallway toward the stairs, unable to move quite as spryly or as rapidly as Chase had moments earlier. "Be careful," Laurie anxiously called after him.

"You bet."

By the time he reached his squad car outside the emergency entrance of the hospital, Chase had disappeared. But Devon's car was no longer parked where Pat had spotted it when he and Laurie arrived. It made sense that since Chase had driven Lucky and Devon from the Tyler place to the hospital, he would still have the keys.

Peeling out of the hospital parking lot, Pat spoke into the transmitter of his police radio and put out an all-points bulletin for Devon's car, describing it as best as he could remember.

"License plate number?" one of his on-duty officers asked through the crackling airwaves.

"Damned if I know," Pat barked. "Just locate the car. Stop it. Apprehend the driver. White male, dark hair, six four."

"Is he armed and dangerous?" another asked.

"Hell, no!" Then he thought about the .357 he'd returned to Chase about a week ago. "Possibly armed." He thought of the Tyler temper. When riled, especially when it involved their women, it was more fearsome than any firearm. "Consider him dangerous. He'll probably resist arrest. Try not to use bodily force. He's got a couple of cracked ribs."

"Sounds like Chase Tyler."

"It is Chase Tyler," Pat replied to the unofficial remark he had overheard one deputy make to another.

"I don't get it, Sheriff Bush. What are we arresting Chase for?"

"Being a hothead."

"Sir, I didn't copy that."

"Just find the car and stop it!"

"Sassafras Street. Sassafras Street," Chase muttered to himself as he headed for the residential neighborhood where he knew the street was located. Sassafras Street. Was it between Beechnut and Magnolia? Or was he thinking of Sweetgum Street? Where the hell *was* Sassafras Street?

The town he had grown up in seemed suddenly foreign territory to him. He couldn't remember which streets ran parallel and which intersected. Did Sassafras run north and south or east and west?

In his mind he conjured up a map of Milton Point, but it was distorted and became an ever-changing grid of streets he could no longer remember, like a maze in a nightmare that one could never work his way through.

He cursed, banging his fist on the steering wheel of Devon's red compact car. Who would have thought that that little weasel, Harrison, had the nerve to terrorize a woman over the telephone? Chase had only met him once, that day in Marcie's office. Harrison had made little impression on him. He couldn't describe him now if asked to do so at gunpoint. He was that forgettable.

That's probably why he made obscene phone calls, Chase reasoned. The calls were his only power trip, his last-ditch effort to achieve machismo. Over the telephone he could be six feet six and commanding. His sibilant vulgarities made his victims gasp and left a distinct impression on them. To a guy like Harrison, revulsion was better than making no impression at all.

"Slimy s.o.b.," Chase said through his teeth. He remembered how disgusted and devastated Marcie had looked after each call.

Why hadn't they consulted a psychologist instead of a law officer? Someone who understood the workings of the human mind might have provided them with character profiles that would have pointed them to Harrison. It was crystal clear to Chase now why he was their man. He had an overbearing, critical wife and a low self-image. They should have gone to a head doctor. Harrison was a sicko. He wasn't a criminal.

Or was he? Maybe talking about sexual perversions no longer satisfied him. Maybe he'd gone over the edge. Maybe he was ready to make good his threats.

"Dammit." Chase stamped on the accelerator.

*   *   *

Marcie's astonishment quickly receded with the onslaught of panic. By an act of will she tamped it down. He wanted her to be afraid. She was. But damned if she was going to give him the satisfaction of seeing it.

"So, you're the pathetic individual who's been calling me. Are you proud of yourself?"

"Don't try to fool me, Marcie. I've frightened you."

"You haven't frightened me in the slightest. Only disgusted me and made me feel very sorry for you."

"If you weren't frightened, why'd you go to the sheriff?"

She tried to keep her face impassive and not let him see her distress. At the same time she was trying to figure a way out of the room and away from the house. Once outside, she could run down the sidewalk screaming, but she had to get out of there first.

If at all possible, she wanted to avoid any physical contact. The thought of his hands on her made her ill. He didn't have a weapon. He wasn't exceptionally tall or strong. In fact, he was slightly built. If it came down to a wrestling match, she doubted he could completely overpower her, but he could hurt her before she could fight him off and that was a major concern.

Not that he would take it that far, she reassured herself. He wouldn't try to rape her. He only wanted to terrorize her.

"Didn't you think I'd know when they put the taps on your phone?" he asked in the taunting voice of her nightmares. "The first time I called and heard the clicks, I hung up."

"Then you must have done this kind of thing before. To be that familiar with police wiretaps and such."

"Oh, yes. I'm quite good at it. An expert. The best."

She forced a laugh. "I hate to dash your self-esteem," she said, hoping to do exactly that, "but you're not very original. In fact, I've had much more, uh, *interesting* calls than yours."

"Shut up!" Abruptly, his voice rose in pitch and volume, alarming her. His face had become congested with blood and his eyes had narrowed to pinpoints of sinister light. "Take off your blouse."

"No." Maybe if she called his bluff, he would get cold feet and run away.

He took three menacing steps toward her. "Take off your blouse."

The empty closet was behind her. Could she step into it, shut the door, and lock herself in until somebody missed her and came looking? She felt behind her for the doorknob.

"That door doesn't have a lock, if that's what you're thinking," he said with a cackle she recognized. Over the telephone it had never failed to send chills down her spine. She experienced them now.

He was right. The closet door didn't have a lock. She glanced quickly at the window. The sill was painted shut. She could never get it open, and even if she could, she couldn't scramble out without his catching her first.

Her only means of escape was through the doorway leading into the hall. He was blocking her path to it. She would have to draw him across the room, closer to her, and away from the door.

Swallowing her repugnance and her pride, her hand moved to the top button of her blouse. Why hadn't she worn a suit today instead of a skirt and blouse? A jacket would have been another delaying tactic.

"Hurry up," he ordered. "Take it off. I want to see your skin. I want to see your breasts."

Marcie slowly undid all the buttons. "My husband will tear you apart."

"Not before I've seen your nipples, touched them. Hurry up."

"He won't let you get away with this. He'll find you."

"You won't tell him. You'll be too ashamed to tell him."

"I wouldn't count on that if I were you."

"Take off your blouse!" he shouted nervously.

She pulled it from her waistband and peeled it down her shoulders. As she withdrew her arms from the sleeves, he released a sigh and actually shuddered orgasmically. Marcie thought she might be sick, but she couldn't surrender to the nausea. She had to get out of the room.

As she had both hoped and dreaded, Harrison took faltering steps toward her. "Now the brassiere. Hurry." He was clutching at his crotch with one hand and reaching out to her with the other.

"You're so fair. I knew your skin would be fair. Beautiful. Soft." His fingertips glanced her chest just above her bra. She recoiled. He took another lurching step toward her. She could feel his rapid breath landing humid and hot on her skin.

"Fondle yourself," he panted.

"No."

"Do it."

"No."

"I said to do it!"

"If you want me fondled, you do it." Her blue eyes haughtily challenged him. "Or are you man enough?"

As she had hoped, he lunged toward her, his hands and fingers forming a cup to seize her breast. She flung her blouse into his face, parried quickly, and ducked under his arm. She scooped the empty bucket from the floor and threw it up at the overhead light fixture, then clambered toward the door at a crouch to avoid the breaking glass that was raining down.

In the sudden darkness she groped for the doorknob. The darkness was to her advantage because she was more familiar with the house than he. She would know how to find her way back to the front door. But first she had to get past this barrier. Having located the doorknob, her fingers had turned to rubber. She couldn't get it unlocked!

From behind, Harrison grabbed a handful of her hair. Her head snapped back. She screamed. He covered her hand and wrested it off the slippery doorknob. They slapped at each other's hands in a battle over control of the lock.

Marcie heard whimpers of fear and draining energy and realized they were coming from her. She had minimized the real threat he could pose to her safety, but had obviously miscalculated. His breathing was the short, choppy panting of a madman. He was stronger than he appeared. Had insanity imbued him with inordinate strength?

She renewed her efforts to escape him, but he gripped her arm so hard that tears started in her eyes. "Let me go," she screamed.

He flung her away from the door and back toward the center of the room. With so much momentum behind her, she reeled forward, stumbling in the darkness over drop cloths, broken glass, and the sack of plaster mix and falling against the sawhorse. It caught her at waist level, and she doubled over it. It toppled over with her, spilling the bucket of paint.

She blinked away the descending blackness of unconsciousness and struggled to her hands and knees. Harrison, bending over her, with his hand on the back of her neck, held her down.

"Bitch, bitch," he said raspily. "I'll show you how much of a man I am."

"Milton seven?"

Pat responded. "Yeah, come in."

"This is Milton five. I've just sighted a red vehicle, license number and make unknown at this time, traveling west on Sycamore at a high rate of speed."

"Close in and apprehend."

"Not a chance, Milton seven. He's driving like a bat out of hell."

"Then follow him. I'm three minutes away. Keep him in sight and let me know any changes of direction."

"Ten four."

"Other units, please converge on that area."

To a chorus of acknowledgments, Pat dropped the transmitter and concentrated on navigating the dark, rain-slick streets.

Chase took the corner close to fifty. Sassafras Street at last! What number? Leaning over the steering wheel, he peered through the darkness, cursing the driving rain and his inability to see beyond the hood ornament.

He sped right past Marcie's car before noticing it. He braked, skidded, and fishtailed, then shoved the automatic transmission into park and opened the car door. The FOR SALE sign bearing her agency's logo was in the front yard. Chase hurdled it in his dash through the pelting rain toward the front door.

He paused in the entrance hall, his blood freezing in his veins when he heard her pitiful cries. But thank God, she was alive. His moves through the unfamiliar rooms and hallways resembled those of a running back going through a horde of defensive players. For every five yards he gained, he had to backtrack two, until he finally reached the closed and locked bedroom door.

He tested the doorknob only once before putting his boot heel to it and kicking it in. From the hallway behind him, light spilled into the room and across the floor, casting a looming, hulking shadow that alarmed him until he realized it was his own.

He dashed inside. Harrison, still crouched over Marcie on the floor, whipped his head around and stared up at Chase with an animal fear so intense Chase could smell it.

"I'm gonna kill you, Harrison."

Reaching from his towering height, he yanked the man up by his collar and shook him like a dog with a dead rat. Harrison squealed. Chase, enraged and unthinking, slung him against the wall. Harrison would have slid down it but for Chase's fist, which slammed into Harrison's midsection, then pinned him to the wall like a nail through his gut. Nose to nose, his lips peeled back to bare his teeth, Chase glared at his wife's tormentor.

"Chase, let him go!" Pistol drawn, Pat Bush shouted the order from the splintered doorway. "Chase!" He had to repeat his name three times before Chase heard him through a fog of murderous outrage.

Gradually Chase withdrew his fist. Harrison, emitting a wheezing sound like an old accordion, collapsed to the floor. One of Pat's deputies rushed forward to see to Harrison while Chase bent anxiously over Marcie. She was lying on her side, her knees drawn protectively up to her chest.

"Chase?" she said faintly.

He placed his arms around her and lifted her into a sitting position, hugging her close to his rain-soaked chest. "I'm here, Marcie. He can't bother you now. Not anymore. Never."

"Is she all right?" Pat hunkered down beside him.

"I think so. Just scared."

"Is she cut? There's glass all over the place. Apparently she broke out the light."

Chase smiled as he smoothed back strands of red-gold hair from her damp forehead. "That's my girl. Always smart. Always resourceful."

"Chase?"

He bent his head down, bringing his face close to hers. Even pale and disheveled she looked beautiful. "Hmm?"

"Get me to the hospital."

"The hospital?"

"I'm bleeding."

His eyes moved over her face, her chest, her exposed midriff, but he saw no trace of blood.

"She's probably cut her hands and knees on the glass," Pat said.

"No, it's not that. Get me to the hospital now," she said, her anxiety increasing. "Hurry, please."

"Marcie, I know you're scared. You've come through—"

"Chase, I'm bleeding vaginally." Her tearful eyes found his. She pulled her lower lip through her teeth. "I'm pregnant."

Chapter Eighteen

It was still raining. Chase looked beyond his own reflection in the window out into the dark, forlorn night. He saw the reflections of his brother and Pat Bush as they approached him, but he didn't turn away from the window until Pat spoke his name.

"I just got back from the courthouse," the sheriff said. "I thought you'd want to know that Harrison is in jail. He'll be arraigned first thing in the morning."

"For assault?"

"Murder one."

Chase's gut knotted. Was this their way of informing him that Marcie had died? He slowly pivoted on his heels. "What?" he croaked.

"I dispatched some men to his house. They found his wife. She'd been dead for several hours. He strangled her with his bare hands. Allegedly," Pat added, remembering his role as a fair and impartial officer of the law.

Chase dragged his hand down his face, stretching the tired, strained features. "Dear Lord."

"Marcie had good reason to be scared of him," Pat said. "Even over the telephone she sensed he was more than just a casual phone freak. I feel like hell for doubting her."

Chase was still too stunned to speak. Lucky squeezed the older man's shoulder. "Don't worry about that now, Pat. You couldn't guess that he was going to carry out his threats. You were there tonight when Marcie needed you." He glanced over his shoulder toward the waiting room at the opposite end of the corridor. "I think Mother and Sage could use you for moral support right now. And vice versa."

"Sure. Chase, if you need me . . . for anything . . . just holler." Chase nodded. Pat ambled off, leaving the two brothers alone.

For a moment they said nothing. Chase couldn't think of anything appropriate to say. He felt hollow. There were no words inside him.

Lucky broke the silence. "Sage made the trip safely."

"So I see. I'm glad she's here."

"She arrived in a mood to celebrate. We had to break the news about Marcie. She started crying. When you feel up to it, she'd like to say hello. Right now, she thinks you'd rather be left alone. Is she right?"

"I don't feel much like talking."

"Sure."

Lucky turned away, but had only taken a few steps when Chase reached out and touched his arm. "I'm sorry this has put a pall on your daughter's birthday."

"It sure as hell wasn't your fault things turned out the way they did. The culprit is in jail. Blame it on him."

Chase's fists flexed at his sides. "He could have killed her, Lucky."

"But he didn't."

"If I hadn't gotten there—"

"But you did. Everybody's safe now."

They didn't mention the baby that Marcie was carrying. There might yet be another casualty of Ralph Harrison's violent madness. Lucky's first child had been born; Chase's second child might die on the same day. He couldn't bear thinking about it.

"Anyway," he said emotionally, "I hate like hell that this had to happen today of all days."

"Forget that part of it. You've got enough on your mind without worrying about that."

The things on his mind were about to drive him crazy. To stave it off he asked, "How's Devon feeling?"

"How do you think? Like she just had a baby. I told her I knew how she felt. I thought she was going to come out of that bed and slug me." He chuckled in spite of the somber mood.

Chase forced a half smile. "The, uh, baby," he said huskily, "how is she?"

"Fine, even though she was several weeks early. The pediatrician checked her out. He wants to monitor her closely for the next few days, but he says her reflexes are normal, lungs and everything seemed well developed." He broke into a wide grin. "She's squalling loud enough."

"That's good, Lucky. That's real good."

Chase's throat closed tightly around the lump stuck in it. He cleared it self-consciously and blinked gathering tears out of his eyes. Lucky placed a consoling hand on his shoulder.

"Look, Chase, Marcie's going to be okay. And so's the baby. I know it. I feel it. Have I ever steered you wrong?"

"Plenty of times."

Lucky frowned with chagrin. "Well, not this time. You wait and see."

Chase nodded, but he wasn't convinced. Lucky stared at him hard, trying by sheer willpower to inspire optimism and faith. The last couple of years Chase's confidence in good fortune had been shaken. Today's events had merely confirmed his skepticism in the benevolence of fate.

Lucky left him to join the rest of the family huddled in the waiting room. The nursing staff had become well acquainted with the Tylers since dusk that day. They now had two Mrs. Tylers in the obstetric ward. One of the nurses was passing around fresh coffee.

Chase turned his back on the well-lighted corridor, feeling more in harmony with the dismal gloom beyond the window.

I'm pregnant.

At first he had just stared into Marcie's anxious blue eyes. Unable to move, unable to speak, unable to think beyond that word, he had mutely gaped at her. Then Pat's elbow had nudged him into awareness.

"Chase, did you hear her?"

Adrenaline assumed control. He scooped Marcie into his arms and carried her past the shattered bedroom door. Pat put two deputies in charge of Harrison and the house on Sassafras Street. He followed Chase through the vacant rooms. "I'll call an ambulance."

"Screw that. I'll make it faster driving myself."

"Like hell you will. And kill yourself, or innocent people? Forget it. If you won't wait for an ambulance, put her in the patrol car. I'll drive you."

So he had held Marcie on his lap in the backseat of the patrol car behind the wire mesh that separated them from Pat. He turned on all the emergency lights and the siren. At intervals he spoke into his police radio transmitter, informing the emergency room staff that they were on their way. Windshield wipers clacked in vain against the torrential rain. The ride to the hospital had taken on a surreal quality to Chase, as though he were watching it from outside his own body.

Because he hadn't wasted time on getting an umbrella, rain had left Marcie's hair damp. There were drops of it beaded on her face and throat. Pat must have retrieved her blouse because Chase didn't remember picking it up. He wrapped her torso in it but didn't bother with working her arms into the sleeves or fastening the buttons. He kept touching her hair, her pale cheek, her throat. She continued staring up at him with tearful and wary eyes. They said nothing to each other.

At the entrance to the emergency room she was whisked away on a gurney. "Who's her o.b.?" the resident on duty asked. Everyone looked at Chase expectantly.

"I . . . I don't know."

Admitting her to the hospital was a seemingly endless procedure of questions and forms to be filled out. Once it was done, he returned to the emergency room. There he was informed that Marcie had been transferred upstairs to the maternity ward and that her doctor was on his way.

Before the gyn even examined Marcie, he asked Chase pertinent questions relating to the attack. "To your knowledge was she raped?"

Feeling bereft, numb, he shook his head no.

"Did he even attempt penetration?"

"I don't think so," he said, barely able to get the words out.

The doctor patted his arm reassuringly. "I'm sure she'll be all right, Mr. Tyler."

"What about the baby?"

"I'll let you know."

But he hadn't. And that had been almost two hours ago. Pat had had time to go to the courthouse and deal with Harrison and come back, and still there had been no word on the conditions of Marcie and the baby.

What the hell was taking so long?

Had they had trouble stopping the bleeding? Was there hemorrhaging? Had she been rushed into surgery? Was her life in danger as well as the child's?

"No." Chase didn't realize he had moaned the word out loud until he heard the sound of his own voice, pleading with fate, pleading with God.

Marcie couldn't die. She *couldn't*. She had become too important to him. He couldn't lose her now that he had just come to realize how important she was to him.

He remembered something that Lucky had asked him earlier that afternoon. That afternoon? It seemed eons ago.

Lucky had asked, "What's the single worst thing that could happen to you, Chase? The worst possible thing?"

Perhaps he had known the answer to that question then. Devon's phone call had prevented him from having to deal with it at the time, but now he repeated the question to himself.

The answer was full-blown and well-defined in his mind. After losing Tanya, after losing their child, the worst possible thing that could happen to him was to love again.

Almost anything else he could have handled. A drinking problem. Getting seriously hurt by bull riding, perhaps permanently injured, perhaps killed. Professional and personal bankruptcy.

Whatever misfortune fate might have hurled at him, he could take because he had reasoned that he didn't deserve anything better. Partially blaming himself for Tanya's death, he had pursued self-punishment. He had cultivated calamity like a twisted gardener who preferred weeds to flowers. Nothing that could happen to him could be worse than losing his family—nothing except loving another one.

That he couldn't deal with.

He couldn't handle caring about another woman again. He couldn't handle another woman's loving him. He couldn't handle making another baby.

He banged his fist against the cool, tile hospital wall and pressed his forehead against it. Eyes closed, teeth clenched, he battled acknowledging what he knew to be the truth.

He had fallen in love with Marcie. And he couldn't forgive himself for it.

Acting a fool, he had rejected her when she needed him

most. He had turned his back on her when she was pregnant and frightened. And why? Pride. No man liked to feel that he'd been manipulated, but the business about the house now seemed more an act of love than manipulation. He'd just been too mule-headed to accept what was so plain and simple. Marcie loved him. He loved her.

If that was his worst crime, was it so terrible?

He examined the sin from all angles, even from Tanya's viewpoint. She wouldn't have wanted it any differently. Her capacity to love had been so enormous that she would have been the first one to encourage him to love again if she had seen what their fate was to be.

Why was he fighting it? What had he done that was so despicable? Why was he continuing to punish himself? He had fallen in love with a wonderful woman who, miraculously, loved him. What was so bad about that?

Nothing.

He raised his head and turned. At the end of the corridor the obstetrician was coming out of Marcie's room. Chase moved toward him, his long strides eating up the distance between them, gaining speed and momentum as he went.

"Listen, you," he said harshly before the doctor had a chance to speak, "save her life. Hear me?" He backed the startled physician into the wall. "I don't care if it costs ten million dollars, do whatever is necessary to make her live. You got that, Doc? Even if it means . . ." He stopped, swallowed with an effort, then continued in a rougher voice, "Even if it means destroying the baby, save my wife."

"That won't be necessary, Mr. Tyler. Your wife is going to be fine."

Chase stared at him, unwilling to believe it. The fortunate twist of fate took him totally by surprise. "She is?"

"And so is the baby. When she fell over the sawhorse, a vaginal blood vessel burst. It was weakened and under unusual pressure due to her pregnancy. There wasn't much bleeding, but enough to alarm Mrs. Tyler. Rightfully so.

"We've cauterized it. I did a sonogram just to make certain that everything was okay, and it is. The fetus wasn't affected in any way." He hitched his thumb over his shoulder toward the room from which he'd just emerged. "She insisted on taking a shower. A nurse is helping her with that now. When she's done, you can go in and see her. I recommend a few days of bed rest. After that, she should experience a perfectly normal pregnancy."

Chase mumbled his thanks for the information. The doctor moved to the nurses' station and left instructions, then departed. Chase's family surrounded him. Laurie was weeping copiously. Sage was doing her share of sniveling. Pat was wiping nervous perspiration off his forehead with a handkerchief and mercilessly chewing a matchstick.

Lucky slapped Chase soundly on the back. "Didn't I tell you? Huh? When are you gonna start trusting me?"

Chase fielded their expressions of relief with what he hoped were the correct responses, but his eyes were trained on the hospital room door. As soon as the nurse came out, he excused himself and rushed inside.

The single, faint night-light behind the bed shone through Marcie's hair, making it the only spot of vibrancy in the shadowed room. Its magnetism drew him across the floor until he stood at her bedside.

"History repeats itself," she said. "I remember another time when you came to see me in the hospital."

"You look better now than you did then."

"Not much."

"Much."

"Thank you."

She averted her eyes and blinked several times, but it did no good. Twin tears, one as fat as the other, slipped over her lower lids and rolled down her cheeks.

"Are you in pain, Marcie?" Chase asked, bending closer. "Did that bastard hurt you?"

"No," she gulped. "You got there just in time."

"He's behind bars." He thought it best not to inform her of Gladys Harrison's murder. "Don't waste your tears on him."

"That's not why I'm crying." Her lower lip began to tremble. She clamped her teeth over it in an attempt to prevent that.

After a moment or two she said, "I know how you feel about having another baby, Chase. I didn't mean to trick you. I swear I didn't. It's true, I should have been more honest about the house, but I didn't lie to you about contraceptives.

"I started taking birth control pills as soon as we agreed to get married, but I guess they hadn't had time to take effect. It had only been a couple of days. It happened on our wedding night."

"But I used something, too."

"It must have broken."

"Oh."

"That happens sometimes. Or so I've been told."

"Yeah, I've heard that, too."

"Has it ever happened to you before?"

"No."

"Do you think I'm lying about it?"

"No. I, uh, I was pretty potent that night when I, you know . . ."

She swung her eyes up to his. "It must have happened then."

"Hmm."

"I'm sorry, Chase." Her lip began to tremble again.

"It wasn't your fault."

"No, I mean about the baby. About making you feel trapped. I know that's how you feel. You think I bound you to me first with money, now with a baby you said you never wanted." She licked the collecting tears from the corners of her mouth.

"You should have told me you were pregnant, Marcie."

"I couldn't."

"You've never lacked the courage to tell me anything else."

"I've never felt so vulnerable before. I found out while you were in Houston. That's why I had no appetite and lost so much weight. That's why I wouldn't take the pill you tried to give me. I knew then and should have told you, but you were so angry about the house. And then that mess with Harrison came up."

She clutched the border of the sheet. "I want you to know that I won't bind you. You're free to go, Chase. I won't hold you to any bargains if you want out of the marriage."

"Are you trying to get rid of me?"

"Of course not."

"Then be quiet. I want to tell you how much I love you." He smiled at her blank, incredulous expression, then lowered his face to hers and sipped the tears off her cheeks. "I love you, Marcie. Swear to God, I do. He blessed me with you."

"I thought you didn't believe in Him anymore."

"I always believed. I was just mad at Him."

"Chase," she sighed. "You mean this?"

"From the bottom of my heart."

Her fingers roamed over his face, his hair, his lips. "I have loved you since I can remember. Since we were kids."

"I know," he said softly. "I realize that now. I'm not as smart as you. It takes me a while to grasp these things. For instance, I still haven't figured out why you didn't tell me about the baby. I could have helped you through this nightmare."

"Could you?"

"Couldn't I?"

"Remember that night I took you home to your apartment, then came back and you were eating chili? We got into an argument when I told you to snap out of your bereavement, that it was self-destructive. You said, 'When you've lost the person you love, when you've lost a child, *then* you'll be at liberty to talk to me about falling apart.'

"I didn't realize until I was at risk of losing you how immobilizing heartache can be, how one does fall apart. I internalized my agony just as you had done then, Chase. I fully understand now how you must have felt following Tanya's death. It's almost self-preservation, isn't it, the way we draw into ourselves when we think no one cares?"

"We won't have that problem anymore."

A radiant smile broke through her tears. "No. We won't."

He kissed her, deeply but tenderly, and wondered why, until now, he'd never recognized the special taste of her kiss as being love. He knew he'd never get enough of it.

"Maybe you were wise not to tell me about the baby, Marcie," he whispered. "I don't think I was prepared to hear about it until today."

"But now that you know, it's all right?"

"All right?" His splayed hand was large enough to cover the entire area between her pelvic bones. "I love the idea of us making a baby. Hurry up and get well so the three of us can go home."

"Home?"

"Home."

Epilogue

"All this fecundity is positively nauseating," Sage commented drolly.

"What the hell's 'fecundity'?" Lucky wanted to know.

"Oh, that's rich," his sister remarked. "Especially coming from you."

All the Tylers had gathered at the ranch house to celebrate little Lauren's three-week birthday. Everyone else had gorged on German chocolate cake. The baby was greedily sucking her mother's breast behind the screen of a receiving blanket. The proud papa looked on, ready to assist at a moment's notice.

"Know what I can't wait for?"

"Careful, Sage." Chase, who'd been twirling a strand of Marcie's hair around his finger while whispering bawdy things into her ear, paused in those pleasurable pursuits to caution his sister. "You never learned when to quit."

Ignoring Chase, she continued goading her other brother.

"I can't wait till some guy makes a pass at Lauren. I want to be there. I want to rub your nose in it, Lucky."

Lucky took the infant from Devon so she could close her blouse. He glowered at his sister. "I'll kill any s.o.b. who even thinks of laying a hand on my daughter. I'll kill anyone who even looks like he's thinking of laying a hand on her."

"How're you going to explain the origin of your nickname to Lauren?" Chase asked, joining in.

Devon burst out laughing. Lucky stopped cooing to Lauren long enough to consign his brother and sister to hell.

"Lucky, please watch your language," his mother said with a long-suffering sigh. "Remember we have a guest."

Travis Belcher, Sage's beau, had accompanied her home for a weekend visit. He had been sitting quietly, either repulsed or dumbfounded by the frankness with which the Tylers spoke to one another.

Chase had noticed the young man registering shock when he had put his hand over Marcie's tummy and patted it affectionately. His estimation of Sage's Travis coincided with Lucky's. The guy was a wimp. Just for the hell of shocking him further, he had leaned over and kissed Marcie's lips.

He got his own shock when she slipped her tongue into his mouth. "Stop that," he had moaned into her ear. "I'm already hard."

Then he had had the pleasure of watching a blush spill into her fair cheeks.

Laurie was jealous of anyone who got to hold her granddaughter longer than she did. Once Lauren had finished nursing, Laurie crossed the living room, plucked the baby from her father's arms, and carried her back to the rocking chair, recently taken out of storage in the attic. It was the chair Laurie had rocked her three children in.

Lucky had offered to buy her a new one, but she wouldn't hear of it. She had said that the squeaks and groans of the wood in this one were familiar and brought back precious memories.

"My goodness, you're getting fat, Lauren!" she exclaimed to the child.

"No wonder," Lucky said. He placed his arm around Devon, who cuddled against him. "She's getting some delicious meals."

"How do you know how delicious they are?" Chase asked with a bawdy wink.

Lucky, not to be outdone, came right back with, "You don't think I'd let my daughter eat something I hadn't sampled first, do you?"

"Lucky!" Devon exclaimed, horrified.

"Lawrence! Chase!" Laurie remonstrated.

Chase threw back his head and roared with laughter, causing baby Lauren to flinch.

Lucky assumed an innocent pose. "But Devon, you begged me to."

"Agh!" Sage jumped to her feet. "You two are *so* disgusting. Come on, Travis. I can't take any more of this. Let's go horseback riding."

She took his hand and pulled him from his chair. "Again?" Obviously the suggestion didn't appeal to him.

"Don't be a spoilsport. I'll saddle a more docile horse for you this time." As Sage dragged Travis through the front door, she called back, "Bye, Marcie. Bye, Devon. See y'all later." While at any given time Sage could strangle either of her brothers, she adored their wives. "Bye-bye, Lauren. I love you. Too bad you've got a reprobate for a father."

"You're a brat, Sage," Lucky hollered after her.

Moments after Sage and Travis's departure, Pat Bush stepped into the living room. "Hi, everybody. I saw Sage outside. She said to come on in."

He was offered cake and coffee and had just taken his first bite when Chase began sniffing the air. "What's that smell?"

He sniffed in Pat's direction. "Why, Pat, I believe it's you!" he said, feigning surprise. "What are you all spruced up for?"

Pat choked on his bite of cake and shot Chase a drop-dead look. Laurie's cheeks blossomed with flattering color. Chase hadn't spoken a word to anyone, not even Lucky, about seeing his mother and Pat in a heated embrace. But the temptation to tease them about it was too strong to resist.

Coming to his feet, Chase pulled Marcie up beside him. Ever since the night following Lauren's birth, he'd slept in the same bed with her, holding her close, verbally vowing his love, but prohibited from expressing it physically.

They'd resumed their torturous game of unfulfilled foreplay. It was making him crazy, but it was a delicious craziness. His body was constantly abuzz with desire. He moved around in a rosy haze of euphoria that made his nights magic and his workdays more tolerable.

Apparently the troubleshooter, Harlan Boyd, had given up on him. Once Marcie was out of danger and he'd gotten around to contacting him, the man had moved on, without leaving word of his whereabouts. It was probably just as well, but that meant he and Lucky needed to get real creative if they were going to save their business.

When he got discouraged, Marcie was his staunchest supporter and cheerleader. Placing his arm around her now, he said, "Well, we'd better be going on home."

"What for?" Lucky's countenance was as guileless as a cherub's. He batted his eyelashes. "Nap time?"

Ignoring him, Chase leaned over his mother where she sat rocking his new niece and kissed her cheek. "Bye. Thanks for the cake. It was delicious."

"Good-bye, son." Their eyes caught and held. He knew she was searching for the pain that had resided in his eyes for so long. Finding none, she gave him a beautiful smile, then turned it on the woman who was responsible for his newfound happiness. "Marcie, how are you feeling?"

"Perfectly wonderful, thanks. Chase takes very good care of me. He will hardly let me lift a fork to feed myself."

Once they were in their car and headed home, she said, "They thought I was joking about your not letting me do anything for myself."

"I've got to protect you and baby. I almost slipped up once." He gave her a meaningful look. "Never again, Marcie, will anyone come close to hurting you."

"You're the only one who could hurt me, Chase."

"How?"

"If you ever decided you didn't love me."

He reached for her hand, laid it on his thigh, and covered it with his own. "That's not going to happen."

The woods surrounding their house bore the virgin and varied greens of spring. Blooming dogwood trees decorated the forest like patches of white lace. The tulip bulbs that Marcie had planted the year before were blooming along the path leading to the front door.

Once inside, Chase moved to the wall of windows and contemplated the view. "I love this house."

"I always knew you would."

He turned around to embrace his wife. "I love it almost as much as I love you."

"Almost?"

He unbuttoned her blouse and pushed the fabric aside. His hands moved over the silk covering her breasts. "You've got a few amenities that are hard to beat."

After a lengthy, wet, deep kiss, she murmured, "I got the go-ahead from the doctor this morning."

Chase's head snapped back. "You mean he said we could—"

"If we're careful."

He swept her into his arms and took the stairs two at a time. "Why didn't you tell me sooner?"

"Because we were invited to Lauren's party."

"We wasted two hours over there!"

Once he had deposited her at the side of their bed, he began tearing off his clothes. Laughing, she helped him. When he was naked, she reached out and stroked him.

He moaned. "You're killing me."

Frantically he removed her skirt and blouse. She was still in her slip when he lowered her to the bed, laid his head on her belly, and nuzzled her through the silk.

"How's my baby?" he whispered.

"Fine. Healthy. Growing inside me."

"How are you?"

"Deliriously happy, so much in love."

"Lord, so am I." He planted a damp kiss into the giving softness.

"Hmm," she sighed, tilting herself up against his face.

He raised his head and smiled down at her. "You like that?"

"Uh-huh."

"Hot redhead that you are." He pulled her slip up by the lace hem, over her middle, over her breasts, over her head. Bra and panties and stockings were quickly discarded. Seconds later, he was gazing at her with loving approval of all he saw.

"They change color a little more every day," he remarked, brushing his fingertips across her nipples.

"They do not. You just enjoy inspecting them."

"That's not all I enjoy."

He bent his head and kissed her breasts, raking his tongue back and forth across the delicate peaks until her tummy quivered with arousal. "Chase?"

"Not yet. We've had to wait weeks for this."

He kissed his way down her body, paused to relish the texture and scent of the glossy curls covering her mound, then parted her thighs and kissed her between them.

She sighed his name and clutched handfuls of his hair, but he didn't temper his ardency until his agile tongue had drawn from her a sweet, undulating climax.

Then he rose above her and slowly, considerately, buried himself within the snug, moist sheath of her body. Mindful of her condition, his strokes were long and smooth, which only heightened the eroticism and prolonged the pleasure.

The pleasure was immense. Overwhelming. Ecstasy eddied around him in shimmering waves that matched the tempo of her gentle contractions.

Yet he couldn't totally immerse himself in it. Because in the back of his mind, behind the physical bliss, he was thinking how marvelous life was, how much he loved living it . . . how much he loved Marcie, his wife.

About the Author

SANDRA BROWN is the author of fifty-eight *New York Times* bestsellers with more than seventy million copies of her books in print. She and her husband live in Arlington, Texas.

About the Type

This book is set in Fournier, a typeface named for Pierre Simon Fournier, the youngest son of a French printing family. He started out engraving woodblocks and large capitals, then moved on to fonts of type. In 1736 he began his own foundry and made several important contributions in the field of type design; he is said to have cut 147 alphabets of his own creation. Fournier is probably best remembered as the designer of St. Augustine Ordinaire, a face that served as the model for Monotype's Fournier, which was released in 1925.